THE PAST WE RUN FROM

MEG JOLLY

Published in 2022 by
Eldarkin Publishing Limited
United Kingdom
© 2022 Meg Jolly
www.megjolly.com

Cover design © Meg Jolly 2022

ISBN 9798517854421

BOOKS BY MEG JOLLY

The DI Daniel Ward Yorkshire Crime Thriller Series:

The Truth We Can't Hide (a standalone novella)

The Past We Run From

The Revenge We Seek

The Mistakes We Deny

The Justice We Serve

The Power We Exploit

CHAPTER ONE

WEDNESDAY

Golden curls caught the dappled sun filtering through the trees that kept the fenced-off play area shaded—not that the children needed shade that day. The sun was a rare visitor, and fresh rain clouds already scudded in from the west—towering cathedrals of grey that dominated the brooding skyline.

Those golden curls bounced as the toddler flew into the air, catapulted by her tiny legs hammering off the trampoline. Her shriek of delight did not carry—lost in the hubbub of a hundred other children thundering around the playground, blazing down the paths of Wibsey Park on skateboards and bikes, or feeding the noisy crowd of ducks by the ornamental pond.

But he was watching. *He* saw—and he imagined that sound. It tugged up the corner of his mouth in a smile. She was so sweet. So young. So innocent.

She ran from the trampoline. Her mother, sat on a bench inside the play park, chatted to another young

1

woman with a baby in her arms. She absentmindedly stroked the girl's curls as the toddler claimed her drinks bottle with gusto, before dashing off to play again, her legs pumping as she ran under the climbing frame to play hide and seek.

The man uncrossed his legs then crossed them again, his only sign of impatience as he shifted on the bench. Beside him, a newspaper lay open but ignored, one he had claimed that had been abandoned on the bench with half its contents missing. The rain started up again, the morning's reprieve over. It was forecast for the next week straight. As if by magic, the park emptied as droves of children and parents rushed home, heads ducked against the pitter-patter.

He watched and waited as the mother stood, fussing over the stroller, and called her over. He watched and waited as they trundled to the adjoining playground to collect her older brother, a taller, stringy lad, probably not even ten, who was reluctant to leave his mates behind. They raucously called after him as he slouched, hands in pockets, head down, back to his family.

He watched and waited as they followed the path towards him, and passed without noticing him on the bench. The mother leaned towards her son, trying to pry any conversation from him—the boy had taken out his phone and refused to look up from it—whilst the girl followed. In their bubble, they were oblivious to the world—and unaware of him, tucked away in the bench between the overgrown bushes.

Courage danced with fear inside him. The opportunity was *there*, right in that moment. The one he had waited so long for.

He offered the little girl a bright smile as she passed, and after a moment of uncertainty, she smiled back, beaming, her blue eyes lit up with a *joie de vivre* that had not yet been silenced by too long in the world. 'Gah!' she squealed, but her voice was drowned out by her mother's curse.

'Oh, bugger. Kian, I left my handbag in the park!' Panic laced the mother's tone. It was a busy park and the purse would probably already have gone. 'Watch your sister!' She abandoned the stroller and legged it back to the play area at a sprint.

If she'd looked back, she would have realised that the boy had ignored her, walking around the pond towards the park gate, with his hood up against the rain, and no thought of his sister at all. But she didn't.

The watcher found his moment. A rush thundered through him. Silently, he reached out his hand towards the toddler, holding a brightly coloured bag of sweets. She toddled closer, and with a brightening of her eyes, a precocious sparkle that made his heart ache with longing, she took one. In a matter of seconds, it was gone. Her pudgy hands reached up for another.

'Alright my sweet, just one more.' In an instant, he swept her up into his arms and covered her with his dark jacket, before stepping behind the bench and through the bushes with careful steps, long prepared. Thick with the swell of summer greenery, the shrubbery shrouded them both in a moment. In the churn of footprints left by the children who played hide and seek in those bushes, his tracks would be lost.

Overhead, the pitter-patter of rain drowned out the rustle of his passage. He whispered to the struggling bundle in his arms. 'Let's go on an adventure, hmm?'

So sweet. So young. So innocent. She *was* perfect.

Suddenly, a piercing shard cut through all other noise.

'Millie!'

In that scream was the visceral fear of every parent's worst nightmare—that their child had vanished. It was already too late for her—for them both. In his arms, Millie became heavier as drowsiness swept over her.

He quickened his step down the deserted nature trail as he took her away from everything that she knew.

CHAPTER TWO

S tanding in the dark of a cold November pre-dawn, in a Liverpool cargo dock, they waited. Thirty of West Yorkshire's finest detectives.

It seemed as though the docks held their breath. Misty plumes erupted before the officers with each fresh rasp, and yet, the silence was absolute. The dread of what they would find within the lorry they circled.

The bolt cutters finally did their work and the sundered locks clanged to the floor, jarring the detectives' already fraught nerves with a crash that carried upon the still air. Two rushed forward to help open the lorry. Whatever state the contents were in...they needed immediate attention. Everyone knew it. The same electric charge rushed through them all, waiting for the go ahead.

The truck door creaked open, screaming on its hinges, and an all-too familiar stench of death rolled out over them all. Detective Inspector Daniel Ward of the Homicide and

Major Enquiry Team gagged, no more immune than the rest of them. Behind him, someone vomited.

He had hoped and prayed, godless though he was, that they were wrong. That every piece of intelligence had not led them there, to this...but Ward knew. And as the air thickened around him with the choking cloud of decay in the air...he had to force his eyes to meet what awaited.

Ward's gloved hand moved so very slowly as he brought up the torch. The officers around him did the same, shining light on a scene that no one ever wanted to see.

In the back of that nondescript white lorry, piled high like limp ragdolls, death waited.

'Search for survivors,' Ward said hoarsely, pulling the medical mask over his face. 'Do it now.'

He knew it was hopeless.

He knew they'd find none.

———

Dawn broke, and Ward watched the light inch into his bedroom, brightening to cast the room in the warm, inviting glow of a new day that the dump of a rental flat didn't deserve. It only served to highlight the cracks, the dirty smears, the picked-at holes in the paintwork on the wall, the scuffed, worn carpet. The whole damned state of his life. But it was light that he welcomed nonetheless.

The dead did not haunt him in the day.

Not if he kept busy.

Ward prised himself up, aching from head to foot

from the restless night, and shuffled to the bathroom, where a quick glance in the mirror was all he could stomach. The nightmares plagued him, but they drove him too.

Time to work.

———

'Christ, sir, you look rough as arses.' DC Jake Patterson's voice was too energetic for DI Ward as the young man practically bounced into the canteen of Bradford South Police Station.

Ward groaned. 'Lord, give me strength to deal with you today.' Patterson was the youngest and newest Detective Constable in the HMET department, and with the merciless budget cuts they had suffered year on year, in Ward's opinion, he was a waste of a place far more deserving of another.

'Rough one, huh? Did you stay out on the lash?'

Ward shot a glare at him, raising an eyebrow. '*Lash*? Is that what you kids are calling it these days? No. It's a weekday.' And anyway, he didn't make a habit of drinking. Nor should Patterson on a week night, if the lad knew what was good for him. DCI Kipling might have been short-sighted enough to hire the lad, but the DCI especially wouldn't tolerate being unfit for duty. None of them would. The lad had yet to earn their good graces, especially Ward's.

A smirk lit up the DC's boyish good looks. The young ladies seemed to like the lad's cheek, but Ward just found it damn annoying at this hour of the morning. 'I forget. You kids can drink anyone under the table with your bottled pops.'

'Ready to take you up on that challenge any time, sir. Bet I can down a pint faster than you.'

Ward guffawed. 'Don't run before you can walk, lad. You might be able to keep pace and get up the next day without a sodding hangover, but Metcalfe can down a pint faster than you can blink. But he'll forgive you for not knowing that, being as you're new and all.'

'Toughest beat around,' Patterson said, grinning. 'S'why I joined.'

'Morning all,' piped up a bright voice. Ward's DS Emma Nowak waltzed in, a cloud of perfume accompanying her 'Is he bothering you, sir?' She pursed her lips in mock exasperation at DC Patterson.

'Like a fly buzzing round my head. Can't get rid of him.'

'But a good-looking fly,' quipped Patterson, admiring his reflection in the glass door of the canteen.

Nowak rolled her eyes. 'Christ, are they hiring anyone these days?' She wasn't much older herself at twenty-six to Patterson's twenty-two, but Ward reasoned the difference in mental age was a good decade. Emma had her own place, a fiancé, and the trappings of adult life. Jake lived at home with his mum, who still washed his dirty kegs.

'Brew?' Emma offered.

Ward answered, 'That's the first good thing anyone's said today. Aye, please.'

The DS took off her coat and wandered to the kettle, Patterson in tow like a puppy.

Ward sighed as he considered the morning ahead. It was going to be a hell of a time given who currently sat in the cells waiting for him. He'd left the man stewing overnight on purpose. The scumbag had gone too far this time, yet again.

'There you go, sir,' Patterson said, interrupting Ward's thoughts and plonking a mug on the table, sloshing it everywhere.

'Steady, son! Ta, Emma,' Ward called. She didn't turn, but waved the spoon in his direction in acknowledgement.

Ward blew on the steaming cup and took a gulp—a lesson of the job. You drank your brew straight away in the force or you drank it cold. There was rarely any in-between. And so, he'd developed a mouth rivalling asbestos to take it as hot as it came.

But not like *this*.

'Ugh!' His tongue shrivelled. He spat it out, spraying the table as Patterson dodged out of the way. The lad's cackling was all the clue Ward needed.

'You salted my brew?' he roared, jumping to his feet. 'I'll have you for that! You don't mess with a man's cuppa!'

But Patterson had already legged it, even as Ward's curses hollered after him down the hall.

———

Detective Inspector Daniel Ward regarded the man sat before him with total contempt.

Bogdan Varga lolled in the hard metal chair of the interview room as though it were a lounger in the sunshine. The fluorescent tube lighting was far from that pleasant. Attitude oozed out of the Slovakian man.

He was well kept and still young by any standards, in his mid-thirties like Ward, but his style failed to reflect the high opinion he had of himself. Garish metal chains hung around his neck, his jet-black hair slicked back and gleaming, with the collar of his purple shirt purposefully open to reveal a tangle of coal-coloured chest hair and a pale scar. Perhaps he thought the myriad women he paid to have in his life found it sexy, but it made Daniel Ward want to heave up his breakfast.

Worst of all was his *face*. The lazy grin and sly twinkle in Varga's dark eyes told Ward everything he needed to know.

The arrogant bastard was going to walk free.

Again.

And he knew it.

'Interview concluded at twelve thirteen pm,' Ward ground out, forcing his shaking hands to still. The urge to punch something—or rather, the *someone* sitting in front of him was becoming stronger by the second.

Beside him, DS Scott Metcalfe stood and cleared his throat. He knew what this case had cost—and still cost—Ward. He knew how Ward felt about it.

'Follow me,' Metcalfe said.

The jumpy young lawyer sat next to Varga pushed

out his chair and stood. The junior appointment had been Ward's first clue. Varga hadn't even bothered to engage his own senior legal team, because he knew it hadn't been a credible arrest and was so completely confident that he wouldn't need counsel. Taking his time, the Slovakian sat forward, pushed to his feet, rolled out his shoulders and let out a deep breath. 'When will you stop wasting my time? I am very busy man, *kukláči.*' Slovakian slang for law enforcement.

Ward shot to his feet, sending the metal chair screeching against the floor. 'When you're behind bars for what you've done, you—'

Scott laid a hand on Ward's arm, the older DS's measured, calming presence exactly why Ward had asked him to sit in on the interview. The two had worked together for ten years in the force and under DS Scott Metcalfe's guidance, Ward had fledged from a newbie DS all the way to a DI, replacing Metcalfe's old supervisor.

It had taken a while to get used to the new dynamic as Ward outranked Metcalfe, but it had soon settled into the rapport they now had, based on respect and a mutual dark sense of humour, Metcalfe's calm surety balancing Ward's more impulsive temper.

'Come on. Out. Now,' the DS said to Varga.

Varga smirked and strode to the door. '*Dovidenia,* Detective Ward.'

DS Metcalfe pushed him out of the interview room before Ward's lid blew.

Behind him, Ward smashed his fists against the table

with an almighty crash. The jarring pain sliced through his fury.

Metcalfe slipped back in a moment later. 'It was tenuous at best, mate. You knew that.' He stopped short of calling Ward a damn idiot for jumping the gun. Even though he deserved it. Ward knew he'd been rash.

They had needed Varga to slip up, to admit it was him on the grainy CCTV footage near the brothel, because they had bugger all else on him this time. Varga would never be so stupid. The man smoothly delivered one 'no comment' after the other in response to their questions, peppered with the occasional smirk or raised eyebrow.

'I know!' growled Ward, eyes flashing with rage. It was all part of the larger case they were trying to build against him, which felt impossible at times. One scrap of evidence here, a little more there...and yet nothing to really pin the bastard with. Nothing to hang it all together into anything that would stand up in court. Varga covered his tracks too well. Used others to take the fall.

Metcalfe took it—he knew Ward's anger wasn't aimed at him personally. They *all* wanted to catch Varga. The bastard ran one of the most sophisticated operations in West Yorkshire. People-trafficking was his forte, but drugs, organised crime...you name it and Varga had a finger in the pie. And yet, they just couldn't nail him.

Varga was a pro at protecting himself. Every loose end cut. Every piece of evidence destroyed. They'd managed to put some of his people away over the years, but they had all been mere scapegoats acting upon his orders. They had never managed to get to the kingpin himself with anything hard—that is, when he was in the country, which was rare enough. If Varga was local, it meant something *big* was going down, something that he wouldn't miss.

Last year, the long-running investigation had cost them one of their own—a fresh-faced lad named DC Toby Saunders. He'd joined HMET at twenty-eight, eager to help on one of the biggest trafficking busts of the year. They'd uncovered a lorry full of bodies—victims of Varga's operation—and gone after those behind it. But it had gone so very horribly wrong. They had been compromised. Someone had leaked the sting.

DI Ward had been in charge of the unit. He had mistakenly gone in at the precise moment their radios had gone down—the error proved fatal. The warning to stand down was never heard, nor the urgent shout to abort. Saunders had never stood a chance. First through the door, first to be shot down.

Varga and his men had sought to escape, not to kill— the vital difference that saved the rest of unit, or the operation would have claimed them too. It was too late for Saunders, though. A shot to the neck—a fraction to the side and he would have survived. Instead, the young man had bled out in Ward's arms.

Saunders was dead before the ambulance arrived. As dead as the people they had found in the lorry shortly after. They'd been too late to save any of them.

It had been one of Ward's worst moments to have to

break that news to Toby's fiancée, to his mother. The guilt soaked into him as the man's mother wept. Ward had sworn that day to devote every waking moment to bringing down the bastard responsible. It didn't matter who had pulled the trigger, not really. He'd nick them too, but it was Bogdan Varga he was gunning for. Varga was responsible for *all* of it. Ward would see him pay if it was the last thing he ever did.

'Come on, mate. Priya just collared me.' Metcalfe broke into Ward's thoughts. 'We're wanted in the incident room. A child's gone missing up in Wibsey.'

If anything could push aside Ward's rising fury, it was that. He rubbed his sore knuckles and straightened. There would be plenty of time to deal with Varga later. He had plenty of nights free now to devote to pinning down the slimy bastard, after all.

CHAPTER THREE

At the door to the Incident Room, DS Priya Chakrabarti ushered Ward and Metcalfe inside. Ward gravitated towards DS Nowak as Chakrabarti cleared her throat and the chatter in the room died down. Light streamed through the blinds onto the blank whiteboard, which ominously awaited their input.

'Right. This one could be a big one,' she started, her Yorkshire-Indian drawl carrying across the packed room. 'Young girl, two years old, vanished from Wibsey Park approximately an hour ago—half past eleven. The mother called it in after a search of the area, with no trace of the lass. We don't have pictures to go on yet but she's Caucasian, about two and a half feet tall with short blonde curly hair, blue eyes. Wearing a navy rain coat, red dress, pink leggings, and red Minnie Mouse shoes. There's been no sightings so far. This is a small, busy area —she should have been found by now.'

She paused, letting them take it in, then continued. 'Working theory is that she's fallen into the large ornamental pond up there and drowned. There's no safety barrier and she was unsupervised close to the water for a short amount of time—enough to fall in and succumb.'

Ward softened, his anger for Varga slowly ebbing as he pictured the missing toddler. Wibsey too—his old stomping ground growing up. It had been an age since he had been to the park.

'All available units have been called in to help,' the DS continued. 'The dog units are heading up and we're combing the area. The divers are on the way. If she's not at the bottom of that pond, then we need to make sure not a stone is left unturned.'

'Yes, DS,' came the reply from the two dozen voices— even Ward's, though he outranked her.

'DI Ward, sir, you're Senior Investigating Officer on this one.'

Ward paused. 'What?'

'DCI's orders, sir.'

'Did Kipling say why?'

Priya adjusted her armful of papers. 'No, sir.'

Metcalfe clapped him on the shoulder. 'I think you can figure it out, Daniel.'

Ward gritted his teeth. DCI Martin Kipling had already warned him about the Varga case just a few weeks ago. Going too hard. Risking losing everything they had by jumping the gun. 'If he thinks he can keep me—'

Metcalfe folded his arms. 'With respect, your ego

needs to step aside. A little girl's missing. When we've found her, you can chase Varga all you like, and we'll be there to help.'

He was right. Ward knew it. Varga would have to wait. For now.

CHAPTER FOUR

When DI Ward arrived at the park with the rest of his team in tow, it was a hubbub of activity, police and civilians amongst the rain that cast a dour tone over the place. Ward and the team parked on the south side of the park, closest to where the child had vanished. Ward had expected a police cordon, not...chaos. A couple of PCSOs were the eye in the centre of the maelstrom and they hurried across with relief on their faces as they spotted the cavalry's arrival.

Ward introduced himself, then got to the point. 'What in the bloody hell is this circus?'

'Locals, sir. Got a few more PSCOs and PCs on the park entrances but we don't have the numbers to stop people, not really.'

Ward swore under his breath. 'Right. Let me handle it.' Well-meaning members of the public were the worst. It was as though the more helpful they tried to be, the less helpful they actually were. They only ever really ended up obstructing, however kindly they meant.

'Victoria Foster is going to kill you,' DS Nowak said behind him.

'She'll have a bloody field day.' The last person Ward needed in his ear today was the head of the Crime Scene Investigation team. But she would be. Vociferously.

'Look at the state of this...' he murmured, glancing around the park and shaking his head. As if it wasn't bad enough that they had to find a child who had seemingly vanished in an already busy park, the helpful locals poking in every bush and behind every fence would obliterate any shred of evidence Foster and her team could find.

'Listen up.' Ward's voice was sharp as he turned to his team and started delegating. 'I want you to enforce the cordon. I don't care what you have to do. Get these people *out* of the park *now*. Take details. If they haven't found her with all this racket, then they won't—she isn't here. We need to piece together her last movements. Hold the fort until the dogs and CSI get here. DS Chakrabarti, you're on point for that.'

'Yes, sir.' Priya, grim-faced, gave a nod.

'DS Nowak and I will interview the mother, find out what we can.' He spied her immediately, sitting on a bench, ashen and completely still amongst the throng.

He beckoned to Emma to follow him.

"Scuse me. 'Scuse me. Coming through. *Police!*' Ward barked sharply, when no one moved. That scattered them. 'This park is now an active crime scene.

Thank you for your assistance. We now request you leave the area immediately. Give your details to the detectives at the park exits on your way out. We'll be in touch if you can help any further.'

They dithered.

'Obstructing a police investigation is a criminal offence. I suggest you move *now*.' He glared in turn at the twenty or so people crowding around the girl's distraught mother and a boy—her son, Ward guessed—clinging to the woman's hand.

The people dispersed, though grudgingly, speeding up as some officers jogged over to help. The mother was mid-twenties, Ward thought—though he sometimes figured the older he got, the younger they all looked— with her thick brown hair pulled into a high ponytail and her skin a tell-tale orange from fake tan, a clash against her pink and grey cropped tracksuit.

The boy, about eight or so years old, Ward guessed, looked utterly shellshocked, staring into nothing. On the woman's other side, with an arm protectively around her shoulder, was an older man with soft brown eyes and a flop of dark hair that was just beginning to thin at his temples. *Her father?* Ward wondered.

Ward stopped just short of the bench. 'Stacey?' he asked kindly, as his eagle eyes watched the retreating hordes, knowing they would be eavesdropping as long as they could.

She gave a large sniff, followed by a wet, thick, 'Mmmhmm'. She couldn't look at him.

'I'm Detective Inspector Daniel Ward. I'm leading the search for your daughter. I take it this is your son?'

Stacey nodded.

Ward smiled kindly at the lad, dropping to his knees so he was on a level with the boy. 'What's your name, lad?'

'Kian,' the boy answered, his voice barely louder than a whisper.

Ward smiled sympathetically, and glanced at the man to Stacey's side. 'And you are...?

The man met his eyes. 'Gavin. Gavin Turnbull.'

'Are you family?' Ward looked between the two adults. There didn't seem to be any resemblance, but that was never a surety.

Gavin shook his head dismissively. 'Ah, no. Family friend.'

'If you don't mind, Mr Turnbull, I need to speak to Stacey alone.'

'Of course,' Gavin replied, his voice subdued. He turned to her. 'Are you sure you're going to be alright?'

Stacey sniffed and nodded.

He squeezed her hand and she looked pleadingly at him. 'I'm just round the corner if you need me. It'll be okay. She'll be found. We'll turn over every stone. Kian, you look after your mum, alright?'

'Yes, Gav.' But the boy did not look up from his lap.

Ward nodded at the man as he passed. 'If you wouldn't mind leaving via that exit there, and give your details on the way out, please. Cheers.'

'Of course.'

Ward turned back to Stacey. 'Can you tell me what happened?'

'I already told the lady on the phone.'

'I know, and I'm sorry to have to go over it again but I need you to tell me exactly what happened in as much detail as you remember. It can really help us.'

After a moment, Stacey nodded, her ponytail swishing. In the sunshine and wearing a smile, she would have looked young, bright, fresh, but her puffy eyes were smeared with the black remnants of her mascara, the dark hollows under them a testament to her fear.

'We were playing in the park. I was chatting to Vicky, my friend. Kian was playing in the big kids' section. Millie—' she choked, her voice breaking on her daughter's name, '—was on the trampoline. It was time to go for her nap, so we left. I only realised when we were halfway out that I'd forgotten my bag.'

'Where exactly were you at that point, Stacey?' DS Nowak interrupted. Her approach was softer than DI Ward's—it often helped draw out more details. Ward stayed silent, trusting her. He'd been slowly letting her take the reins. She was a promising new DS to his team, proving with every case her adaptability and competence. *Let's see how she handles this one*, he thought, watching her.

'Umm...there. Sort of between those trees there and the pond.' Stacey pointed, and both DI Ward and DS Nowak turned to look. The park wall lay beyond.

'And then?' DS Nowak prompted.

'I ran straight back over here. I told Kian to watch her.' The boy had ducked his head, his lip quivering, before her grief-stricken ire could turn on him—and the blame that laced her accusing tone falling upon him once more. 'Vicky had my bag. Thank God. She'd seen it right away, and no little scrotes had 'ad their hands in it. I must have been a minute or two, maybe three, tops. I just stopped to thank her and...and then when I got back to Kian...'

Her lip wobbled. 'He'd wandered off, left the bloody stroller in the middle of the path, good thing there wasn't owt worth nicking in that, and she was *gone!*' Fresh tears leaked from her eyes as her shoulders heaved, and she curled into herself, cradling her face in her hands. 'We looked everywhere she might be, all the bushes, but she was gone!'

'Forgive me, but we have to consider the possibility that there may have been an accident,' Ward said. 'Do you think it's possible she fell into the water?'

Stacey's eyes gleamed as she glanced up at him. 'N-no. God no, *please* no.'

That was a 'yes' in Ward's experience. The woman's grief told her it couldn't be possible—because she couldn't cope if it were to be the case.

'And you started searching then?' Ward said.

Stacey's eyes lingered on the dark water, thirty feet away, before she forcibly dragged her attention away. 'Yes,' she said. 'Other people helped too, more and more chipped in...but no one found her. I rung 999. I didn't know what else to do.'

'Did you find anything? Any trace of her, any of her belongings?'

Stacey shook her head, her shaking hand covering her mouth. 'She didn't have anything. Just what she wore.'

'Which was?'

Stacey described the outfit but with no more detail than Ward had already been given. There was nothing more that he could go on. He knew if he glanced around the park, he would not see a tell-tale flash of red. Millie was long gone.

'Does she have any history of wandering off?'

'No, never.'

'Could she have gone to a stranger?'

Stacey gaped as the weight of what Ward suggested sank in. 'M-maybe. She's so friendly. Trusting.' She crumbled again.

Nowak glanced at Ward, who nodded, understanding. Millie's mum needed a softer touch or they'd be here all day, though Ward was already growing impatient. Every second they wasted was another second Millie might come to harm.

Nowak spoke kindly but firmly. 'Stacey, I need to take a few details from you to help our search. May I do that?'

When Stacey did not reply, Nowak pushed on. 'I need to take your prints, Kian's too. I also need a sample of your DNA—a cheek swab will be fine—and an item of Millie's so the dogs can track her scent whilst it's still as fresh as possible. Is this blanket hers?' She gestured to the tatty-edged blanket that lay scrunched in the stroller.

'Yeah,' Stacey croaked. 'That's hers. She can't sleep without it.'

'Please may I take it? For the dogs?'

Stacey nodded.

'I'll do it. You stay here,' Ward murmured. He pulled a pair of latex gloves out of his pocket, before picking the blanket up and carrying it across to the dog team.

'Afternoon,' Ward greeted the dog handler. 'DI Ward. SIO.'

'Afternoon, sir. Where do you need me to start?' Her tone was business-like, the German Shepherd beside her eager to do its service, though it did not stray from her side, completely obedient.

'She went missing around there—' Ward pointed to the spot, '—according to the mother, almost a couple of hours ago now. This should be good for a scent.' He passed her the blanket.

She grimaced and Ward saw the way her attention strayed around the park. She would have calculated the same conclusion that he had—it was a busy park, well used, and the rain would not help. The chance of isolating that tiny trace in a maelstrom of clashing scents was a tall order, even for a highly trained police dog.

'Right. We'll do our best.' She reached out and took the blanket from Ward, who stepped back to give the dog space. 'Let's get to work, Bingo,' she murmured, bending to offer the loyal hound the blanket.

Before he returned to DS Nowak, Ward jogged over to DC Jake Patterson, who was guarding the exit and seeing, at last, the final stragglers out of the now deserted park. 'Good work, DC Patterson.'

'Blimey, did you just give me a compliment, sir? Are you feeling alright?' The young DC grinned at Ward.

Ward growled at the young reprobate, 'Don't be expecting a medal, son.'

'No, sir,' Jake agreed affably. 'A cup of tea will do nicely, thank you.'

'It sure will. Now you've cleared the park, find somewhere for a brew, will you? White coffee for me. DC Shahzad can stand in for you for now. Thanks.' He beckoned the other constable over.

'No! I didn't mean...I was...'

'On your way, Detective Constable. Don't forget DS Nowak's usual too. And DC Shahzad here. What're you taking, Kasim?'

DC Kasim Shahzad grinned. 'Oh, if you're offering, Jake, I'll have a flat white, cheers.'

'I'm not offering,' Patterson grumbled.

'Aye, well off you trot, sunshine. Should be a cafe up near the roundabout somewhere, or try the petrol station.' Ward smirked as Patterson slouched off grumbling unintelligibly, before turning to his colleague. 'Did you get all the details?'

'Yessir,' Shahzad replied. 'Names, telephone numbers, email addresses, life stories.'

Ward snorted. 'Of course. Can't do without those. Any word on CSI?'

'No, sir. DS Chakrabarti said they'd be up shortly, and the divers will be here within the hour to check the, y'know...' The young DS trailed off, glancing at the giant pond behind them, so large it had an island in the middle. It lurked, a dark, ever-present reminder of the most likely place they would find Millie Thompson.

'OK. I'm taking a trip to the victim's house to see what we can get there. Oh—and when Patterson gets back, keep him in line.'

Shahzad rolled his eyes. 'I can only try, sir.'

By the time Ward made it back to DS Nowak, she'd already finished chatting to the boy.

'Kian didn't see anything either, unfortunately.'

'Too busy on that bloody phone! Your dad's to blame for that,' Stacey's face twisted with dislike. 'Won't pay maintenance, doesn't give a shit, but thinks a second-hand iPhone makes up for it all, and now look what it's done.'

'This isn't Kian's fault, Stacey—we don't know what's happened. We'll all be working as hard as we can to find Millie safe and well. Can you show us your usual route home? You said you come here often and little ones are so much smarter than we give them credit for. She might have made her own way home. We've sent a unit already but it never hurts to retrace steps.' Emma's voice—warm, friendly, soothing—had the desired effect.

Stacey turned away from her son and the hostility fell away. 'Yeah. Sure...we always go that way. There's busy roads though. Oh God, if she's out there right now...' The thought galvanised her into action and she sprang to her feet, dragging Kian with her by one arm. She grabbed the stroller, and then released it as though it had stung her—

the fresh realisation that what did she need it for, when the toddler she'd normally push in it was gone?

Nowak gently moved it aside. 'If you don't mind, our Crime Scene Investigators will need to take a look over that—mind if we leave that here for now? It'll be kept safe.'

Stacey nodded, her eyes already on the park exit and the road beyond it. She was off without another word and Ward and Nowak had to jog to catch up. Ward grimaced at the strengthening drizzle that seemed to permeate through every level of his clothing like cool, clammy hands.

As they left, the dog team was disappearing into the wooded area next to the path, while ahead, a contingent of divers arrived, laden with equipment. Seeing them, Stacey wavered, her face going slack with horror as she realised why they were there. They would be dredging that huge pond for the body—*the body*—of her daughter.

'We should go,' prompted Ward.

'I can't...what if...' Stacey gaped, her eyes bulging as she stared desperately at Ward.

'It'll take a while, I'm afraid. Let's retrace your route home for now.' Before Stacey could break, Nowak ushered her past the police tape cordon that had finally been established.

'Stacey?' Just outside the park, the man—Gavin Turnbull, Ward recalled—waited. 'I hope you don't mind me waiting, I wanted to make sure you were alright.' His attention strayed to the two detectives behind Stacey. 'I'm sorry, I didn't do anything wrong, did I?'

'Not at all,' Ward said, glancing more closely over the man. Where Stacey was petite, he was taller and had a natural stoop to him. He was tidy—clean shaven and his hair fresh, his jeans and hoodie unassuming—and otherwise average. None of the warning signs, visual or instinctive, that Ward usually looked for. 'Do you live round here?'

'Yeah, just by the park—Park Square, as it happens. S'why I was able to get here so quickly when we heard the commotion. Everyone knows everyone here—when I heard Stacey's name mentioned, that she was in trouble...' He glanced at Stacey and his face fell further. 'I came right away.'

Ward glanced at Nowak, and she nodded almost imperceptibly.

'What house number is that, sir?' she asked innocuously. 'Just for our records.'

'Oh, er, number twenty.'

Nowak smiled and jotted it down.

'You mentioned 'when *we*' heard the commotion?'

'The neighbours and I. I was out front clearing some stuff in the garden. I was chatting to the Irving's a couple doors down on and off all morning—they were out doing their garden too. News passes fast around here.'

'You weren't working?'

Gavin wrinkled his brow, and narrowed his eyes, though he looked more bemused than annoyed at the peppering of questions. 'Not until later. I work at the school. After school hours.'

'Look, can we go, please?' Stacey asked, edging away. Her hands tangled together.

'Apologies. Of course.'

'Do you want me to come with you?' Gavin asked.

'Yes,' Stacey answered quickly.

'Sure,' said Ward a second later. Stacey would need the support if they didn't find her lass soon.

After a momentary flutter, Stacey collected herself, turned a sharp right outside the park, and headed along Wibsey Park Avenue with Gavin and Kian behind, and Ward and Nowak trailing at the rear. She didn't speak— neither did her son or Gavin—as she charged down the pavement, looking left and right frantically for a sign of her girl. Calling her name until she was hoarse.

Kian, Gavin, Ward, and Nowak looked too, for any trace of red or pink out of place amongst the gardens lining the wide road. They bloomed with flowers of every colour, but most cruelly it was the red ones that stood out, stark like fresh blood spilled against the grey light cast by the rainclouds that seemed to wash every other colour from the detectives' field of vision. By the time they were a mile away on Farfield Avenue, having crossed over several side streets and the main road, Stacey halted outside a row of terraces, the two-up-two-down, age-blackened, Victorian-era terraced houses that were a staple of Bradford's Industrial Era architecture.

Her shoulders crumpled as she sobbed once more, and Kian clung to her in quiet shock, as she realised that Millie, by some miracle, was not sat waiting on the front step after all. Gavin hooked an arm around her.

'Ssh, she'll turn up. It'll be alright,' he murmured, though he glanced around the street all the same, his brows furrowed, as though he hoped to find her in their periphery.

DI Ward cleared his throat. 'Stacey. We'll need to have a look inside, please. In the meantime, DS Nowak, will you ask around?'

'Course, sir. I'll try the neighbours and I'll check at that shop up the road too.' They could only hope that a kindly neighbour might have taken her in. With the growing possibility that she had drowned, or worse still, abducted, growing by the second...it was the ending they needed.

Stacey fumbled with the PVC door, her keys crashing to the floor twice as her hands shook, before she eventually got it open. Kian dashed in, shouting for his sister. Ward's heart sank at his optimism that a toddler, a two-year-old, might have miraculously made it home, and through a locked door.

Stacey gestured for Ward to follow her inside, and he squeezed past the clutter she'd dumped in the hallway, barely managing to shut the door behind him. He followed into a small living room, cluttered with toys that were presumably Millie's—dolls, building blocks, teddies, and a battered old sofa and matching chair. Stacey had just managed to fit a small flatscreen TV by the side of the chimney, where a gigantic, blue, plastic doll's house with a *Frozen* banner obscured the original Victorian fire from view. Ward eyed it for a second—he had no idea what kids did for fun these days, what was trending. Whatever *Frozen* was, he supposed.

Kian did not come back downstairs again, and Stacey shuffled through into the kitchen, cracking open the kitchen window as she did so and followed by Gavin. The tiny house was stifling, bottling up the heat. Ward tugged at his collar, hoping Nowak would be back soon. He didn't have her deftness when it came to these situations. He turned to Stacey, who had slumped in a wooden chair and was clutching a soft toy doll to her chest.

Gavin cleared his throat. 'I'll go see to Kian. Just shout if you need me.'

'Cheers.' DI Ward stirred. He wasn't best equipped for this—not emotionally. 'Stacey. I'll need to take a quick look around—is that okay?' The child wasn't there. They all knew it—but he still had to do his job. See if there were any obvious signs. CSI would be sure to comb over the place too, to find anything that the passing eye could not see.

She nodded dully, stroking the doll's wool hair.

Ward slipped upstairs but there wasn't much to see. There was a small double bedroom with a cot crammed at the foot of the bed. Nappies and piles of Stacey's and Millie's clothes towered on top of an overflowing chest of drawers. A half-eaten bag of babies' rice crackers lay open on the unmade bed.

Across the tiny hall, there was a tiny box room for Kian. Ward hovered outside the door for a moment.

'It'll be alright, Kian. Your mum's not mad at you, she's just worried.' Ward could hear Gavin murmur.

Ward nudged open the door. Bright red football bedding hiding a Kian-sized lump lay atop a single bed. Gavin looked up from where he perched on the side of the bed, his legs bumping against the wall, and smiled sympathetically, his hand on that lump, trying to offer some wordless comfort.

Ward backed out, pulling the door closed once more, and edged into an even smaller bathroom, so old and unloved that the varnish of the wooden panelling had long peeled.

There was barely room to swing a cat upstairs, let alone hide a toddler, between the piles of unfolded clothes and stacks of detritus.

With a sigh, DI Ward retreated downstairs. 'Thank you, Stacey. Now, the next step is that someone will be along from the Crime Scene Investigation team. As DS Nowak said, they'll need to collect DNA samples and prints from you and Kian and take a proper look over the house—a formality. I need you to stay here until they've been, and I promise you, every single resource I have is out there finding your daughter.'

There was a rap at the door. 'Millie!' Stacey shot to her feet and ran to it, wrenching it open. But it wasn't Millie.

'It's just me, DS Nowak,' Emma said kindly. 'May I come in?'

'Have you got her?' Stacey was shaking like a leaf as

the shock started to give way to the trauma of what had happened.

'I'm sorry, Stacey, no, not yet.' the DS stepped inside. 'But we're doing everything we can.' She shook her head at DI Ward who had stuck his head into the small hallway. 'Nothing, sir.'

'Do you mind if we ask a few questions, Stacey?' Ward asked as they entered the lounge again.

Stacey shook her head, not meeting their eyes as she sank onto the single couch.

Ward nodded at Nowak to take the chair, and remained standing by the window, propping himself up on the sill instead. 'Thank you. How long have you lived round here?'

'A few years. Since Kian was a baby so...Seven, I s'pose.'

'Do you have family or friends around here?'

'Yeah. My sister Sammy lives in Woodside.' The estate to the south of Buttershaw.

'Any other family?'

'No. Rest of 'em are in Elland.'

'How come you moved here, then?'

Stacey sniffed, and wiped her nose with her sleeve. 'D'you need to know this?' She glared miserably at him.

Ward shifted. 'We're just trying to build up a picture of your life, and Millie's. It can help our investigation.'

'I was with Kian's dad, but we split up. He were a dickhead. Used to treat me like shit. It got nasty and I left. I just wanted to go somewhere where I wouldn't see him. This seemed like far enough, and with Sammy 'round the corner, I knew I'd be okay.'

'I'm sorry.'

'Don't be,' she muttered darkly. 'The twat's inside now for dealing.'

'Is he Millie's father too?'

'No.' Stacey coloured. 'I din't expect...Millie came along, but her dad wasn't interested. It were never serious.' She straightened, and lifted her chin. 'I manage well enough myself. Don't need them.'

The scratch of Nowak's pen broke the silence.

'What do you do for a living, then?'

'I work down Tesco.'

The house was located a stone's throw from the local supermarket. 'I see—do you get any help with childcare from any friends?' Any other parties who might be interested in the toddler.

'My sister takes them. We manage between us. She has three an' all.'

'Where's your sister today?'

'Working. I can't get hold of her. She works at the tanning bar on Wibsey high street,' Stacey added as Ward opened his mouth to voice the question. 'Dave'll be watching the kids for her. He doesn't work. Lazy good fer nuthin' that he is.'

'Alright, so you manage with your sister. Any other family or friends nearby?'

'The girls from work...they live Buttershaw, Woodside, Wibsey...don't see them much outside work, though. Don't have the time.'

'And Gavin?'

'Yeah. He was a friend of my brother.'

'Was?'

'My brother lives in Manchester now, don't see much of him. They knew each other from school. Gav always looked out for me and Sammy. We stayed in touch.'

'Did you ever have a relationship with him?'

Stacey pulled a face of disgust. 'No! He's like family.'

Ward chuckled. 'We have to ask these things, sorry.'

Stacey relaxed slightly and nodded, pulling a weak smile. Her gaze snagged on the Frozen toy, and that smile faded quickly.

'Does Gavin ever help out with the kids? Kian seems to like him.'

'Oh yeah, every now and then. Think Kian just likes having someone to look up to, you know? He's a lad...I know he'll gimme hell when he hits teenage years.'

'Sounds like you're in good hands for now, then. Is there anyone you know who holds a grudge against you, or might have wanted to take Millie—anything at all you can tell us might be helpful.'

'No. I just don't understand. She were right there, and then...she were gone.' Stacey's lip was beginning to wobble again, as reality crashed down upon her again. She jumped to her feet and paced to the kitchen, leaning over the counter as shuddering sobs took her once more.

'I'm sorry to upset you, Stacey,' Ward said. 'DS Nowak, I need to return to the park to help coordinate our enquiries,' Ward said. 'Would you mind staying until CSI arrive? I'll make sure we have a liaison for them.'

'Yes, sir.'

'Thank you for your time, Stacey. I'll ring you if we have any update.' Yet, instinctively, Ward knew there would be no update. If they had not found the girl already, she was gone...or dead. Trouble was, he hadn't a clue which.

CHAPTER FIVE

Ward returned to the park, where officers were out in force doing door to door enquiries. The park itself was empty, the divers already busy in the pond, and CSI on site, sweeping for evidence. Ward ducked away, not wanting to interrupt them and face the wrath of Victoria Foster, senior investigator for the CSI team. There was no love lost between the two of them.

Instead, he retraced part of the journey and turned onto Reevy Road, heading on the outskirts of the park towards his old school just a little way up the road. He had a closer destination in mind. Park Square. It sounded callous, but he had to consider that the girl had been taken by someone who knew her, or perhaps even her mother was involved. It was not unheard of, after all. Innocent until proven guilty, said the law, but everyone was a suspect until proven otherwise first.

A flat expanse of grass with a dozen or so trees on it separated the square from Reevy Road, which was often used as a fast rat run from Odsal to the top of Buttershaw, avoiding the traffic of Wibsey. Five semis sat in a line. He noted an '8' sign by the first one, and counted along. Turnbull's house was the second to last semi.

Two police officers in fluorescent jackets had already started door to doors at numbers eight and ten. Ward strode up to the other end of the square and started at the corner house, number twenty-four. An older couple were already out in the garden, gawking at the fuss.

Ward flashed his warrant at them. 'Detective Inspector Daniel Ward. I have a few questions, if you don't mind.'

'Aye, we've heard the news about the missing nipper,' said the man from twenty-four.

'Just awful, isn't it,' said his missus, her short silver perm wobbling as she shook her head. 'I hope they find her.'

'I'm here in connection with the disappearance of a two-year-old named Millie Thompson. Blonde hair, and wearing a red dress and shoes, with a navy raincoat perhaps. May I take your names, please?'

'Barry and Joyce Irving,' the man answered. Ward's ears pricked. Irving. The name Turnbull had mentioned.

'Whereabouts were you this morning between eleven and twelve?'

'Well, here. We were tidying the garden and washing the car before the rain came to take a punt at it.' Barry jabbed a thumb at the Vauxhall Astra on the paved drive.

'And then you went inside?'

'Yes, briefly. Came out again just after quarter to

twelve to start again, but we heard the fuss soon after, so we didn't finish.' Ward could see the vehicle was half freshly-cleaned, the passenger side and the wheels still dirt-flecked. A bucket of soapy water stood by, a bright yellow sponge floating within. By the front door behind the car, he could see secateurs and a trowel with some gardening gloves and a kneeling pad.

'Have you seen or heard anything in that time that might help us find Millie Thompson?'

'No, I'm afraid not. We'd have noticed her coming past, from that description, especially if she was on her own—we would have stopped her to make sure she was alright.'

'Right, thank you. I'll try twenty-two.'

'Oh, Doris is deaf as a post, she won't hear you.'

'I still have to try,' Ward said, smiling wryly. 'Do you know the chap who lives at number twenty?' Ward glanced at the house—just another nondescript eighties semi.

'Oh, Gavin?' Joyce answered. 'Gavin's *lovely*. Always so helpful and polite. You know, we could do with more of that. Some of our neighbours aren't so considerate. Sixteen are a nightmare.'

'So, you know Gavin well, then?' Ward prompted, steering her back.

'Oh, well I mean he's lived here a few years, nowhere near as long as us two old codgers though. Quiet chap. No wife or girlfriend—well, or husband, I suppose I should say these days. I don't know why, he seems like such a nice fellow.'

'Was he here this morning?' Ward didn't need to know Joyce Irving's analysis of Turnbull's life in such detail. Not yet—unless their interest fell upon him. He was interested, of a sort. The man lived right next to the park where Millie had vanished, and was a close family friend. If anything, that made him more likely to be a suspect, no matter how nice he appeared to be.

'He was here too. Trimming his hedges—he came round earlier to borrow our clippers. Think he's been at it ever since. Good thing too, they're wild this year,' Joyce sounded indignant that Turnbull had let his hedges go.

'What time did you see him?'

Barry frowned before he answered after a moment of thought. 'Well, he was out here at the same time as us, I mean...I wasn't watching him. But he was there, I'm sure of it, at least since ten.'

'We definitely saw him after,' prompted Joyce. 'Do you remember? He popped his head out and asked what the fuss was, when those police cars drove past with all their noise and lights.'

'What time was that, Mrs Irving?'

'Oh goodness, I didn't check. Around twelve? Just before?'

Ward chewed his lip. Not enough to put Gavin out of the picture, but not enough to put him in it either. The neighbours had seen him, however, in the timeframe needed, to verify his alibi.

'When we heard what had happened from people coming out of the park, he went there straight away.'

'Did that seem unusual to you?'

'No, not here, son,' said Barry. 'Everyone knows everyone.' Ward knew that well enough. Back in his day, it had been the same. The Irving's were from that era of Buttershaw—a true community. 'Turns out he knew the girl and her mum by name,' he said, when we found out who it was. He wanted to go help.'

'Such a nice young man,' Joyce murmured.

'Well, thank you for your time.' Ward handed them a card. 'If you do have any information, please call me at once. I'll pop down to eighteen and—'

'Oh, they're on holiday, they won't be in,' said Joyce quickly. 'They went off to Tenerife for the week.'

'Lucky them,' said Ward, glancing up at the steely sky. 'Thanks, again.'

'We hope you find her,' Joyce called after him as he left.

CHAPTER SIX

Millie Thompson stirred. In the darkness, she curled, her legs folded to her chest, arms wrapped around them, cramped into the small space. She wriggled, and there was some give, but she could not uncurl. She whimpered, and it turned into a muffled screech of annoyance as she kicked out unsuccessfully.

Botbot...

It was not so much a thought as a *need*, gnawing through her urgently. Where was her juice? Mama had her botbot. Where was Mama? She was just right there, in the park...Now it was dark. Millie did not understand.

An ache of hunger added to the thirst.

Want chick nuggs and dip dip...

'Ma...mmmm...ma?' she tried to say, but it was hard. Her voice wouldn't obey her, her tongue thick.

Mama? Kian?

Tired...

Where blankie?

CHAPTER SEVEN

The Incident Room was crammed full. DCI Kipling had called in everyone who could make it to assist in the growing hunt for the missing toddler.

The pond had been dredged, and aside from three shopping trolleys and a plethora of junk, there had been no trace of Millie. A relief, though a double-edged one. They could be reasonably certain she hadn't drowned in it, but it meant they had no other leads to go on.

The dogs had found no trace of her at all in the messy tangle of scents in the park, though their handlers combed the grounds for hours. The search had drawn up nothing. The park was a wide expanse of land without CCTV as a result of the old system being down whilst it was replaced, and the local village—a small hub surrounded by sprawling suburbia—was similarly lacking in anything helpful.

There had been no sightings, no witnesses, and as far as CSI was concerned, the whole crime scene was a disaster. The park had numerous exits, playing fields, paths, bushes, landscaped gardens, even a nature trail, but they had managed to find absolutely nothing they could call *evidence* anywhere.

Ward knew the place like the back of his hand—or, at least, once upon a time, he had. He'd grown up on the Buttershaw Estate. He'd attended the school beside Wibsey Park in his teenage years, though more accurately speaking, the park had been his first home. He hadn't exactly had the cleanest of records at school.

The park was where they'd all gone to doss when they didn't fancy maths, science, or a detention. He hadn't been there—the school, or the park—in a while, though he'd attended crimes in the local area. The park had changed—a new playground, an outdoor gym, the skatepark improved, and the like—and yet it felt the same, only as though he looked at it through a window, from a different time.

The immediate neighbouring properties to the park had been canvassed though there were still plenty more to check. Ward had found nothing on his work at Park Square. The Irving's description of Turnbull's activity that morning seemed to check out, and so gone was an easy suspect there. Doris at number twenty-two was indeed deaf as a post and had chewed his ear off about council tax increases and falling bin collections, and it had taken him a while to escape her. Gavin had not returned home in the time he was there, though Ward would have liked to search his property to be sure, and number eighteen was vacant as the Irving's had told him.

The rest of the square seemed to be out at work from the unsuccessful attempts of the PCSOs to get ahold of anyone, and the couple that were at home had been out at the time and only returned later. No one on the square had any information. Ward hoped that some of the other door-to-doors would turn something up. There were plenty of residential streets around. But for now...

'So, all in all, it's a shit show,' DI Ward said through gritted teeth as he stood in front of the empty board. A picture of Millie, taken from Stacey's front room, now sat right in the middle.

'Pretty much,' said DS Scott Metcalfe, the only one of them who dared to state it out loud without DI Ward tearing him a new arsehole.

'She's probably not had some kind of accident. She would have been found by someone by now.' The room was a sea of nods.

'I checked the hospitals—BRI and Calderdale. They've had no one matching Millie's description in. None of the local GPs within a mile have had a walk-in either,' offered DS Norris.

'Great. Thanks, David. She probably didn't wander off. The roads are busy, so again, she would have been seen, and with the very public nature of that street, it's likely if she was found there...well, we'd know her where-abouts already and we wouldn't all be here.'

Another round of murmured agreement.

'That leaves us with only one logical conclusion,' DI Ward said sombrely, staring around the room at the faces before him, grim with the knowledge of what was coming. 'Millie was abducted.'

Silence.

Abducted. The word hung between them all.

'Does anyone disagree?'

Silence.

Shaking heads.

Downcast eyes.

Ward pursed his lips. He had hoped someone would have a brilliant theory, but this was what they were left with. Somehow, in a busy park, in broad daylight, the girl had been snatched. 'Next steps then?'

DS Nowak stood. 'She's officially a *misper* until we know otherwise. Her image is already in circulation nationwide and we have a television appeal lined up tomorrow if she hasn't been found by then. Press department says that all the local TV and radio stations have agreed to broadcast it in their news throughout tomorrow's cycle, and it's going in all the papers too—digital today and paper tomorrow.'

'Good. In the meantime, I want background checks on every man and his damn dog. The mother, any family members, friends—anyone connected to that child. Do we have any instincts on whether mum could be involved, for example?'

He looked around, but no one spoke up.

'It could be random, or it could be someone who knew her. She went without a fuss, no screaming or crying if someone snatched her...so perhaps she knew them.' He knew some of them would remember the infamous case of Shannon Matthews in 2008. One of the largest searches in police history...and she had been under everyone's noses all along.

The nine-year-old had been the target of a hoax kidnap. She had turned up four weeks later, having been concealed by her mother and mother's boyfriend, in an attempt to fraudulently claim huge reward money for later finding her.

DCI Martin Kipling and DSI Diane McIntyre would have Ward's balls for a screw up like that. They could leave no stone unturned.

Ward continued, 'Mobile records, financial records... anything irregular or suspicious.' The DCs in the room were already taking notes.

'Sir?' DS Chakrabarti spoke up. She was holding out her phone.

'What?'

'I think you need to see this. The *Bradford Herald* has a headline out already...but it's not the one you're asking for.'

Ward marched over to the DS, who handed the phone over to show him.

Ward read the headline—and then a second time, to make sure he'd not mistaken the words.

MISSING CHILD: Possible new victim of CONVICTED CHILD KILLER AND PAEDOPHILE. EXCLUSIVE! Michael Green spotted in the area where toddler was last seen just HOURS before her disappearance. This convicted child killer and paedophile was recently released after serving his sentence, taking on a new identity in Bradford to avoid detection, but local vigilantes have exposed the criminal in a bid to save little Millie from harm. Should this dangerous man ever have been released, should he have been allowed to change his name, and has he already abused and killed again?

'DS Chakrabarti, what the shite is this?' Ward bellowed. 'Who spoke to the press?'

A shaking hand went up at the back. DS Kasim Shahzad. 'Sir, I briefed the press department. Only the official line was given out—we have no idea where this came from.'

'Then find out, immediately! I'm not having this investigation turn into a media frenzy. And how the bloody hell did we not know Michael Green was out of prison and living locally?'

'He's not registered in our area, sir. The article suggests Green changed his name to Stephen Tanner by Deed Poll. Our records show that he's apparently still residing in Derbyshire since leaving prison.' Which meant he'd breached the terms of the Sex Offenders Register by not registering a move with his new local police station.

'Or not. Damn it! We have a missing child, with no other leads, and a known child killer and paedophile is in the same area just before her disappearance, flying under the radar. Coincidence? Not a fucking chance. I want everything there is to know about Michael Green on my desk in the hour, and evidence he did it within two.'

———

Ward sat in his office, the door pushed closed, and afforded himself a sigh as he slumped in his chair and dragged a hand over his face. He felt chilled to the core with the fragmented picture now emerging.

He typed into the search bar: *Michael Green child killer* and clicked through the first few results. All news headlines, sensationalised, posted years ago. The internet had barely existed when Green was put away, but there had been reviews, even twenty years later, with the full story of his heinous crimes, to keep the story selling.

They all told, however, the same, grim tale.

Michael Green was a monster who demonstrated the darkest edges of human nature. Over three decades ago, another little girl had gone missing—and her face now stared solemnly up at Ward from the screen, the image faded, taken from a scan of an old photo. Big brown eyes stared out of a pale round face framed by a bob cut of glossy chestnut hair. Those eyes were almost accusing, the little girl's rosebud mouth pursed with displeasure. How long after that photo had been taken had she died, Ward wondered?

Sarah Farrow was not seen alive again. The three-year-old had been abducted using sweets to bribe her from her parents' side at a park in Nottingham. A huge search had been conducted, but she had vanished. It only came to light after her body was discovered weeks later, poorly hidden out in the woods, what had happened, and how she had come so very close to being saved during the course of the investigation. That catastrophic failure had led to several overhauls in policing when it came to missing children—forces began to work more closely together, and the case fed into the creation of the nation-wide police computer system to help forces from different areas avoid such a tragedy again by pooling data.

Forensics had led back to Michael Green and the monster had been unearthed—a man who had suffered a traumatic childhood filled with abuse, who already had previous convictions for assaulting a prior girlfriend, and several more dropped charges to his name. He had also been reported for attempting to lure another child away from their family in the same manner, whilst on holiday in Cornwall the year before.

Yet, under a different police jurisdiction, he had never been flagged to his local police at the time of Sarah's disappearance. That alone would have made him a prime suspect. Would have maybe given Sarah a chance.

When Michael's flat had eventually been searched, the true depths of his depravity had been discovered. A small, hidden compartment in his wardrobe had served as the place of Sarah Farrow's death. She had died of asphyxiation—allegedly after Michael had hidden her there to answer the door to the police searching the neighbourhood in a routine sweep, unaware of the monster lurking in that neighbourhood. The sock inside that compartment was still soiled with her saliva from where he had gagged her. Scuffs haunted the inside of the box, echoes of where she must have tried desperately to get out.

If they had only searched inside his residence, she

could have been saved—*would* have been saved. Yet it was only after the discovery of Sarah's body in the woods had led painstakingly back to Green, that the police—in the time before the Internet, and digital records—discovered the physical collection of underage pornography in a shoe box in his bedroom. Only then that they had uncovered the local ring of child molesters that Michael Green called his friends. Only then that they had discovered the truth of it all. He—in fact most of them—had never even been on the radar.

Due to the state of Sarah's remains, they had never been able to discern whether or not he had violated her, but the circumstances were more than enough to show intent. Michael Green had maintained ever since that her death had been accidental—even dragged her family through the indignity of an appeal to get his murder conviction downgraded to manslaughter on the basis of diminished responsibility due to abuse he had suffered as a child.

A spike of anger surged in Ward as he read that. He already had a bitter tang in his mouth from the story, but this was a whole new level of cowardice—Green not even having the courage to face up to his crimes as an honest man, with whatever integrity he had left.

Ward knew all about abuse. He, his mother and his brother had all suffered at the hands of his alcoholic father. Ward and his brother didn't speak now. The pain of the past filled the void between them. The man—Ward refused to think of him as a father, for it was a violation of the word—had shattered their family.

Yet that had not destroyed Ward, it had *made* him. Unlike Green, who had hidden behind the excuse like the coward he was, Ward had used it to fuel a desire to protect. He had his father to thank for one thing—the burning cause to join the force so that he could stop others from being harmed in the same way that he, his brother, and his mother had.

Ward scratched his beard and scowled. He needed to turn his thoughts away from the monster that was his father and back to Michael Green. In the end, Green's conviction had been upheld. The man had spent the prime years of his life in jail—but every sentence came to an end. Somehow, without the country realising, Michael Green was loose once more...and now another little girl was missing.

'Sir.' DS Chakrabarti nudged the door open. She was uncharacteristically quiet.

'Are you alright?'

She swallowed. 'No.'

'Jasmine is Millie's age, isn't she?'

'Yes.' Priya's two children were her pride and joy, and she protected them as fiercely as a lioness guarded her cubs. He saw the determined glint in her eye. A mother's instinctive compulsion to protect. Ward knew she would be feeling as though her own children were missing, compelled as only a mother could be to protect her young —and by extension, Millie.

'What have you got?'

'No doubt the same as you.' the DS jerked her head towards Ward's computer screen, where Sarah Farrow stared reproachfully out at them. 'But also, some inter-esting details that won't have made the press.'

'Go on.'

She strode to Ward's desk and dropped a sheaf of papers. 'Green's prison records. Flawless. But due to the nature of his crimes, they deemed him ineligible for parole.'

Ward nodded. That was to be expected.

'He was approved for release after serving his full sentence, however, and here's the thing. They were more than happy to sign him off as fully rehabilitated. How on earth was he considered *safe to be released*?'

Ward sighed. It happened all too often.

Some crimes were too dark to come back from, weren't they? That was a question that Ward asked himself time and again. Were some crimes beyond salva-tion, redemption, forgiveness? How could anyone who had murdered a child—and possibly committed unspeak-able acts to them beforehand—ever be safe for release? Ever *deserve* release?

And yet...Green had served the punishment that the law deemed fit for his crime. They could not hold him any longer, not without good reason.

'How did the press get hold of this? They must have had a tip. Hell, we didn't even know, and he's wandering around in our ward!'

'Shahzad chased it up. The paper won't reveal their source, but they said it was information from a credible informant.'

Ward growled. 'Sons of...'

'I know, sir. I pressed as hard as I could but they're not giving me anything. Not without a warrant.'

'Then get one. I don't care what it takes. One way or another, we're speaking to that source.'

'Yes, sir.'

Ward followed Priya as she left his office, barking at DC Jake Patterson, who lounged with his feet on his desk, thumbing mindlessly on his phone. 'Feet down!'

Patterson practically jumped out of his chair.

'This is a critical investigation—you don't have time to be checking bloody Facebook.'

'I'm on my lunch break!' Jake insisted.

'It's four o'clock.'

'Yeah, and I didn't get any lunch, alright, sir? Busy briefing and searching at the park, remember?'

Ward's stomach rumbled in agreement. He hadn't eaten either, but he ignored it. 'We don't have time for breaks today, DC Patterson. Eat up and get back to it. Every single minute counts.' His mind tortured him, imagining poor little Millie with her blue eyes desperate and filled with tears, bound and gagged in a small, airless space, just like Sarah Farrow had once been.

For once, DC Patterson didn't joke, didn't push him, didn't rise—as though he realised that now was not the time. Instead, he sat up straight, tucked back into his desk and got back to work. 'Oh, sir?'

'What?'

'I might have something. Kasim and I have been digging into some online chatter.'

'Is this that Reddit thing again?'

Patterson tactfully turned away to hide his grin. 'Yes, sir. Reddit, the dark web, and—'

'—Alright, I know, you're smarter than me on this stuff, get to the point.'

'We monitored the usual channels and Shahzad found some other little hidey holes. It turns out we have quite an active community of Hunters in the area, sir.'

'Hunters?'

'That's what they call themselves. They're vigilantes—'

Ward interrupted with a groan. 'Don't tell me. Paedophile hunters.'

'Yup.'

'Right. Go on.'

'It's pretty simple. Nationwide, they hunt down paedophiles—those they suspect, those that have been convicted, anyone they think is a legitimate target. They can get pretty violent too. Some down south were involved in a nasty business last year. Beatings. Assaults. Nothing was proven, charges dropped...sounds like they intimidate anyone they think is involved with anything of that nature. Fancy themselves crime fighters, I suppose, above the law. Their motto is '*justicia fiat*' which is Latin for 'justice is served'.'

'Thugs.'

'Some of them, yes.'

'So how do they connect to Green?'

'From what we can see, they know he was released from prison, and they've been working hard across the country to discover his new identity, since he doesn't go by 'Michael Green' in public anymore, presumably for obvious reasons. A week ago? They did.'

'What does that mean?'

DC Patterson shook his head. 'I'm not sure. But the headline you saw...I reckon the Hunters are the source of it.'

'But you don't think they're done with him, do you?'

'No sir, we don't.'

Ward muttered, 'That's what worries me.' He smoothed his close-cropped beard with a palm. 'Right. Patterson, you and Shahzad are on this. I want usernames, IP addresses, home addresses, whatever you can find out. They're involved in this somehow. If Michael Green abducted Millie and they've been tracking his whereabouts, they may know something useful.'

'Sir,' Priya lifted her head from the desk across from Patterson's. 'You want help from these people?'

'We have a missing child, a known child killer and paedophile, and no other leads yet, DS Chakrabarti. Vigilantes or not—we need all the help we can get.'

CHAPTER EIGHT

Within the hour, DI Ward had what he wanted—everything there was to know about Michael Green, right from the abusive childhood at the mercy of a wife-beating alcoholic father—which sounded uncomfortably too familiar for Ward's liking to his own upbringing—to the chilling details of Sarah Farrow's autopsy.

He clicked out of the browser and stood, unable to look at the dead girl's face again after what he had read, the Pot Noodle he'd just wolfed churning uncomfortably in his stomach. It made for nauseating reading. But he knew one thing for certain. He had to get Michael Green into custody as soon as possible. And first? That meant finding him.

'DS Nowak,' he called across the office the rest of the team shared. 'It's time to go and pay Michael Green a visit.'

'Are we bringing him in, sir?'

'I'd say so, yes.'

'Do we have an address?'

'Aye, thanks to Patterson and Shahzad.'

'Did you hear that?' said DC Patterson. 'That's the third nice thing he's said to me today. Pigs'll be flying!'

'Watch me chuck you out of the window and see if you fly, son,' grumbled Ward. Ward snatched up a set of keys and beckoned to Nowak. 'Come on. Let's see if we can get to him before the Hunters do.'

It was a relief to slip into the unmarked BMW and fire up the air conditioning, perhaps the one redeeming feature the car had. Ward was a fan of cars but only arse-holes drove BMWs, in his opinion. At least it wasn't a Merc. He shoved the stick into gear and slid out of the car park. 'Do we have anything else of note?'

'There's a Facebook group, sir, that DC Shahzad's found, for Hunters in the Bradford and West Yorkshire district. Private, and we've managed to gain access—well, Kasim has. He's already pulled a list of group members and is running them against the database.'

'Do you have it?' Ward accelerated to make the lights before they changed to red, flying across the crossroads before slowing to thirty miles an hour to avoid the speed cameras ahead.

'Yes, sir. I don't recognise anyone on what I've seen so far, but there are almost a thousand members.'

Ward's eyebrow rose. 'A thousand?'

'Yeah. Seems our community has a lot of vigilantes...'

'I doubt that. For every one that acts, there are nine that won't but are happy to cheer along. They'll all probably support the ideology—feel important, like they have a cause—but if push came to shove, I bet plenty of them would be too scared to actually do anything.'

'Still though, sir. A thousand names. That's a big network—and that doesn't include anyone else who's on the dark web, who are far more likely to be hiding.'

'Hmm.' Ward swung a right, turning up Great Horton Road and slowing. The road was packed with the usual crowd of vehicles—an artery in and out of the city, a hub of blended cultures in the densely populated terraced streets that climbed out of Bradford city centre.

'Kasim's concentrating on the group admins. They might be higher up in the organisation—or it might be a dead end. They could just be fans. Anyway, he's seeing if any of them have any priors, where they're located, and if they tally to any members on the dark web and the forums, though that's more difficult as they don't exactly use their real names.'

'Good. And DC Patterson?'

'No doubt hindering at all opportunities,' Nowak answered wryly. 'Shahzad will set him to task, and Metcalfe's there to make sure he's not slacking off.'

'And as long as he's not in charge of the kettle, they'll all be alive when we get back,' Ward said.

'Sorry, sir.' Nowak flushed red and looked out of the window to hide her embarrassment. 'I didn't even think...'

'I didn't think the station coffee could get worse. I was mistaken, apparently. Not your fault. I'll make him pay; don't you worry.' Ward's voice held a smile of grim prophecy.

'Just leave his fingers unbroken, sir. He does need them for his job.'

Ward guffawed at her dark humour. 'I might leave him one or two.'

Having turned off the main road, Ward pulled up by the curb on a street lined with the small back-to-back, age-and-pollution-blackened stone terraces that lined Bradford's hillsides. 'This is us.'

They got out of the car and scanned the street. The hubbub of the main road lay behind them, traffic thundering up and down, and the smell of the exhaust fumes was a welcome mask for the fetid stink emanating from the piles of rubbish bags and overflowing green wheelie bins.

Children played on the street, screeching and shouting, but at the sight of Ward and Nowak, they fled, whooping and hurling choice abuse.

'Charming,' Nowak muttered. 'Where do they learn words like that?'

Ward watched them go with narrowed eyes. 'They're getting a thorough introduction to the English language, it seems.'

'I don't remember my parents teaching me *that* when we came to England. My mum would have killed me if she heard me talking like that. She probably still would,' Nowak chuckled. Born to a Polish father and an Irish mother in Warsaw, her parents had uprooted to England when she was two years old.

DI Ward quickly passed the festering trash, with DS Nowak close behind—holding her breath too, he suspected—before they turned down one of the alleys that lined the back of the houses. It was a warren of small streets, cut throughs and bolt holes that made it an excellent neighbourhood for chasing suspects on foot—if you were the suspects. Plenty of easy ways to lose the police.

This time, however, they weren't looking for a runner, Ward hoped. He strode along the wall-lined and dog-shit-filled alley. Gates and openings leading to dwellings punctuated it. Ward chased the numbers he found occasionally on the poorly maintained houses until he could find one close enough to what he sought, and count manually from there. It was deserted, save for two figures loitering at the other end. He paused to stare at them—they seemed out of place loitering in the neighbourhood, though he had nothing but a honed police instinct to go on.

'Here, sir. One hundred and twenty-seven.' Nowak said, pointing into an ajar gateway, to a tiny garden lined with broken flagstones and a sea of weeds, testament to the long, slow decay of Bradford from its Industrial Era boom to the current poverty-riddled skeleton of a city, long abandoned by Government policy to its fate.

The two strangers seemed to be busy on their phones and had not seen Ward and Nowak. 'What's going on with those two?' Ward wondered to Nowak, then he entered the garden.

Downstairs windows yawned, thin and tall, tired openings betraying nothing of their interior, covered with stained brown curtains. Ward glanced up—the upstairs windows were covered with what looked like bedsheets hung across the window and tacked into place in each top corner. The house was filthy, the yard unattended, but oddly, the front door was sparkling clean as though recently scrubbed, for he saw dirt caked the very top of it, where it had not been washed off. *Strange.*

Green's address was Flat 127B—upstairs. Ward approached the solid door and bent to peer through the letterbox. Empty stairs covered in a threadbare grey carpet and a pile of unopened mail at their foot greeted him. He rapped on the door, the signature police knock echoing.

'I don't think Michael Green is home,' Ward mused, stepping back to look at the upstairs window again. 'But is it a coincidence, or is he running?'

He sucked the inside of his cheek, considering his options, but really, they didn't have any. Not without a warrant. Much as his fingers itched to batter down the door and charge in, they had no probable cause, no evidence...nothing but coincidence. The man was innocent until proven guilty, no matter what had happened in the past.

'Sir...?' Nowak said. The hesitation in her voice had Ward's attention in an instant.

'What is it?'

'The two at the end of the alley, sir. They're coming back this way.'

'Let's have a nice chat, then.'

They exited the yard to find the couple only ten metres away. Upon seeing them, the man bloomed red, right up to the top of his balding pate, whilst the woman glanced down, up, *anywhere* that wasn't at them.

Ward's instincts—a sixth sense that had never steered him wrong and saved his life on more than one occasion—tingled as they drew close. Both sported crisp summer attire—he, chinos and a polo, her a flowery summer dress of cornflower blue to offset her highlighted wavy hair just so—and they were middle aged, Caucasian. They did not seem lost, yet did not seem to fit in, either. *So what on earth are they doing here?*

'Good afternoon,' Ward said pleasantly, planting himself in the middle of the alley so they couldn't pass.

He did not miss the way their eyes flicked over his shoulder at DS Nowak flanking him. And then to the upstairs flat at number one hundred and twenty-seven.

'Good afternoon?' the woman said. Her voice was soft, simpering even, but her brown eyes were cold and calculating, the smile on her lips not reaching all the way to her crow's feet.

He pulled out his warrant card. The smile froze on her face. 'Are you lost?' He affected a polite tone, his expression unreadable as he scanned them for any hint of a threat—but they appeared harmless enough. It only fuelled his questions.

'No, thank you,' she replied sweetly, holding her closed umbrella in the crook of an elbow.

'Hmm.' Ward straightened, taking a deep breath, and his eyes narrowed. 'I just wondered, as I don't usually see folk such as yourselves loitering in the back alleys of Great Horton. What's going on?'

'Nothing, sir,' the man jumped in. He wilted under the withering stare his partner gave him, his jowls wobbling as he seemed to shrink back into himself.

She calls the shots then, Ward noted.

'Neighbourhood Watch, officer,' the woman cut in smoothly.

'Oh, right?' He heard the rustle behind him as DS Nowak pulled out her pocketbook. 'Whereabouts do you live?' At their silence, he cleared his throat. 'Your address, please?'

They exchanged a glance. 'We live in Clayton Heights,' she answered.

Ward raised an eyebrow. 'Bit far to be in your Neighbourhood Watch down here, isn't it? What're your names?'

Another cagey silence, and he saw her jaw twitch with frustration. 'Jillian and Andrew.'

'Jillian and Andrew *what*?'

Jillian looked at him with barely concealed venom, the loathing in her eyes clear. She clearly knew not to withhold details when facing an officer of the law but resented it. At her side, Andrew squirmed, caught between the wrath of his partner—wife, Ward presumed, by the flash of gold on his finger—and a police detective.

She opened her mouth, but no sound came out. 'Do I have to give you my details?' she eventually said, her voice rising in pitch. 'I mean, we haven't done anything wrong. It's not a crime to walk down an alley. We're free people, you know!'

Behind Ward, Nowak cleared her throat and stepped to his side. 'Jillian and Andrew Broadway?'

Jillian's attention snapped to the other detective, like a rabbit caught in the gaze of a hawk, she froze.

'I'll take that as a yes, then.' Ward could hear the satisfaction in Nowak's voice. How had she done it? It took a second before he unworked her logic. *The Facebook group. Of course.* He liked to think he understood how clever and resourceful Nowak was, but the truth of it was that she continually surprised him. And it meant his instinct was dead on. They didn't fit in Great Horton at all—they were there with an ulterior motive.

Andrew Broadway nodded glumly, his eyes falling to the cracked tarmac beneath them, where old cobbles and weeds peeked through.

'You're Hunters.' Ward's voice was matter of fact, his stare hard.

Jillian swallowed, but then she rose before him, straightening out, lifting her chin, and when her reply came, it was filled with defiance. 'Yes. What of it? It's not a crime.'

'Perhaps, perhaps not. Let's not pretend. Why are you here? Or to be clearer, *who* are you waiting for?'

The man flinched but Jillian's mouth thinned. She was clearly unused to being called out.

'It is not a crime to watch tha—that *paedophile monster*,' she burst out, 'to make sure he doesn't hurt anyone else.'

'You're watching Michael Green.' He had to hear it confirmed from the horse's mouth.

'Yes,' she hissed, her mouth turning into a hideous snarl.

'May I remind you that no matter your personal view on the man, he was convicted of his crimes and served the punishment set out by the letter of the law. He's a free man now, Mrs Broadway, and you would do well to remember that. He is entitled to live as a free man—not being surveilled or stalked,' Ward warned. 'Whatever your feelings, you have no right to serve what you feel is justice. That's our job. We look at the evidence, and the courts decide. The *law* decides. We don't get to take that into our own hands.'

Ward could tell from the balls of red on Jillian's cheeks that she was about to launch into a tirade. He held up his hands to forestall her. Cutting a tall figure of darkness against the light of day, it was enough to give her pause. To think about who she spoke to.

When she spoke again there was a cunning glint in her eye, and though her voice held an edge of ragged anger, Jillian Broadway was in full control. 'If you're here, that must mean you suspect him.' He heard the satisfaction in her voice—she must have deduced Michael Green's possible involvement in Millie's disappearance.

'I can't comment on any ongoing investigation or individuals.'

'Obviously, because he's guilty.'

Irritation spiked in Ward, and he gritted his teeth. Good god, the woman was like a dog with a bone. 'We have to pursue any and all lines of enquiry—especially if an individual is at risk.' He glared at them pointedly.

Jillian had the wiliness—and perhaps good sense—to wilt before him. But her eyes glittered with ferocity still. 'How can you protect a *monster* like that?'

'It's our job to protect everyone,' Nowak piped up, her voice as strong as her stance. 'Remember, in our court of law, it is innocent until proven guilty.'

Jillian scoffed. 'He was already proven guilty.'

'And he served his time. He is innocent of any further wrongdoing until proven guilty, Mrs Broadway.'

Jillian jabbed a finger at them. 'You know, that's exactly what's *wrong* with this bloody country! You're all too damn soft. Why do you think we exist? Because we can't trust you or the law to protect us, our children, our loved ones, from these *demons*. We make sure they face justice when you won't.'

'That's enough!' Andrew snapped, stepping before his wife and glaring at her, before turning his attention to the police.

Ward raised an eyebrow, surprised by the man finally finding his balls. But perhaps he could understand why the man had snapped. She was toying with the line, dancing too close to incriminating them in something deeper and darker than anyone could guess.

'Look,' he said, his voice steady and hard. 'A little girl is missing and it's critical we find her. I don't have valuable time to waste speaking to you for loitering about, or arresting you for stalking, or whatever you might think is an appropriate measure of response to an individual you *think* is guilty of something, without any proof. I'm going to ask you to move on now and you'd better go, or I'll do more than take your names.'

Jillian bristled at the threat.

DS Nowak stepped forward. 'Millie Thompson is missing. She's only two.' Her voice was pleading, urgent. 'Wherever she is, whatever has happened, she needs to be back with her mum, safe and well. If you have any information that can help us, please, tell us now, but I urge you not to take matters into your own hands. Trust us to bring Millie home, and if anyone is responsible for her disappearance, they'll be punished appropriately.'

Jillian still brimmed with righteous fury, but she held Emma's gaze, and nodded jerkily. She swallowed. And glanced at the ground. 'We've been monitoring this address twenty-four hours. Not us personally,' she added quickly. 'I mean...'

'The Hunters.'

'Yes. He's not been here in that time.'

Ward shared a glance with Nowak, the message passing wordlessly between them. If it was true that Michael Green hadn't been seen at his home address for twenty-four hours, it meant, at the very least, that Millie Thompson couldn't be inside flat 127B.

'Thank you,' said Ward, more than a tad grudgingly.

'Please,' Nowak urged. 'Contact us if you have any further information.' She fished out a card with her direct line on it, and gave it to Jillian. 'Your information might be incredibly valuable in helping us bring that little girl home. Can I take a phone number—just in case we need to chat?'

Jillian's anger was softening now, as Emma's focus on the missing toddler pulled Jillian's away from Michael Green. She nodded, and Emma jotted down a telephone number on the back of her hand. Ward wondered if the woman had children of her own. He pitied them if she did, based on the woman and the spineless man he had just met.

'Now go,' said Ward, prompting Andrew to jump again. God, judging by his wife's short leash, Ward almost pitied the man. *He probably doesn't even get to shit in peace...*

He waited as they turned and walked away, slowly at first, and then more quickly, with Andrew giving them a single backward glance.

'Good work,' Ward said with a sigh of relief as the couple rounded the corner and passed out of sight.

'Luck, really,' Emma mused, glancing back towards Michael's flat. 'I'd started reading through the names in alphabetical surname order...I'd only just reached the C's.'

'Hmm, well I'll take it. That got us valuable information. The Hunters clearly know all about Michael Green, and they're watching him—or worse, hunting him.'

'We have to find him first.'

'Aye. It'd be in his best interests if we did. Anger aside, those two seemed tame enough, but the same can't be said for all the Hunters. They'd just better stay out of our way.' Ward's voice fell to a growl. 'I'm not having them balls up our investigation with their witch hunts.'

'Yes, sir, but remember, they could also be an incredible asset. They know about Michael—they might help us find him. Look at the snippet of information we received there. I'll still put the warrant in so we can search the place, but we now know there's little chance of Millie being in that flat, if what they said is true.'

'If,' Ward highlighted ominously.

'We can't trust them.' Emma sighed, as they began trudging to the car.

'We can't trust anyone.'

CHAPTER NINE

Back in the car with the engine fired up, Ward rang the station.

'Get me DC Shahzad.' He waited. 'Hi, Kasim.'

'What's up, sir?' Kasim's voice echoed around the car on the Bluetooth, as Ward pulled back onto Great Horton Road and turned the car down the hill, back towards the station for the end of an exhausting—and fruitless—shift.

'What time do you clock off?'

'Not 'til eight tonight, sir.'

'Good. Get up to Great Horton, will you?' He gave Michael Green's address to the DC. 'The Hunters are already closing in on Michael. We have to make sure we find him first.' The threat of what Michael faced if the Hunters uncovered him before the police did didn't bear thinking about. 'I want you to watch the flat. If he comes back, bring him in. If he doesn't...well. See who comes by. There are some sore thumbs wandering around.'

'Yes, sir.'

'Any other updates, by the way?'

'No, sir. DS Metcalfe sent a few of us out to check on Green's haunts as identified by the Hunters, but so far... nothing. It's like he's disappeared.'

Ward's heart sank. Innocent men rarely disappeared. 'Alright. Thanks, Kasim.'

'Bye, sir.'

Ward drove, with Nowak in companionable silence. The sun was still high above the clouds even though rush hour was over. The street was busy, the many shops hawking fresh exotic fruits, clothes, jewellery, and all the wares of the bustling Asian and Eastern European communities, still open with their customers filling the pavements, clogging the road with vehicles. On the surface of it, it was Bradford as it always was—brightly multicultural, gloriously bustling with life, continuing in the same day-to-day humdrum it always did. Life didn't stop, even when a little girl was missing.

Yet, lit by the unforgiving sun peeking beneath a fissure in the clouds above, the chink shining for a bare minute before the sky closed off once more, it appeared there were still shadows to hide in. Every person who seemed to glance at the unmarked police car as it passed —some with hard eyes, inscrutable faces. Were they Hunters too? Could they have snatched Millie? *You're getting paranoid, man.*

But how many Hunters *were* there in his city, hidden behind ordinary faces, watching, waiting, stalking their prey? There were more layers of shadow to this city than even he realised, at times. And he did not like that thought.

––––––

Ward pulled up outside Gavin Turnbull's house on Park Square once more. It was quiet now, and crowded with cars. Folks were home inside for the evening, and with the ever-present on-off rain that week, it was not a night to be striking up barbecues in the back gardens.

The office had called ahead, but not by much, only to check that Gavin Turnbull was once more home and available for an informal chat. Daniel had the niggle and he had to see it addressed. The alibis appeared to check out, but he had to have it on file from the horse's mouth itself.

Turnbull opened the door a few seconds after the knock. 'Hi, come in.' He stood aside to let them past, glancing up at the darkening sky. 'In here,' he added, pointing to a tidy living room.

As Ward entered the living room, he took a sly glance into the next room, a kitchen diner, and the extent of the downstairs. All simple and clean, though dated. The living room held a sofa and chair, a TV in the corner, and a TV cabinet stuffed with DVDs. The cream walls and brown carpet were bare, hardly a hint of soul or person- ality in the place. Not that Ward could judge with his current arrangements, he supposed.

'What can I help you with?' Turnbull didn't offer them a drink, Ward noted, as many often did, but it had been a long day, and perhaps Turnbull wasn't feeling too sociable. Ward could understand that. 'Please, sit.'

'We just have a few questions to ask you, if that's alright,' Ward said as he eased into a grey armchair. Beside him, Nowak perched on the edge of the sofa, and Turnbull sat on the arm furthest from them both.

'Sure.' Turnbull looked tired, drained.

'Where were you between eleven and twelve today?'

Turnbull looked taken aback by the question, and he paused before he replied, as though he realised the weight of what they asked. 'I...uh...I was here,' he said quickly. 'I was working on the garden this morning—it's grown a little wild, and Mrs Irving keeps complaining. I thought it would be easier to just prune the bushes, to keep on her good side.' He smiled, but it was more of a grimace.

'She can be a little bit of a battle-axe when she wants, you see. I borrowed her clippers, as mine broke a few weeks ago, and I'd forgotten to get some more, to be honest. I was out there from probably...ten-ish until I think just before twelve? I heard the news from the park and left straight away. I think that was just before twelve.'

'Thank you. And how do you know Stacey Thompson and her children?'

Turnbull shifted on the sofa arm, leaning his fore-arms on his thighs and loosely lacing his fingers together. 'It's been years, to be honest. I used to knock around with her brother at school. I don't see much of him anymore, since he moved away, but I've always been pretty close with Sammy and Stacey.'

'Where are you from? Your accent sounds southern?'

'Nottinghamshire. I don't remember it much, though. Moved up here when I was a kid.'

'With your parents?'

A shadow crossed his face. 'Yes.'

'Are they still local?'

'They passed away a lot of years ago,' Turnbull said, with a pained smile.

'I'm sorry.'

'It's fine. It was a long time ago—but you never really get over losing your mum and dad.'

Ward recognised that hurt. 'How old were you?'

'Hmm, about eighteen when mum went. Dad, a few years later. It was hard,' Turnbull acknowledged, 'but I've made a life for myself of sorts now.'

'And you don't have any other family?'

'No. We didn't really have a big one, and they were all down south. Since my folks died, I don't really know where to find anyone. I was really grateful for Stacey's mum. She took me in, you see. She knew things were tough at home, and she made sure I always had somewhere to go if I needed it.'

'So they're like your family now?'

'Aye. I suppose so. Closest thing I have to one, anyway.'

Ward shifted. 'Well, thank you for your time. I appreciate your help.' All through their conversation, he'd been listening, ever so carefully, for anything that might hint Millie was there—it would have been so nice and neat. The family friend who lived right next to the park where she was last sighted, the culprit. But it was silent aside from their conversation.

'Do you mind if we take a look around?' he asked, just on the off chance. It was cheeky—he didn't have a warrant—but if Turnbull let him, then he could at least put the doubt to bed.

Turnbull's face tightened. After a moment of pause, clearly uncomfortable with the thought, he said, grimacing, 'Sure—I mean, I haven't tidied, you might find some boxers on the floor in my room.'

Ward chuckled. 'We don't judge.' Ward certainly couldn't. Half his meagre belongings were still in boxes or suitcases, half-unpacked in his flat.

Turnbull followed Ward upstairs, leaving Nowak in the living room. Two double bedrooms—complete with a small pile of mucky washing on the floor in the master room—and a bathroom. A loft hatch.

Ward glanced at it pointedly. 'Mind if I...?'

Turnbull shrugged, and pushed open the loft hatch, grabbing a pole sitting in the corner of the landing and handing it to Ward, who tugged down the ladder. He poked his head up.

'Light switch by your head on the right,' Turnbull called up.

Ward flicked the light on. A loft sparsely boarded out with a few bin bags and cardboard boxes, and the smell of damp. But, otherwise empty. He climbed down and retreated downstairs whilst Turnbull reset the ladders and closed off the loft, taking a glance into the back room, a kitchen diner, and the cupboard under the stairs.

'Do you have any out buildings?'

Turnbull grimaced. 'There's a shed out there, but I don't have the key, sorry. It's the landlord's.'

He showed Ward outside nonetheless, to a small back garden covered over by the canopy of trees from the park. Ward eyed the bolted and padlocked back gate briefly, and peered into the spiderweb-shrouded window all the same. It was silent and gloomy within, and the door didn't look like it had been touched in a long while from the detritus and spider webs sealing it shut.

'Thank you. You've been very helpful,' Ward said, fixing Turnbull with a polite smile. There was nothing there. No sign of Millie Thompson. *Damn it.*

———

Ward clocked off reluctantly at the station. He'd checked there were no major updates—a double-edged knife. He would have had to finish for the day regardless, and he hated leaving loose ends, but at the same time...some news would have been better than the yawning silence of nothing.

The Big Board still lay relatively empty. Depressingly empty. The minutes ticked by. The crucial minutes adding up to hours that marked the likelihood of Millie being found alive diminishing with each moment that passed.

CHAPTER TEN

D aniel Ward returned home—not that it was any sort of a home, really. The first-floor rental flat was empty and lifeless—a vacuum of the soul. Across the city, his hopefully soon to be ex-wife resided at their former shared home. A quaint three-bed post-war semi in a good neighbourhood—where they'd planned to lay down roots, start a family, and have the normal life that society told everyone to sign up for. Marriage, two point four children, respectable jobs.

'Join the force, get a divorce,' was the slogan. Daniel laughed dryly. It had worked for him.

Daniel remembered what his cynical father had once told him. The only certain stages in life were birth, life, taxes, and death. At the spike of hatred, he turned his thoughts away from that man at once. His father was not a man, but a demon who overshadowed his every move.

His father was the reason he'd joined the police. That was how he and Michael Green were different. They shared an abusive, alcoholic father who'd beat their mothers and terrorised them as children. But that had made Daniel determined to protect, serve, prevent...not sink into a pit of despair and vile vices the way Michael Green had. Their pasts didn't make Daniel Ward and Michael Green blameless products of circumstance. They were responsible for their choices, how they chose to act in the face of adversity. Michael Green had crumbled. And Daniel Ward had...risen from the clutches of that darkness. Or tried to.

Yet, had Daniel really ended up any different to his father, in the end? He'd pushed Katherine away with a different sort of abuse, if he really considered it harshly. He'd abandoned her. He'd put his cause, his job, at the forefront of everything. It consumed him—and the ashes of their marriage had burned in its wake. Anger stirred—at himself and at her as a part of him bucked at the blame staring him down like the barrel of a gun. Blame that he couldn't bear to face, so raw still was all the pain.

Katherine hadn't cared enough to help him, because God it had been tough fighting all by himself, for justice, for salvation—for himself and others—working all hours, giving everything to make sure others didn't have to suffer pain like he had. She hadn't understood. She'd resented him for it—and how dare she?

It wasn't as though *she* were blameless. Over the years, her controlling nature had tightened around every choice he'd made. At first, innocuous things—not letting him pick a new furnishing, or organising their schedule to her needs—but he had realised upon leaving their

marriage for good just how much she'd starved and strangled him of everything and everyone he had loved.

One by one, all his friends, cut off without him ever
realising, until he only ever socialised superficially in her
circles with the people she preferred—and lord knew, she
hated anyone in his life who brought up memories of his
less than middle-class upbringing on a former council
estate. Her snobbery had cost him his social support, and
never allowed him to try and bridge the void with his
estranged brother, Sam. *Another* product of his past that
she disliked. Ward had started texting Sam again weekly
now, but he hardly ever got a reply. It stung, but he
understood all the reasons why.

It had also cost his hobbies. Ward hadn't played
amateur rugby in years, his once weekly release, or gone
to watch the Bradford Bulls play. Long gone were the
days he'd held a season ticket for them at Odsal. He
couldn't remember the last time he'd been for drinks and
snooker with the lads, either. Not that he spoke to any of
those lads these days. It made for a lonely existence—one
that he avoided acknowledging by working as much as he
could.

He was mad at her for it all, but equally frustrated at
himself for not seeing any of it as it happened. Daniel
growled aloud to the empty room. It was stiflingly hot.
The south-facing windows had soaked up an insane
amount of warmth. The sun balefully glared in, still too
high above the hillside to offer any respite. It was an oven,
cooking him alive. He supposed he ought to be grateful at
least that it wasn't raining anymore. Outside, the rolling

green hills of the outskirts of Bradford gave way to wild, windswept moors.

He stripped down and threw on a pair of shorts, and left his torso blank. The scars of his career stared back at him from the mirror—stab wounds and blemishes, each with their own story. Opening the windows onto the sun's fading rays, he sank onto the couch.

His unconscious mind waited for the dog to bound up as he always did, but Oliver wasn't there, only his ghost, a missing hole by Ward's side. Ward's anger at Katherine grew for that. She wouldn't even let him have the dog that she hated, just because Daniel loved him. She was punishing Daniel with everything—keeping the dog, the house, holding it all like a chain around his neck, dragging him down into the dark depths. She would control him, even after they'd split.

He eyed the bottle of scotch on the counter in the corner of the open plan room that the estate agent had had the gall to refer to as a 'kitchen'. Half-drunk already, the lid not fully screwed back on from the previous night. The only way to take the edge off any of it was to drink to forget, even though he knew it didn't help.

It only made him feel worse. More like his father than he wanted to be. He knew he shouldn't, but he needed the release—his one vice. He had nothing else...Thinking of his father had awoken the need. He wrestled the urge down, knowing it would return. Before he could change his mind, he strode over to the bottle, opened it and poured it down the sink.

He pulled out a bottle of lime cordial instead. Not quite the same.

He didn't even have a bed yet, the old mattress from the spare bed at their former home the only thing he'd persuaded *her* to part with. It saw him sleeping far too close to the carpet left by the previous tenant, which stunk of weed, piss, and smoke. He'd had to take the flat—it was that or sleep in his car. But he regretted it now. Still, only for six months, until he got back on his feet, until they sold the house. Then, he'd start afresh, he hoped. Until then, he'd be wiping his feet on the way out.

Anger fuelled him once more as he remembered the heated argument—trying to separate out some things so he could start up again, and then the dog—how well *that* didn't work out for him. Daniel grabbed a chipped mug. He hadn't bought anything yet, having only recently moved in. He hadn't had time to shop. He didn't like it. He didn't want to. However, if he was being honest with himself, it was more because he didn't feel like this was home—so why settle in? It wasn't like he was expecting any company there. Ever.

The mug had been one of the few things she'd made him take—and he only needed one, he reasoned. It wasn't one of the good ones of course, but one she'd always hated that said '*dickhead*' on the bottom so that when he drunk from it, folks got a titter. Ward supposed it was fitting. Perhaps he was a dickhead. But she was still a cow.

And somehow, despite trying to do his best for everyone—for his city, for his force, for his wife, he'd ended up alone and angry in a shitty little flat in south

Bradford with a second-hand couch, an old mattress, and an empty bottle of scotch to his name. He could have laughed at the irony of the contrast between his image at work—competent, ranked, respected to a point—and the image of him at home, standing in a shithole of a flat, drinking cordial out of a chipped 'dickhead' mug.

It was only when he stumbled out into the hallway later on his way to the bedroom—half drunk from exhaustion—that he spotted the envelope on the floor. Crumpled, where it had been pushed under the door. His eyebrows crumpled in a frown as he processed that sluggishly. Whoever had put it there had been inside the building. He'd never heard a peep from any of the neighbours. Not one had welcomed him there in the past few weeks—not that he really cared. It was easier to be left alone, and right then, he was even less of a people person than normal, given his personal circumstances.

The post boxes were downstairs, so it definitely wasn't a bill. What did one of his neighbours want? Curiosity had him reaching for it, picking it up, turning it back and forth. A plain brown envelope, letter size, not named or addressed. A few small, loose pieces of paper inside, by the feel of it. He tore it open to rifle through the contents, already walking to the kitchen, ready to throw it in the bin. Whatever spam someone had posted him, he wasn't interested.

Daniel Ward pulled out a stack of polaroid photos.

And halted dead in his tracks.

The room was stifling. But all of a sudden, he felt cold to the core.

A photo of his front door—taken from *inside* the security-protected building. The door under which the envelope had been pushed.

The next—a photo of his pride and joy, his white VW Golf, parked, the registration clear. It wasn't parked outside the flat. It wasn't parked at work, even. It was parked outside Katherine's—his old home. And from the peeking suitcase in the corner of the shot, Ward knew exactly when it had been taken. The day he had left their marital home for good.

His fingers shook—not from the tiredness, but with adrenaline rushing through him as he turned to the last photo. It was of *him*. Taken at a terrible angle and blurry in the car park outside—but him. Last week, as the sun rose on his return home from an overnight shift. He'd had to change out of his work attire that night after it had been covered by a spewing drunkard, and as a result had to sport a hideous orange Hawaiian shirt left over in Scott Metcalfe's locker from a staff Christmas party.

Ward gaped.

All thoughts of Katherine and his anger toward her were gone. He rushed to the window, looking out on the car park below, the other apartment blocks close by. Deserted of people. Empty cars parked like silent sentinels. None he did not recognise—he was careful in those first few weeks, with his copper's nose, to keep watch on his surroundings. But, in an unfamiliar neighbourhood, far from his usual beats, he could not vouch for every single person he had seen. Or not seen.

Unease curled through him.

There was only one person able to get this close without him realising.

Ward closed every window, then, no matter that it was so hot he was already despicably sweaty, and double checked the door was locked and bolted.

Bogdan Varga.

The envelope—and its contents—were a threat.

And if it came from the crime lord, it was a serious one.

Ward leaned against the wall, flicking through the photos again under the dim light of the piss-poor energy-saving bulb dangling above him that he'd not yet got around to replacing.

There was no mistaking the content of the photos. Varga shouldn't have known where Ward lived. Ever. However, the man was following Ward—and he *wanted* Ward to know. Ward knew exactly what Varga was trying to say. *Stay away.* That if Ward got too close, pushed too far, didn't back down...There would be a price to pay.

Ward's hands still shook—but not with the fear that Varga had probably sought to provoke. It was fury. That the slimy, arrogant, cruel bastard thought he had the power to intimidate the police into not throwing every-thing they had at him. That Varga thought he had the power to intimidate *Ward*.

Daniel wasn't about to let him go so easily. It would take more than a well-targeted threat to get him to back down. The man was responsible for almost all the people trafficking into the county, from brothels to slave labour to child exploitation—Ward thought again of that lorry of nightmares—and no doubt more that he didn't even know the half of.

He paced to the kitchen, a captive beast checking for weaknesses in its cage—checking that everything was shut and locked. Not that it would stop Varga. Ward wasn't so naive. But if the Slovakian came calling, Ward would be sure to hear Varga's men smashing their way through a window or the door.

He gave the photos one last glance before tossing them in a kitchen drawer on top of bills, spare keys, batteries and other junk. His heart thundered as he shut the drawer, retreated to the bedroom and prepared himself for another sleepless night.

Who would have dominance over his waking night-mare—Bogdan Varga or Michael Green?

———

The nightmares gave him no peace again that night.

The creak of that lorry door opening was forever embedded in his deepest, darkest torment. Time seemed to slow, stretching out over a minute as the full horror of the lorry's contents were revealed. Piles of bodies—people who had once been living, breathing humans.

They were arranged haphazardly, almost like rag dolls, across the container floor, where broken crates littered amongst their bodies. Their mouths were wide in horror, their bloodshot eyes still open in endless stares that chilled DI Ward to the bone.

Men.

Women.

Children.

They had suffocated to death in that lorry—it had been an airless void that became their tomb. He could see the agony on their faces, did not need to try to imagine the fear and pain they had endured in their final moments—for it clutched viscerally at him too, like a ghostly imprint imparted from their very souls.

A clutch of despair had stilled his lungs, threatening to take him to his knees, at the horrifying scene before him.

CSI were already on hand—they'd been called to photograph the lorry, the contents, but...not this. Not bodies. They had expected to find Varga's human ship-ment alive, if not all well. There were ambulances waiting with kind-faced paramedics on call and ready to attend, with stacks of blankets—foil and fabric—emergency rehy-dration and food sachets, medical care. But, they would not be treating anyone. They would be ferrying to the morgue.

DS Emma Nowak had pulled open the door, with DC David Norris on the opposing leaf. She turned to face him, her face slack, the desolation in her gaze finding a mirror in his own. Her latex-gloved hands rose to her face. Norris stared at the lorry's contents, steely-eyed. Middle-aged, it wasn't his first rodeo, but even so...one needed a stomach of iron to not baulk at what they faced. For DS Nowak...it was her first major enquiry. The young woman was fresh out of her constable rank.

Complete silence fell across the tarmac until DCI Martin Kipling's voice cut across them all. He rarely got involved in field work, but this was the biggest case on the Homicide and Major Enquiry Team's books. He was heading up on DSI Diane McIntyre's orders—specifically, no fuck ups—Ward could still hear her, yelling it at them. And this time Ward was glad to let him, in the face of a lorry full of dead bodies.

'Paramedics here now. Divisional Surgeon needed to confirm end of life. CSI to the front—Nowak, Norris, out of the way. Quick forensics photographs of the scene as untouched, and then we start pulling them out. I want everyone in full PPE. Not a drop of forensics to contaminate this. Bag them, label them, and get them out of here—with respect, understand?'

A murmur of assent came from all gathered there.

'These poor people need to be treated with dignity, even now.'

Ward suspected it was more dignity than they had been treated with on their doomed journey to the United Kingdom.

White lit up the night as the bright flashes of CSI's cameras went off, capturing in macabre glory forevermore, the latest victims of Bogdan Varga.

The roaring in Ward's ears intensified.

What fresh hell had they uncovered?

CHAPTER ELEVEN

The man's finger idly lifted a curl of Millie Thompson's hair as she slept. No one would find her. He'd made sure of that. It had taken a lot of work to orchestrate, but it would be worth all the pay off. The time he spent with her, before he had finished with her, would be worth it.

For now, he'd given her some comforts. A place to sleep, crude though it was. Toys. Nappies. It made things easier, in the sparing moments she awoke, though drowsy even then from the pills he crushed into her milk, and crying for her mama.

She lay curled into a ball on the mattress with the duvet half over her, her legs folded to her chest, and arms wrapped around them. Oh, if she had known how sweetly close it was to how she had come into the world, a foetus tucked in her mother's womb, uncurled from that same stasis to arrive bloody and screaming into life.

He held a teddy in his hands, as he watched her

sleep, sat next to her on the floor. It was a simple item—a brown, furry bear, a nondescript staple of so many children's homes. It took him back to another time, and another place. Another young girl, too, much like Millie.

Longing stirred within him.

It had been so long.

Too long.

CHAPTER TWELVE

THURSDAY

Ward's nightmare shattered as his phone rang. Ward scrambled to find it in the dark. *DC Kasim Shahzad* flashed up on screen, next to the time. Just after midnight.

'Yes?' Ward said hoarsely and cleared his throat.

'Sorry, sir. I've taken Michael Green into custody.'

'What? Seriously?'

'Yes, sir.'

Ward exhaled slowly. 'I'm on my way.'

Bogdan Varga haunted DI Ward's steps all the way to work, as unease concentrated by his nightmare warred with the urgency of Shahzad's development. Ward triple checked he'd locked his apartment door. Scoped out his car before he approached it. Did a quick sweep for a tracker or a bug...and all the way, chastised himself for letting the criminal rattle him. It was exactly what Varga would have wanted.

Then, he ducked into the car and raced off, hoping

that Varga would leave it at that. That whilst they investigated Millie Thompson's disappearance, Varga would take it as a sign Ward had backed off.

He arrived to the changing of shifts as tired officers who had patrolled all of Wednesday night up in Wibsey village as they searched fruitlessly for Millie Thompson before handing over to the Thursday early morning shift.

'Morning sir. Sorry about the late-night call,' DC Kasim Shahzad said, smiling tiredly at his senior officer.

'You were supposed to clock off at eight, DC. What happened?' It was now approaching one in the morning.

'I know, but I had some hours to make up—and a hunch. I thought I'd stay just a little while longer. I was watching the property, saw someone enter Green's yard just before eleven o'clock. Recognised him from the mug shot, sir.' The pride on Kasim's face was evident. 'He's shaved his beard off, like, and he had a baseball cap on, and a black eye—for a second, I wasn't sure, but turns out he wasn't completely upset to see me.'

'How d'you figure that?'

'Practically begged me to put the cuffs on him,' Kasim's face fell, trouble creeping into his triumph. 'He's afraid, sir. Says someone's after him. I'm not sure if he's our guy—I mean the story the paper told fits neat, like, but...I don't know. Something's not right.'

'The Hunters have him running scared, that's what's not right,' growled Ward. 'They're running interference. It's like they're the bloody police and we're nothing more than bodies getting in *their* way. And we can't do a damn thing about it.'

Ward straightened his jacket and set off down to custody with Shahzad in tow to interview Michael Green.

———

Green took an age to settle himself into the cold, hard chair. The baseball cap gone, he had no place to hide, and it showed in his cowed posture. Before Ward sat a broken man—or one who acted broken to excellent effect. Ward couldn't be sure which.

He was still Michael Green, recognisable from the mugshots in the press decades ago, but his hair had thinned until his scalp was visible through the sparse sandy strands. His warm skin had paled to grey and wrinkles lined his aging face. Deep grooves of grief and time carved into his visage. He was no longer strong with youth, but thin and wiry, his clothes slack with the decay of his form. A black eye bloomed in stark contrast against his waxy pallor, angry and purple, already fading to yellow-green around the edges.

'Now then, Michael. How'd you get that?' Ward asked, cocking his head to admire it. He suspected the answer. Regardless of what the man might or might not have done, if the Hunters had overstepped the mark, Ward would be the one hunting them.

Green set his jaw and did not answer.

'Interview commenced at 1:07am. Present are DI Daniel Ward, DS Kasim Shahzad and Mr Michael Green.'

Michael eyed him darkly, his black eyes darting to Kasim too. He was right to be wary of police, Ward supposed. They hadn't exactly had a storming relationship over the decades.

'Michael,' Ward said, leaning forward in his chair and clasping his hands together on the table. 'Can you tell me where you were yesterday morning between nine and eleven thirty A.M.?'

'Out.' Michael's curt tone gave nothing away.

'Where?'

Michael squirmed, his hands writhing together. Hesitated. 'At a friend's.'

'Which friend and where?' Ward probed. Beside him, Kasim started jotted notes, though his pen moved slower than DS Nowak, who Ward was far more used to teaming up with.

'I—I can't say.'

'Can't, or won't?'

'I don't want to drag anyone else into this.'

'Into what?' Ward cocked his head.

Green gave a nervous cough. 'I know what you think I've done. I've heard the news. But I didn't do it.'

'Didn't do what, Michael?' Ward stared him down.

'That kid...Millie something...I didn't take her.'

'Then you need to prove that, Michael. You have to understand—the coincidence is unfortunate at the very least. You're in the wrong place at the wrong time. If you took that little girl, then you need to make this right and help us find her. Let this not be like last time. Like Sarah Farrow.'

Michael's eyes darted away as Ward spoke her name.

'I'll ask you again. Who were you with yesterday—Wednesday—morning?'

Michael remained silent, his shoulders hunched and his eyes troubled under wrought brows.

'We'll be obtaining a warrant to search your property shortly. I don't need to tell you what that means.' Ward said.

'You won't find anything.'

'I hope that's the truth.' Ward flexed his fingers before re-clasping his hands.

'Look, I just don't want to get anyone in trouble,' Michael muttered, his gaze downcast.

'And you won't. Assuming you weren't doing anything you shouldn't have been, then you have no reason to fear telling us.'

'I was with a friend—Liam Chapman. He lives in Armley. Look, there's probably CCTV footage of me on the buses home. I was on the X6 and then the 576, between seven and nine last night. Had to wait at the Interchange for a while between too.'

Ward half-took in the bus details—at his side, Kasim scribbled furiously. It was the wrong time of the day, for starters, but the name snagged. Liam Chapman—he knew that name. It made him look at Michael Green with more darkness clouding his judgement. 'Liam Chapman is a convicted and registered sex offender. Why were you with him?'

Michael looked away again. 'We're friends, that's all. A social visit.'

'Nothing illegal?'

'No. Nothing like that. Look, we're...involved. It's none of your business.'

'Right you are—unless either of you are doing anything to break the law.'

Green glared at him. 'I don't do anything I shouldn't now. I did my time.' As he clenched his jaw and turned his head to the side, Ward discerned the pale silver scars on the man's neck. Prison had tried to end Michael Green more than once, he guessed. Even criminals had standards. No one held love for paedophiles and child killers.

'You did,' Ward agreed, though he felt the sentence would never be enough to make up for the lives Green had ruined. The law, however, was not his to make. 'Why did you go to Liam's?'

Green snapped, 'We're involved. It was a social call. You fill in the blank for God's sake.'

Ward raised an eyebrow. 'So where were you yesterday morning, between say, eleven and one?'

'I just told you.' Green's voice was venomous.

'No, you didn't. You told me where you were between seven and nine yesterday evening.'

Green gritted his teeth. 'I was at Liam's.'

'So, you can't prove it?'

'No,' Green admitted at last, folding his arms tightly to his chest.

'Alright. Let's park that for now, then. When did the Hunters first make contact?'

Green went from blazing defiance to fearful subsidence in an instant. 'About a week ago,' he said quietly. His eyes darted to the locked door.

'You seem afraid of them,' Ward commented. 'Is there anything you want to share with us? Maybe the story behind that shiner?' He pointed towards the black eye Green sported.

Michael's eyes widened—or, one of them did. The other was still too swollen to do much. 'Have you not seen what they're capable of?' He gestured to the scar on his neck, long healed. 'They did this, you know. The inmate that shanked me told me so. Told me he'd stab extra hard because he fucking hated me, but that the money, the means, and the opportunity came from the outside...from them.'

'That's a very serious allegation to make.'

'I know. They'll never be caught anyway. I survived. I learned a lot from that. Learned how to protect myself.' Michael shrugged, but the scowl that crossed his face contradicted the nonchalant gesture. Old wounds still festered inside.

'But they found you a week ago?'

A nod.

'How?'

Michael shook his head. 'I don't know. One minute, I'm minding my own business...the next, this.' He gestured to the black eye. 'I look over my shoulder wherever I go. Doing time...being rehabilitated—it doesn't change anything for some people. They see what they want to see. I thought if I looked like no one they might be interested in, that's exactly what I become to them. People didn't pay me a bit of notice. Not in a place like Bradford, where everyone comes and goes, and no one gives a shit about their neighbours in a street like mine. No one knew me. It was a fresh start.' He fell silent.

'What have you been doing since you got out?'

Michael shrugged. 'I got myself set up again. Changed my name to Steven Tanner by Deed Poll. No one knew any different—no one cared. Let's face it, I didn't have anyone here.'

'When did you move here?'

'Couple months ago.'

'You're on the Sex Offenders Register. Why didn't you register your move?' They would have known if Green had registered in the area, under his name or a new one. There hadn't been any alert out in either name, so Ward deduced Green hadn't missed one of the regular check ins at his former local police station as required by the terms of his inclusion on the register. Yet. The day would be inevitably coming.

Green shrunk away. 'I didn't want to. The whole point of coming here was a fresh start.'

Ward forced his face to remain blank, though he seethed at Green's avoidance of the law. 'That's a criminal offence, Michael.'

'I've not missed an appointment.' Michael had the good grace not to respond with anything that might damn him further.

Ward moved on. 'But you made friends? You met Liam?'

Ward saw the momentary hesitation before Michael nodded.

'You knew him already, didn't you?'

Michael swallowed. 'We were inmates together. He got out first. We stayed in touch. He helped me get set up on the outside.'

'A stroke of luck, then. But he knew who you really were, didn't he?'

'Yeah.'

'And you trust him with that information? Trust him not to leak that?'

Michael opened his mouth but stopped short. He frowned, thinking it through. 'I...I mean I do. I think. I'm not sure. He had no reason to tell anyone who I was— look at who he is. He keeps a low profile too.'

'But still. It's possible he could have leaked your identity.'

Michael sat forward in his chair, resting his head in his hand. 'Yeah. S'pose.' The answer was muffled against his palm. Ward knew Michael was wondering if he had misplaced his trust. Could you ever really trust anyone?

'Tell me about your eye. For the benefit of the tape, Mr Green is sporting a black eye, which appears to be recent from the colour of the bruising. What happened?'

Michael's tongue darted out to wet his lips, and he folded his arms, as though they could protect him from any of it. 'About a week ago. I was walking home from Tesco. I'd gone for beer and fags. It was late, just gone dark. And a bloke shouted 'paedo' across the road at me. But when I looked, there was no one there. I know I didn't imagine it. I didn't sleep that night. Got myself back to the flat, locked the door, wedged a chair under the handle.

'The next day, I was walking down the road to town. Someone shoved me into the road in front of a bus! Nearly shit myself. Managed to get out of the way —the bloody bus almost crashed swerving out of the way...but there was no one there when I looked. At least no one who looked like they'd just pushed a man in front of the 576.' Michael shuddered. 'It was a good, hard shove. Two hands right in the middle of my back. No way was that an accident. And I knew...I knew then.'

His voice dropped to a mumble. 'I knew my identity was out. I didn't know who, not then, but I knew someone was after me. When I got home the next day, someone had sprayed a red crosshair on my front door. Fucking shit me up that did. Knew the Hunters had found me.' Ward watched as the blood drew from the man's already pale skin.

'The crosshair is their 'logo', sir,' DS Shahzad murmured.

'I see. What happened next, Michael?'

'They got me whilst I was scrubbing it off the door. Like I need any trouble where I live, with who I am, didn't need that on my front door. Three of them, all wearing balaclavas—men/ Couldn't see anything of them, not enough to recognise them anyway. It was all noise and pain, they just kept coming and punching, and, well...I had a knife on me.'

Ward drew in a breath, and his chair creaked as he sat up.

'Look! You would too if you were me. I have to, for protection. I'd never use it—but I'd be dead if I hadn't. I fought my way out of there.' With the knife, Ward read between the lines.

'And then?'

'I ran.'

'Where?'

'Went to Liam's. Been holed up there all week. I only came back to get my stuff...thought...if I hadn't been for a few days, maybe they'd forget, maybe they'd get bored of waiting, I don't know.'

'They didn't,' said Ward grimly. Michael met his stare, eyes wide, and swallowed audibly. Ward owed Michael nothing.

'And then you bumped into me,' DC Shahzad said, looking up from his notebook. 'No wonder you were so keen to come quietly.'

'I haven't done nothing wrong,' muttered Michael. 'This is safest place to be, isn't it? In 'ere.'

'It sure is,' said Ward, leaning back in his chair, and folding his arms.

There came a knock on the door. 'Sir?' A voice, muffled, came from the other side.

Ward rose and crossed to the door, opening it just a crack. 'Yes?'

A female DC stood outside. 'There's been a development, sir.' She passed him a note. He scanned it and his jaw fell. 'No...'

'Yes, sir. This was made yesterday evening, but we've only just made the connection.'

'Shit...' Ward breathed. 'Thank you.' Ward's jaw tightened as he prowled back to the table and stood there, arms folded. Slowly, deliberately, coiled with energy waiting to be unleashed. 'It seems you haven't been telling us the whole truth, Mr Green. The picture, please, DS Shahzad.'

Kasim reached inside the beige folder under his notepad and pulled out a photo. He slid it onto the desk and Millie's bright face stared up at them.

A gleam passed over Michael's eyes but then it was gone. Ward frowned. 'Do you recognise this girl, Michael?'

'No,' the man said too quickly.

'For the benefit of the recording, DC Shahzad is presenting Mr Green with a photograph of Millie Thompson.'

'There are two reported sightings of a man matching your exact description, around Wibsey park, at the time of her disappearance. Both from different, unconnected sources. How can that be, Michael?'

'I don't know,' he said sullenly, and his hand fiddled with the toggle on his hoodie. 'It's not me. I wasn't there. I told you, there's CCTV of me on the buses—'

'At eight that night!' Ward growled. 'Millie Thompson went missing around eleven in the morning. I don't give a shit where you were at eight that night, unless it's connected to my investigation, but as it stands, you can't prove your whereabouts at eleven yesterday morning, and the only word you can offer me is your own, or that of a registered sex offender and fellow convicted criminal. Forgive me if I'm not rushing to believe *that*,' he spat venomously.

'You don't have any evidence.'

'We'll be the judge of that.'

'I know you don't, because I didn't do it!' spat Michael, suddenly blazing, and he met Ward's glare with ferocity. 'I'm only here because those Hunter bastards shat me all over the press and faked those sightings! Someone's setting me up!'

Ward shook his head. 'Lies, Michael. Lies. You've danced this dance before, and we're not doing it again. Last time, Sarah Farrow *died* because you were too cowardly to come clean. Last time, her family were *destroyed* because of what you did. I won't let you do it again.' He slammed his palms down on the table with an almighty crash. 'Where is Millie Thompson?'

Michael blinked rapidly, swallowed, that defiance rearing its ugly head again. And then he looked dead ahead, through DI Ward, and when he spoke, his voice was void of all feeling.

'No comment.'

CHAPTER THIRTEEN

W ard was still shaking with fury. Green had said nothing else. Given no clues. Absolutely nothing. 'Damn it all!' Ward roared at the sky above. He sank against the limestone brick wall behind him, the fire escape door propped open with an extinguisher. The quiet of the un-overlooked corner of the police station was his solace away from the crushing pressure of it all.

It was dark, the early hours of Thursday and sirens wailed across the city, carried on a soft breeze. Ward breathed deeply—the fresh air brought him back to himself, reminded him that there was hope, and that he had a job to do. That people were counting on him not to crumble. Those deep breaths saved him every time the abyss threatened.

Ward afforded himself a few more minutes of calm, then he slipped back inside, carefully closing the door behind him. He couldn't control how Green responded, or what the man had done, but he could control himself, and he knew with certainty, like he always did, that he would do everything within his power—and that had to be enough. It had to be enough, else he'd never be able to live with it all. The cases that went unsolved. The ones that left families destroyed while criminals walked away.

Ward fixed the image of Millie Thompson in his mind—those blue eyes staring at him with all the precocious innocence of youth—and promised her silently that he would do everything possible to find her. Before it was too late.

He grabbed a few hours fitfully napping in his office before the department awakened around him and it was time to begin again. The team were combing through any leads they had in a bustling Incident Room.

Ward took a cursory glance at the burgeoning Big Board—and the picture of Millie staring out while information and queries wove around it like a nest. Michael Green's mugshot showed the man with a lip curled in contempt, and hate in his eyes. He looked every inch the paedophile and child killer he'd been convicted as. Next to Millie, it was a stark contrast. One that turned his stomach.

DS Chakrabarti's notes were neatly lettered on the board, with some in DS Nowak's slanting hand too, and others in DC Norris's neat block capitals. The drowning theory. The leads with Michael—his alibi already queried on the board. The reported sightings to verify by CCTV, some still waiting for an answer. Ward knew that they would all more than likely turn out to be dead ends.

He forced down the spike of rising frustration. This

ought to have been an open and shut case. Would they have to do the same as the last time Michael Green had been caught and put away? Would they have to painstakingly build a case against him, then find a body by sheer luck more than skill, before they could link him to the crime? Not on his watch.

Ward had already tasked DC Shahzad straight out of the incident room with following up the CCTV from the bus company. It wouldn't exonerate Green, but it would mean they could verify where he got on the bus. And perhaps, it would show if Green had been anywhere plausible to hide a two-year-old...or dump her body, like he had with Sarah Farrow all those years ago in that cold, dreary, lonely woodland.

———

'You look like you need a coffee, sir,' Nowak said sympathetically at Ward as they walked out of the Incident Room. Her neat hair—slicked back and coiled into a regulation bun —flashed fiery auburn with each strip light they passed under, and as usual, her appearance was impeccable.

Next to her—with the grizzle of decidedly *not* regulation stubble lurking around the edges of his beard—Ward felt decidedly dishevelled. He'd let his grooming go a little since Katherine, he supposed. Even Oliver's fuzz was in better shape than his. A night awake at the office had not helped.

He grunted at her. 'Got anything stronger?'

'At this time of day?'

'It's afternoon somewhere in the world.'

She rolled her eyes and diverted him into the canteen, where DCs Patterson and Shahzad were already lurking by the overpriced vending machine, picking out their next sugar overdose.

'I wish this thing did ice cream,' Ward heard Jake mutter.

At Daniel and Emma's entrance, Kasim looked up and grinned, then returned his attention to the vending machine.

Jake pulled a face at the sight of Ward. 'Christ sir.'

'What?' Ward growled, not in the mood to put up with any flak.

'Well, sir, not to put it too politely, but you look like shit.'

Kasim burst out into a guffaw of laughter.

'I'm not prepping for bloody Vogue, lad,' Ward retorted. 'I've got a case to manage in case you haven't noticed. I don't have time to do my make up like you whilst your mum ties your shoelaces of a morning.'

'I don't wear make up!' Jake drew himself up, affronted.

'You don't need it,' Kasim assured him, pinching his cheek. 'You're gorgeous just the way you are, sunshine.'

'Oi!' Jake batted him away, glaring.

Ward grumbled, 'It's no wonder I'm always picking up after you two clowns. You never get anything done—too busy mucking around.'

Nowak crossed to the kettle, pursing her lips primly.

'Good thing you have immigrants like me coming over and taking all the jobs, sir, isn't it?'

'Oh aye. God forbid the natives do any work.'

'Don't I know it!' DS Scott Metcalfe's warm, homely voice boomed across the canteen as he entered with a glass to refill. 'That's what they always say in Lancaster. If you want the job doing *right*, never trust a Yorkshire man.'

Ward scoffed as he rifled through the cupboard for a clean mug. 'Like a bloody Lancastrian'd know what a hard day's work was if it punched him in the face.'

'I was working when you were still in nappies, son,' Metcalfe said, jabbing a finger at Ward and looking him up and down. 'My hard work props this place up.'

'It sure does,' Ward said, staring pointedly at Scott's growing paunch. 'I don't know how your desk would stand up if it didn't have your belly to sit on.'

'You cheeky sod!' Metcalfe's face, already pink, went a shade of lobster.

'If I didn't keep you on your toes, Metcalfe, you'd be dozing at your desk.' Ward didn't know how anyone could. After a few hours in his office chair, every inch of him hurt.

'Keep me on my toes? I spend half my time sorting out your messes. Oh, watch out for Kipling by the way. He's still on the warpath after the Varga incident yesterday. He collared me, but to be honest, I just blamed you.'

Ward groaned. Fallout from his ill-timed attempt to pin Varga was the last thing he wanted to deal with. He'd already given himself enough crap for it. He didn't need

DCI Kipling piling it on too. Not to mention the photos— he hadn't mentioned them to anyone, and he wasn't sure he would. What would it prove? 'Good thing it's not DSU McIntyre, I suppose. Kipling, I can handle.'

'Oh, I dunno, Daniel. He's *extra* beige today. Might bore you to death with a lecture.'

'Well in that case, least I won't have to deal with Katherine. Silver linings.'

Scott had the good grace to wince as he filled up his glass with water. 'How's that going?'

'*Fantastic*, mate. Really love divorcing. Getting kicked out of my house, moving into a shithole flat that stinks of scrotes, with no furniture...Oh, and now all my money? I get to pay to a lazy shite of a solicitor who bills me five hundred quid every time I want to send a sodding letter, and they don't even bloody proofread it properly before it goes out. It's as fun as a hole in the head. You should definitely try it.'

'Did you get any further with, you know, getting anything?'

'Don't be daft. I have the luxury of the old, knackered couch and the spare mattress—and that's too handsome a reward in her eyes. God forbid I'd get any of the furniture I paid for in that house.'

'What about Oliver?'

Ward ground his teeth. 'Don't even go there.'

'That bad, huh?'

'Mmmhmm.'

Metcalfe clapped him on the shoulder. 'Hang in there, mate. It will get better.'

'No, it won't,' said a clipped, nasally voice behind them.

Ward steeled himself and turned, plastering a tight smile that was more a terrifying grimace across his face. 'Good morning, sir.'

He faced DCI Martin Kipling. The man was a head shorter than him and dressed in a crisp suit of dark beige, a burgundy tie neatly perched at his throat. His salt-and-pepper hair was neatly combed, not a strand out of place, but he was no less intimidating than Ward's burly, unkempt self to the uniforms in the building. It was not through physical prowess, but the hiring and firing power he possessed—and the ability to make Ward's life exceedingly unpleasant.

'Don't 'good morning' me, DI Ward,' Kipling snapped, marching across the canteen, his polished brogues flashing with each step. Like mice seen by the neighbourhood cat, DCs Shahzad and Patterson slipped out and bolted down the hall, their snack haul rustling as they went.

Kipling jabbed a finger at Ward. 'What the hell were you thinking yesterday?' he blazed.

'I was doing my job, sir,' Ward said blandly.

'No, Ward, you weren't. In fact, I'd go so far as to say you were doing the exact opposite. You know you need *evidence* to bring someone in if you're going to have any chance of charging them.'

'I did have evidence sir.'

'No, you didn't. Some blurry CCTV footage taken vaguely near the scene of a crime, and a prostitute with a random tattoo gives us absolutely nothing to go on. Of course, the man's not going to fess up to anything when he knows that. In fact, I'd say it gives us even *less* than nothing to go on, as you know damn well. The moment you flushed Varga out prematurely, he'll have doubled back and covered his tracks. Anything we could have got from that brothel? It's gone. Congratulations. You just helped him. How does it feel?'

'I thought we had enough to make him sweat,' Ward growled at him, hackles rising, unable to stand there and take it. Yes, he knew he'd massively cocked up, yes, he'd jumped the gun, but it had been with the right intent. 'I want that bastard taking off—'

'Watch your language,' Kipling warned.

'—the streets as soon as is humanly possible. Sir, you didn't see the state inside that place. You wouldn't have kept rats there, let alone people.'

'And did you *get* any people?' Kipling's retort was a sharp barb. He knew damn well that the brothel had emptied as they raided it. They'd managed to get only one of the girls, who had panicked and locked herself in the toilet. Just seventeen. Branded on her chest with the crowned 'V' tattoo that marked all of Varga's sex-slaves and prostitutes.

'V' for Varga. His property. Owned like chattel. To be used at his pleasure.

'V' for '*vernost*'. The Slovakian word for loyalty. A reminder of the price of breaking it.

A crown for the shadow kingdom Varga ran, seemingly beyond reproach from an inconvenient thing like the law.

The girl would be safe now. Ward could still smell her—stale sweat, cheap perfume, sex. Still see the fear in her wide, blue-green eyes, the way she shrank away as though she expected a beating. And, her skin, so much of her half-starved form bared by the neon pink crop top and black PVC miniskirt she wore that left nothing to the imagination. Her ribs had poked through, her stomach caving in a hollow between her jutting hip bones. It had made Ward want to vomit.

He had used what broken Slovakian he had learned on the force to reassure her. '*Ahoj—je to v poriadku. Som tu, aby som ti pomohol...Si v bezpečí.*' Hi—it's ok. I'm here to help you. You're safe.

She had still looked as though she wanted to bolt, but there was nowhere to go in the tiny room with an even tinier window. Ward had raised both his hands in a gesture of reassurance and peace, restated the broken Slovakian—hoping he had not misspoken—and gestured to DS Nowak beside him. The girl would not react kindly to men, he figured. Not after what she had endured. At Nowak's smile and reassuring gesture, the girl had come, shaking every step of the way out of that dump.

He'd never even seen animals treated as badly as Varga treated the people he trafficked. A bruise on the girl's cheek, a raw sore around her ankle from where she had recently been chained. No doubt she would be too terrified to testify—too scarred both on the skin and under it to build any kind of normal life without serious intervention.

'No. We didn't get any of Varga's people. We saved one of his girls, though.' And, despite the fact the girl had nothing to her name, DS Nowak, gem that she was, had managed to track her identity, verify her as a European citizen, and find emergency accommodation for her with a women's domestic abuse charity in Bradford to begin her rehabilitation. Her statements, translated from Slovakian by the police translation service and identifying Varga as a regular presence there, had formed the bulk of Ward's decision to move against Varga, when the man had been spotted on CCTV returning to the now cleared brothel site.

'And did you charge Varga?'

'For God's sake, you know the answer,' Ward longed to retort. 'No,' he ground out instead. *He said, she said* would never prevail in a court of law, especially not between a possibly illegally immigrated prostitute and an alleged crime lord. Ward didn't need Kipling to tell him that he'd buggered it up, letting a hot head of anger incited by the girl's disgusting state and treatment get the better of him.

'Then it was damn near *pointless* then, wasn't it, Ward?'

Ward did not answer. He didn't need to. And he wouldn't solely to satisfy Kipling's ego.

'Your recklessness has endangered lives. Bringing him in puts more people at risk and it makes him even more dangerous. We look like fools. You're lucky I don't suspend you for this.'

'If you want to suspend me, sir, then I'll respect your decision.' No, he wouldn't. But he couldn't say that or the vein pulsing in Kipling's forehead might well actually explode.

'Don't be a smart mouth, Ward,' Kipling spat, his eyes narrowing. Kipling sliced a hand in front of him. 'I won't have this any longer. You're becoming a liability over Varga. I expect better. If you can't do your job, I'll give the case to someone who can handle their basic emotions. Perhaps you should consider a break—when was your last week off, anyway?'

Ward couldn't remember.

'You're no good to me if you're dead on your feet and pulling stunts like this. Consider this your last warning. The next time that man comes into this station, he'd better be getting charged with concrete evidence, or you're finished.'

He shot down any reply from Ward with a glare. 'And get a bloody shave!' he added scathingly. 'You're a disgrace to the force looking like that. You look like you've been kipping on the street. Go and tidy yourself up *now*. You're a DI and you ought to know better.' With a last glare, Martin Kipling raised his chin, turned, and strode out.

Ward and Metcalfe shared a glance. Scott waited until the door slammed behind the DCI before he let out a sigh. 'Blimey. You don't half know how to push his buttons, mate.'

CHAPTER FOURTEEN

Ward returned to the Incident Room, where DS Chakrabarti coordinated leads and resources with DC David Norris, who was known for his meticulous detail.

'Where are we with the warrant on Green's place?' Ward asked.

Priya looked up from where she sat poring through a sheaf of papers and typing at lightning speed into a laptop. A sheen of perspiration cast her face with a dewy glow. Strands of her dark hair had escaped in flyaway wisps, tortured by the humidity. 'Got it. CSI have already entered the property but there's been no updates yet.'

Which likely meant that Millie Thompson wasn't there. Ward sighed. 'No devices yet then?' Criminals' digital footprints were beyond valuable—an extension of the self, most folks didn't realise quite how much they shared.

'Not yet but if he has anything there, they'll find it.

Fingers crossed.' Ward had no doubt Green's devices, if he had any, would be a dark hole of grim content. Rather the digital forensics team going over it than him, he thought.

'Anything else?'

'Plenty, sir. We're cross-checking the members of the Hunters' group on Facebook with the forum members on the dark web. Slow going, trying to match up usernames, IP addresses and the like, but there may be something there to help us pin Green for this. I've tasked DC Patterson on it, and DC Shahzad can join him whenever he's done chasing up for you.

'Patterson found interesting chatter on one of the forums anyway. I've scanned through your interview transcript. I can verify the timings Green gave you for the incidents he's reported from what I've already read on the forums. Looks like the Hunters uncovered him about a week ago.

'There's enough chatter on there to corroborate the attack at his home address too, sir. A user called 'TheRealJustice' claims responsibility, and they tagged in a 'GuardianHunter' and 'Hellbent1994', so we might have our three perpetrators there. They're not daft though, Patterson said. They're using VPNs—naturally—so we can't see their IP addresses to narrow them down. But we're working on it.'

'Good.' Ward meant it. The Hunters were circling like sharks over blood in the water. Nowhere and yet everywhere. 'I'm not sure how they're connected to this— whether it's coincidence, whether they have information that can help us, or whether they're just getting in the damn way, but we need to identify as many of them as we can. I want known contacts of Green too, anything we can get on him. He may not be working alone.'

'We're on it, sir.'

'Any update from liaison?'

Priya sighed, and paused her typing. 'Mum's struggling. To be understood, given the circumstances. We're coming up to twenty-four hours now with no news—and of course, on our end...we don't have any concrete leads yet. It's not looking good.'.

'Aye.'

'There's not been anything useful turned up there yet. Obviously, Millie hasn't miraculously appeared out of the blue, but we haven't received any actionable information either.'

'No suspicion that mum is involved?' They had to rule it out. It wouldn't be the first time a guilty mother had been overlooked.

'She seems to be in some financial difficulties, going by her financial records. She doesn't have the best credit rating and there are some long-term debts against her name, but she is making payments on all her accounts every month and there are no large or unusual transactions that we've found in her accounts. I don't *think* there's anything there.'

'Hmm. Well, that's good I s'pose.'

'There are some unusual activities on her phone, though. She's been making a lot of calls and texts to the same phone number since Millie disappeared. There's no indication these messages were responded to, or calls picked up, but it's the only thing that strikes me as unusual, sir.'

Ward cocked his head and frowned. 'Show me?'

Priya handed him a multiple page print out showing calls and texts made and received, with over twenty calls and about the same number of texts going to the same number.

'Did you run the number?' Who did Stacey need to contact so desperately?

'Yes, sir, but nothing came back. Unregistered, and currently off the network.'

'Hmm. Ok. Did you manage to find out about Millie's dad?' According to Stacey, the man had walked away from his child—but that didn't mean that he hadn't come back to claim her. They had to explore the possibility.

'He's moved, it seems. Currently living in Doncaster. I've found a place of employment for him—a building site down there. He was working yesterday, all day.' Which meant he could not have taken Millie.

'Right. Leave it with me. Liaison's readying mum for a TV appeal shortly. We're taking this county-wide on all the broadcasters, it's going in every publication we can get it into. By lunch time, Millie's face is going to be everywhere in Yorkshire—and maybe that will be enough to jog someone's memory. After that's done, I'll have a word with Stacey about this.'

'Yes, sir. Other than that, the community is back out in force, looking for her, and so are we. Uniforms are still up in the area, mainly on door-to-door, seeing if there are any witnesses—if anyone saw anything suspicious. I'm collating the statements as they come in, but we've already done hundreds of houses and there's nothing.' Ward could hear the edge of despair in Priya's voice.

'If there's nothing else, sir...' Priya glanced pointedly at her laptop, an ancient, slow beast which was whirring angrily with threats of overheating.

'No, thanks, Priya. I'll follow up this phone thing with Millie's mum—oh, and chase CSI.'

Priya snorted. 'Nice knowing you.'

Ward winced. It was his least favourite job—well, second only to reporting anything less than stellar to DSI Diane McIntyre, that was.

———

'Oh God, not you.'

'Yeah, believe me, I don't want to be here either,' Ward said. He leaned against the wall outside Victoria Foster's office, where he'd been waiting impatiently for her to return from Green's place after she'd curtly cut him off when he called for an update.

Foster huffed and tossed her head, her pristine blonde pixie cut not moving a millimetre, as she fixed Ward with a glare through bright aqua glasses. 'We *just* walked in the door. For goodness sake, you're like a child, or a *dog*—no patience. I told you I'd update you when we got here.'

'And here you are, and I am. I've got a missing toddler to find, Victoria.'

Victoria softened a little but she still narrowed her eyes. 'I suppose I ought to be thankful you didn't come and trample all over my scene today, shouldn't I?'

'Yes, you should,' Ward said, jumping on the suggestion. 'I was going to, as well. You're welcome.'

'God, you're insufferable. Does being such an arse come naturally to you, or is it a perk of the job?'

'Born and bred, love, born and bred,' Ward said, affecting a broader Yorkshire accent and daring to offer her a wink.

She huffed in disgust and marched away. Ward followed.

'Hey! It was years ago. When are you going to drop that? It's petulant to hold a grudge, you know.'

'I'll stop holding a grudge when you stop being such an incompetent clod,' Victoria said with venomous sweetness. Nothing new there, then. Ward swallowed a retort. It was not the time to spar with her, much as he enjoyed their spite-filled banter.

'What did you find?' he asked.

At the change of tone, Victoria turned to him, all business once more. Much as there was little love between them, when push came to shove, they were both experts in their fields.

'An absolute pig sty. Disgusting hovel, but I'm not here to judge.'

Ward snorted.

'Place hadn't been cared for. Don't think he'd ever used the kitchen. Instant noodle and microwave meal kinda guy, by the looks of it.'

Ward winced. That struck a little close to home, still finding his feet in his new flat, he was an 'instant noodle and microwave kinda guy' right now too, as it happened. Once upon a time, before he'd gotten in too deep in the force, he'd liked cooking. It was one of the ways he'd wooed Katherine. Sort of. In that his cooking was terrible, but his attitude and eagerness endeared him to her.

'—And a stack of beer cans that could have built the great pyramids,' Victoria continued, oblivious to his response. 'Nothing much to go on. Living room was messy, a sofa, a small TV, an old laptop which we've seized. Nothing untoward in the bathroom though we took water samples and swabs in case any matter was passed down the drains. The bedroom...'

Victoria wrinkled her nose. 'Well, put it this way, it made the rest of the place look like a show home. And the smell. God.' She pressed her hand to her stomach for a moment, as though to steel herself. 'There was plenty of semen and DNA in the bed. We took samples from each room, dusted for prints...you know the score. We'll probably confirm that Michael Green was there a lot but that's likely it, to be honest. It wasn't a place you'd like to find yourself, Daniel.'

Ward started. She hardly ever addressed him by name. *Christ. It was that bad, she's being civil.*

'So you didn't find anything of Millie?'

Victoria shook her head. 'You'd have been the first to know if we had. Nothing obvious—like I say, perhaps DNA will turn something up but...there's nothing there of hers, and she's certainly not there. We turned the place upside down. Believe me—I didn't leave a stone unturned. I'm sorry. If there was something to find, we would have found it. The laptop is probably your best bet of finding out what Green's been up to. But I don't think he took Millie there.'

Ward's shoulders sank. He had come to a similar conclusion himself, but he'd still held out hope that she would be inside that flat. That unlike Sarah Farrow, this time, they would have found the girl in time. Alive.

'I'm sorry.' Victoria sounded genuine—and she was. Perhaps not for Ward, but for the little girl at stake.

'Is there anything else from the park?' Ward stood tall. There was no time to mope. It had been a full twenty-four hours. No trace of Millie. Time was running out, and the most critical hours had already vanished.

'Nothing,' Victoria said. 'It's bad enough that it's a park, to be honest. That makes it difficult, but by the time we got there, the local search party had trashed anything we could have hoped to find. We've got a couple of sweet wrappers, a half-dissolved newspaper, and a collection of partial footprints taken from in the bushes near where she vanished, but honestly, they probably all belong to the clods who trampled the whole place before we could get there.

'I've examined the dive team's findings too—again, nothing we can tie to Millie. Random pieces that have probably sat at the bottom of that pond for years.'

'Damn.'

'Yeah.' He could hear the irritation in her voice. It was a matter of personal pride that her team hadn't been able to turn up anything of consequence—a matter she counted as a failure.

'Well, let me know what the laptop turns up. And anything else you find.'

'Yes, your Lordship. Anything else?'

'A brew would be nice.'

Victoria snorted, and brushed past him to open the door as a pointed hint for him to clear off. 'Make it yourself.'

'Always a pleasure,' Ward muttered as he headed back upstairs to watch Stacey Thompson's no doubt tearful TV appeal for her daughter. Those things never got any easier.

CHAPTER FIFTEEN

Ward leaned against the back wall of the conference room, which had been filled with rows of chairs for the press conference. They were all filled, giving a heavy expectancy to the room, a weight of attention entirely focused on the empty row of tables at the front of the room, with three chairs behind them, and against a backdrop of police blue, West Yorkshire Police's crest proudly emblazoned upon a standing banner. Another tall banner stood beside it, with a giant picture of Millie Thompson and the helpline number upon it.

Nowak filed in with Shahzad. 'Alright, sir?' she said.

Ward nodded in response, tightening his folded arms as at the front of the room, through a separate door, DCI Martin Kipling entered, leading Stacey Thompson and her sister.

Stacey Thompson, dressed in a simple white long sleeved top and jeans, sat in the middle chair, flanked by her sister—a few years older, but the spit of her, Ward thought—and the DCI.

Kipling cleared his throat, as the room leaned forward expectantly, bristling with handheld microphones and recording devices and pens. Red lights blinked on a couple cameras in the front row.

'Thank you all for coming today.' The DCI began, his voice calm, measured, and clear. 'As you know, we're here to make an appeal for a missing girl, Millie Thompson, aged two, whose current whereabouts are unknown. It is our current belief that Millie was abducted.'

A frisson of whispers fluttered around the room, and notepads rustled and pens flashed as the journalists wrote.

He described Millie's appearance, last known location, and time of her disappearance, before turning to her mother. 'We are seeking her return safe and well at this point. Millie's mother Stacey Thompson has prepared a short statement for you all.'

Stacey looked pleadingly at her sister, who grasped her hand and gave it a light squeeze. It was as though she had aged years in the past couple of days. She'd made herself up, but even so, Ward could see the dark hollows underneath her eyes, and the weak trembling of her lips. Stacey Thompson was a broken woman—and she would be until her daughter came home. *If* they found her. Ward shifted on his feet, guilt prodding him again that they still had no idea where Millie was.

When Stacey spoke, her voice was thick. 'Please,

baby. Mummy loves you so much, and I'd do anything to have you back with me right now. Kian misses you and he wants to give you the biggest hug. Everyone is waiting for you. We just want you *home*, Millie.' Her voice broke on her daughter's name, and tears streamed from her eyes.

Beside Ward, a sniff emanated. He glanced down to see Nowak's eyes welling up. Their role was to be impartial to a point, but they were all only human, as exquisitely beautifully painful as it was. It was hard to face such loss and not be moved—but Ward did not allow himself to crumble. It would not help Millie. And he expected Nowak to do the same—wobble if she needed, but then to pick herself back up and carry on doing her job to the best of her abilities.

DCI Kipling leaned in to whisper to Stacey, who shook her head, then nodded, and cleared her throat. She blew her nose noisily with the tissue her sister offered her, and placed a shaking hand upon the prepared statement on the table. Her eyes scanned left to right, trying to find her place again. Beside her, her sister wordlessly clasped her other hand.

Her voice was clearer, steadier, more distant as she read aloud, 'Every second my baby girl is missing, the pain grows. I can't imagine another moment without you. I know that someone took you, but I don't understand how anyone could separate a little girl from her family. I want to reach out directly to the person that took her, to appeal, please, bring my little girl home, to her family, where she belongs. Please bring her home safe and well.

We need her. She needs us.' Stacey dissolved into tears, turning into her sister, who embraced her as her own tears fell. Stacey's sobs grew, half muffled.

DCI Kipling sat straighter. 'It is imperative that Millie Thompson is returned safe and well. If you have any information on her whereabouts, please ring the helpline number at once. If you find her, please contact 999 and request immediate assistance.' He looked around gravely.

'Millie Thompson is two years old. She cannot fend for herself. We must find her safe and well, as soon as possible. I would like to personally implore to the person or persons who took her, to please return her to her family. For the moment, our investigations are ongoing and we are following strong leads. Thank you. That'll be all for today.'

DCI Kipling stood, and ushered Stacey and her sister, both still crying, outside. Ward watched them go, his eagle eyes evaluating both women. The cynic in him watched them for tells, or a slip of the mask. Were they telling the truth? Were they uninvolved? He had to ask the question.

Ward huffed under his breath. 'Come on. Back to it. Nowak, come with me please—I need you for an interview.'

'Sir?'

However, Ward was already leaving. He caught up with the DCI at the end of the corridor, where Kipling spoke in the foyer with Stacey Thompson and her sister in hushed voices.

'Sir. Sorry to bother you. Might I have a word with Ms Thompson?'

They turned to him, Stacey with a tear-streaked face. 'Of course,' answered Kipling. 'We were just finishing. I'll get back to the investigation now, Stacey, Sammy.' He smiled—though it never seemed to reach his eyes—and left.

Ward held back a tut. Like DCI Kipling was involved in the ground level investigative work. 'Thank you. Stacey, I need to speak to you under caution. You do not have to say anything. But, it may harm your defence if you do not mention when questioned something which you later rely on in court. Anything you do say may be given in evidence.'

Stacey froze, aghast. 'A-Am I under arrest?'

'No,' Ward smiled—infusing his voice with warmth and reassurance. 'I just need to ask you some questions on record. If you'd rather not chat here, we can nip to an interview room?'

'OK,' she said quietly, glancing at her sister.

'I'll wait here,' Sammy replied, her eyes narrowed as she watched them walk away.

————

'Hopefully this is just a formality, Stacey, thank you for your time.'

Ward sat back in the chair. He glanced to Nowak at his side, poised to note take. 'We have to look at every possibility in your daughter's disappearance, Stacey, leave no stone unturned. That's what you want of course, right?'

'Yes.' Stacey huddled miserably in the chair.

'Unfortunately, that means we also have to examine Millie's family and friends to see if there's any involvement there.'

Stacey's brow wrinkled in confusion.

'That means we also need to look at you, Stacey.'

Stacey stilled as his words sank in. 'You think...I took my own daughter?'

'We don't think anything, Stacey. We're investigating the evidence available to us. We do, however, have to consider it.'

Stacey shook her head. 'You're kidding, right? How can I have done it? I was right there in the park! What is this?'

Ward had spooked her—already upset and unsettled in the wake of the TV appeal, it was a good time to catch her on the back foot, but he did regret the callousness of how investigations went. Sometimes, the timing was never great, and it wasn't like he set out to cause distress.

He raised his hand to placate her. 'I just have some questions regarding your phone records, Stacey.' He pushed a copy of Priya's paperwork across the table to her. 'This is a record of all calls and texts made or sent to and from your phone. There's a reasonable amount to and from your family, which is to be expected, especially at a time like this. However, if you look at the highlighted lines here, we're not sure who this person is. Who have you been trying to contact so desperately since your daughter disappeared and why, Stacey?'

'Her dad!' Stacey burst out. 'I had to get ahold of him. I wanted him to know, and I wanted to know if he had anything to do with it, because I've been trying to think who'd want to take my little girl and no one I know would do it!'

'So, you wondered if her father had maybe taken an interest in her at long last?'

'Yes,' Stacey said, bursting into tears again. 'I can't get hold of him though. I don't know what that means. Whether he's changed his number, or whether he has done something to her...I just don't know.' She looked at Ward. 'Please, can you find him?'

'So, to confirm, this number here is his contact number?'

'Yes! Look—here.' Stacey pulled her phone out, scrolled through her contacts, and showed Ward the number attached to her ex's name, which Ward recognised from the information they'd already taken.

'And you don't have any other way to contact him?'

'No.'

'Do you know where he lives?'

'He moved and I can't find out where.'

Ward sighed. It looked as though Millie's father was a dead end, and possibly her mother too. 'Alright. Thank you. It looks as though this phone number is no longer in use. We have tracked down Millie's father, but he was confirmed to be working all day yesterday—in South Yorkshire. I hope that offers you some comfort?'

Stacey nodded, and sniffled.

'That's all, anyway. Thanks for your time.' Ward smiled reassuringly, though inside, frustration rose. He still had no damn answers.

CHAPTER SIXTEEN

W ard sat back in his chair and stretched his arms to the ceiling with a yawn, trying to fight off the tired fuzziness the office stifled him with.

Green's laptop contained little to no forensic evidence of use to Victoria, so she had handed it over for technical examination by digital forensics. That had yielded *interesting* results—but nothing to connect Michael Green with Millie Thompson. Ward had hoped for a cornucopia—searches on kidnap, or concealment, murder, location. Anything to pin the man to the missing child. But still nothing. What the hell were they missing?

Mind, Ward thought, stroking his beard. Michael Green had kidnapped and killed Sarah Farrow—and done whatever else—in the world before the Internet. He could still be an analogue criminal—whether accidentally or intentionally.

It didn't mean the man was innocent, just that perhaps they wouldn't find anything on his laptop. Ward glanced at the clock. Late afternoon. Only a few more hours left before they would have to release Green without charge. A wildly inflammatory press article and a couple of anonymous sightings was hardly enough to hold someone in for a kidnap or murder that may not even have happened—Millie could, however shrinking the chances, have wandered off and come to entirely accidental harm. *Or be safe and well,* Ward reminded himself. However non-existent he thought that was now. A two-year-old could not fend for herself for so long.

Ward gritted his teeth and returned to the content reports. Unsurprisingly, they'd found a lot of porn on Green's ancient laptop, both on the hard drive as the ghost of deleted files and rescued from the deleted Internet history. Plenty of niche stuff—some rough, some kinky—and plenty of young women and men that Ward would have considered to be girls and boys, but all a legal age and consensual...just. It looked like Green had been very careful not to stray over the line—at least not on that device.

Michael Green hadn't even had a smartphone when he'd come into custody, just an old Nokia, which provided nothing of use, save for a limited contact list that Ward had immediately authorised to be traced. If the man had a network for anything nefarious, they needed to know about it.

The list had already turned up a number of associates, local and further afield, tracing back to inmates he'd served with, or those who shared his particular sexual interests. Judging by the messages, Liam

Chapman wasn't the only social call on Michael Green's list, though he hadn't had physical contact with any others in the past few weeks.

Chapman was the only one of Michael's network, it seemed, in contact with him physically and otherwise in the time around Millie's disappearance. *A possible accomplice, or just a coincidence?* Ward wondered.

It wasn't enough to go on. He longed to bring Chapman in, but the memory of Kipling's rage drove sense and protocol into him. *Not yet, not unless they had something to pin on him.*

Ward exhaled, a long, slow breath.

Where was Millie Thompson?

Ward knew they were missing something—but time had run out.

Without any further grounds to detain Green, he was only allowed one more interview.

Another hour of 'no comment' followed from Michael Green, until his twenty-four hours in custody were up, and DI Daniel Ward had less than the square root of sod all to charge him or keep him with.

Ward watched as Green was returned his personal belongings and signed out of custody. Ward prowled behind Green as he left. Green opened the door and turned to look at him. Green said nothing. His face was entirely closed, but his eyes held dislike. Dislike that Ward mirrored right back at the bastard.

Yet, Ward did not miss the flicker of fear running through the man. Green might not have wanted to be in custody, answering to Ward, but there had been a reason

Green had come so willingly with Shahzad the night before, and as he paused on the threshold of the station, seemingly not so eager now to leave, Ward could see that fear of the Hunters resurface again.

The moment passed.

Green stepped outside and walked away.

A free man.

CHAPTER SEVENTEEN

D I Ward stormed out of the station shortly after Green's release that Thursday evening, a storm brewing inside him. His blood roared through him, amplifying his pumping fury, that the bastard had walked free, that they hadn't had enough to charge him.

Oh, they had warned him he was on bail, not to go far, and that they'd be keeping an eye on him, but Green knew as well as they did, it was all idle threats. They had nothing on him. As long as he didn't screw up, he'd get away with it. Green wouldn't be so daft as to lead them to Millie—not like they had the manpower to put a tail on him in case he did. He was guilty, Ward dared to believe, but Green wasn't stupid. Not this time. He'd learned from his mistakes.

The more Ward thought about it, the more he believed it could not be coincidence, that Michael Green, convicted paedophile and child killer had appeared in precisely the right neighbourhood at precisely the right time to abduct Millie Thompson. Planned or opportunistic, it hardly mattered. It was off the grid, just like before. And Ward, it seemed, couldn't do a damn thing about it. Not one damn thing to help her.

He understood the Hunters' anger and their crusade, though he could never professionally admit it. No, he did not believe anyone could be redeemed for the kind of crime that Green had committed. No, he did not think that languishing in jail at Her Majesty's pleasure ever truly measured up as a price against a young girl's life and God only knew what else had been done to her.

Yet somehow, it was up to Ward to stop it happening again, before it was too late. It was hard not to feel like the justice system had failed when he had a missing toddler, Green sighted in the locale, and absolutely nothing concrete to connect the two—or at the very least, keep Green off the streets and under pressure until the man cracked and admitted what he had done.

Ward was certain Green had done it. Liam was nothing more than a poor alibi no one could verify—Michael knew that as well as they did. Yet, until they had more evidence, they couldn't act.

Innocent until proven guilty.

Daniel got into his car and slammed the door. He fired up the engine—the throaty roar of the VW Golf R's turbo diesel engine a soothing reassurance and familiar comfort after the day he had had, and always a relief after having to drive the force's BMW. He allowed himself to soak it in for a moment, drowning out his punishing inner monologue, before he slid it into gear and drove it out of the car park.

For once, he wished he was going back to his crappy flat with his crappy kitchen-diner and crappy instant noodles.

He had a far worse job to do.

The text that had been waiting for him all afternoon had been the spark that had lit the match of rage within him.

'*Papers here from solicitor. Come and sign them today. K.*' Katherine, his—for now—wife.

No pleasantries, no kindness in her message. Those days were long gone. Anger surged, soon replaced by a positive emotion he almost couldn't recognise in the tempest of frustration that had been his day—the thought of Olly. At least he'd get to see his little best pal, even if it was only for five minutes. Maybe Katherine would even let them go for a walk.

Daniel followed Canal Road through the valley bottom, past the heights of Bradford City football stadium rising to his left, under the bridge, and out towards Shipley. It was dead at that time of night, except for the occasional taxi, the day gone. Katherine would no doubt moan about the late hour, but he wasn't in the mood to hear it.

He crossed the busy Shipley intersection, followed the road across the Leeds-Liverpool canal and then the Aire River, and turned up the hill towards Baildon. It was a small, middle-class village on the outskirts of Bradford. Katherine had stalked Rightmove and every other local estate agent for almost a year to find their perfect home there. One that they could afford, in the pricey area.

The perfect home ended up being a three-bedroom, post-war semi and in the five years since, Katherine had decorated it tastefully. Ward had left her to it. It kept her sweet and she didn't welcome his input when he had an opinion to offer in any case. She had seemed happy there but he wasn't sure it had ever felt like home—so clean and clinical, with none of the homely touches he remembered his mother trying to inject into their house of abuse, to disguise the darkness that lay beneath the surface.

Until his father had broken his mother's hand in a drink-fuelled rage, after which it had never healed right, she had painted. Beautiful landscapes and scenes from sprawling Yorkshire, using whatever paint she could get her hands on or afford with the money she had saved in her knicker drawer. They had hung on the wall in the hallway, in the kitchen. She had even painted a mural in his bedroom of his favourite TV characters, the Teenage Mutant Ninja Turtles.

As a boy, Daniel Ward had known, had seen the light in her soul that only her boys and her painting brought—a refuge from the suffering his father brought upon them. He couldn't even think of the monster's name without feeling the mental scars, as fresh as the moments they were inflicted.

How he longed to see his mother again too. He could barely think of her name without cracking open. It had been so many years since he had felt her arms around him. Seen her shy smile. Felt the familiar waft of her homely scent wash over him, welcoming him home. The fading paintings were all he had left of her now.

Katherine hadn't let him put up one of his mother's artworks in their new home. Not one. Maybe that was why it had never really felt like home. Instead, they'd been banished to the loft at her insistence, so they wouldn't 'clutter' the house. Half of those precious few pieces had rotted away under a leaking roof tile before he'd realised. Daniel wasn't sure he'd ever forgive her for that. It reminded him to take those that had survived, though. At least he'd have something of his mother, something that felt like *home*.

Perhaps home wasn't a place—perhaps it never had been, Daniel wondered. Perhaps it was a *feeling*. One that he'd never truly shared with Katherine.

And as he pulled up outside the house that Thursday night, it felt like a stranger to him all over again.

CHAPTER EIGHTEEN

'Where've you been?' Katherine hissed, as soon as the door opened.

'Work.'

'I texted you at lunch time!'

'And I've been at work since one this morning, Katherine. I'm knackered, I've had a shite day, and I'm no mood to get it in the neck from you. I came as soon as I could, alright?'

She glared at him, and then beckoned him to come inside with a sharp gesture.

It felt so strange, to be invited into his own home —*house*—as though he were a guest. He didn't live there, but he still owned half the place until the sale and divorce went through. He'd noticed that there still wasn't a sign up in the front yard. 'I thought you were putting it up for sale?'

'I haven't had time,' she snapped, wheeling around so he was forced to stop dead in the porch.

Her hand lay on the door knob, the door still closed before her.

Ward scoffed, a mirthless chuckle. Katherine Ward liked to think she was a busy person, but she was a fusser more than anything. She liked to look productive but she never actually got anything done. 'I'll sort it if you can't.'

'I'm doing it!' Her eyes flashed in anger. Exactly as he knew they would. Katherine was controlling by nature. She wouldn't let him near any of the necessary tasks with a bargepole. He'd been happy—foolishly so—over the years to cede to her. Now, he wondered if that had contributed to his downfall and the predicament he was now in, thinking, like with everything else, unconsciously, that the continual papering over the cracks in their relationship would fix it. He had given her the power. Of course, in the final throes of their marriage, she had no interest in sharing it. Not when it would not benefit her.

'Then get it done this week. You might be fine here but I'm in a shithole dump and I'd like my money so I can get set up somewhere else.'

'Not my problem,' she said sniffily.

'I can move back in here, if you like, since it is my home,' he said icily.

She gaped at him in wordless horror.

'Christ, no one would ever think you'd loved me with a face like that. I'm not a monster, you know that. I just want what's mine, and I want to move on.'

'You've found someone else? Already?' In an instant, she had changed, suspicion and bitterness closing her perfectly made-up face.

'It's none of your business.'

Wrong answer. She paled with rage.

'I haven't, for the record.' He laughed darkly. He needed to at least try not to get his head ripped off before the divorce was finalised. 'Like I even have the time.' *Or inclination.* His obsession with the crime lord Bogdan Varga was one of the things that had driven them apart in the end. All-consuming. Engulfing. At all costs. He wasn't proud of that, his inability to separate work and home. It had been the final wedge that had irrevocably driven Katherine away. Perhaps, in part, because it was the one part of him that she couldn't control.

She scoffed, then stormed into the house—and shrieked as a brown-and-white-and-black blur shot past her, nearly tripping her up.

'Olly!' Daniel fell to his knees as the dog barrelled into him, tail wagging furiously, raining stinging blows on his arms as he swept the beagle up into a giant cuddle. 'Hey, little bud, I've missed you.'

He spoiled the dog for a minute, checking over every inch of the pup. He was in good condition, so Katherine was clearly doing the bare minimum in looking after him, even though she hated the animal. Like everything else, Oliver was nothing more than collateral damage to Katherine. A way to hurt and punish Daniel for everything.

'The papers are in here.' Katherine's cold voice cut across Oliver's whimpers and whines as the dog tried to burrow his way into his beloved human and lick every part of Daniel's bearded face.

'Alright, bud, alright.' Ward grinned, his anger and frustration washed away for a moment by the dog. He braced himself as the force of the beagle's love pushed him backwards, and then got to his feet and followed the hallway through to the kitchen, with Oliver jumping around his ankles at every step.

'Here.' Katherine held out a pen and jabbed her finger at the paperwork in front of her. 'For engaging their services.'

Ward had a good mind to read them, but he honestly couldn't summon the brain power after the day he'd had. He sighed, scanning the papers briefly. Something about engagement terms and fees. Solicitors were always banging on about fees. The down payment just to engage them had been eye-watering. Ward took the pen and signed next to Katherine's flourishing signature at the bottom. His was jagged, spiky. She always said it matched his personality.

'I want to take Olly out for a walk.'

'It's too late.'

Ward glanced out of the window. 'Still light.' It was technically true, if somewhat of a stretch. The very last remnants of the late sunset clung on the horizon, the rest of the sky star-filled. 'Anyway, he's my dog too. Save you the bother of having to go out for the toilet with him, won't it?'

'Fine. Hurry up, then. I'm going to bed at eleven.' It was already well after ten.

Daniel grabbed the lead from by the door—where it had always been, on the lowest coat hook—and a chewed-up tennis ball that lurked in the corner. 'Come on, boy!' he called, infusing an excitement into his voice that did not come naturally. 'Walkies!'

The dog shot at him in a hail of barks and Ward clamped his hands around Oliver's muzzle as the dog jumped up. 'Oi! Quiet, bud, you'll get us in trouble.' He clipped on the lead and slipped outside. It was a short walk down the street and through a snicket to the steep, open fields and beyond that, Baildon Moor soaring high above them.

Oliver knew the way and dragged Daniel into the darkening fields along the line of the wall bordering onto the edge of Baildon and its residents' back gardens. Daniel unclipped him a minute in and Oliver raced off into the grass, bounding around the field in loops, weaving through the rising and falling terrain as he picked up exciting scents here and there.

Ward whistled quietly, and at once, Oliver was alert, his eyes focused on the ball in Daniel's raised hand. Daniel lobbed it, and once more, Olly was a blur as he pelted after it. In a minute, he had returned to drop the ball at his master's feet, already jumping up in anticipation. Ward lobbed it again. And again. And again. Laughing as he watched Oliver run loops around the field, giddy with happiness, the dog's simple pleasure infectious, the cascading warm rays of the setting sun a balm over the day's darkness.

It was a relief that he desperately needed. It seemed that darkness consumed him now, whether at work or outside it. Daniel couldn't remember the last time he'd felt so at ease, a smile curling his lips without effort, and the natural tension in his body drained away.

Oliver returned the ball, and Daniel saw that the battered thing had finally given, split under a hail of Oliver's unrelenting chewing. Nevertheless, he held it up once more as Oliver expectantly waited. His arm lashed forwards—in an imitation of a throw—and at once, Olly was off. Ward chuckled at Oliver's gullibility at his misdirection, the sorry, soggy remnants of the ball still held firmly in his palm as Oliver chased across the field, hell bent on finding it.

Eventually the dog returned, trotting happily towards him, his tongue lolling out, and leapt upon Daniel as he realised that his master still had the ball.

'You daft git,' Daniel said fondly, stroking Oliver's head, his silky soft ears, the coarser hair across his back. 'Come on, then.' He sighed. 'Best get you back.' He'd ask again. He always did, on the rare occasions they met these days. She'd say no. But he had to try.

Oliver obediently walked to heel as Daniel returned him to Katherine, cocking his leg one last time as they left the fields. She opened the door to his knock, but didn't step aside for him to come in. Daniel supposed there was no reason for him to go inside again. He handed the lead to Katherine, along with the remnants of the ball, which she stared at with disgust, her lip recoiling as she took the soaking item.

Olly whined softly as Daniel stepped back. He

dropped to a knee to give the dog a stroke, his fingers lingering on the scruff of the beagle's leg. 'Please can I take him, Katherine?' he asked quietly.

Already, his good mood had faded, the freedom and lightness he had felt in the field watching Oliver play had shed with each step back to reality.

'No. Oliver, heel.'

And with a whine, Oliver's mournful eyes turned upon Daniel.

Katherine reached forwards and grabbed his collar, hauling him inside. Oliver yelped as she choked him. Daniel gritted his teeth, that familiar dark anger surging again. He turned and left without another word, storming down the driveway and out onto the pavement where he had parked. He heard the door close and lock behind him. She would not be able to see him shaking with frustration, but she would know. *It'll make her damn day.*

Everything she did now was to hurt him. Like it had all been his fault. Like any of what had passed between them was on purpose. They had fallen in love. They had tried. And they had failed. Daniel just wanted to close the chapter and move on. Why did she insist on picking open the scabs? On digging in the knife further, twisting it each time they spoke?

He slipped into his car, started the ignition, over-revved it, and roared away.

———

The shipping yard had become a temporary morgue. The cold November night was a blessing, chilling the bodies as they were removed, one by one, from their resting place. Now, rows and columns of body bags waited, each one needing to be confirmed dead and then sealed up and transferred to the morgue.

They had all pitched in to help, donning full-body suits, masks, goggles, gloves...A painstaking labour, to carefully remove each of the victims, for many of them were tangled together and had to be uncoiled from where they had fallen. With the movement of the truck, DI Ward could see how it had swept some of them from their original positions, bodies stiffened in a seated position were on their sides. Thrown about like waste.

These people had given everything, their families' life savings, to make the journey from Syria to the United Kingdom, where they had hoped to finally escape the conflict that had torn their country to shreds. Many would still have family back home. Waiting, praying, and hoping they had made it. Knowing that at least some of their number had been saved, that they could at least be at peace with their loved ones in a safe haven. The United Kingdom meant hope and a chance for a better life away from death and destruction.

And now, they were all dead, through no fault of their own. They had given their all, and endured unimaginable hardships to reach these shores. Dead because Bogdan Varga had exploited them with no thought to their safety or wellbeing. He had been paid. What did he care whether they lived or died? They were wastage. Like any production line.

Not one of them was a person, a human to be valued or treated with dignity and compassion, to Varga. They were merely a product to be shipped from A to B. Many of them would have paid the fare and ended up bonded to him in servitude or cheap labour, trapped in a new life of hardship and poverty far from the life they had been promised. Farm hands, cleaners, sex workers, child labour. It did not matter. They were only there to make Varga more money.

It disgusted Ward to his core. He forced another breath through the suffocating mask and turned back to the devastation to pull out the next body, and the next, and the next, whilst behind them in the lot, the divisional surgeon moved from body bag to body bag to tell them what they already knew as each was closed by the CSI team in turn. ROLE: Recognition of Life Extinct. Every last one of them was long dead.

Some were inexorably locked together. DS Emma Nowak had had to take a moment upon the discovery of a young woman holding a child tightly in her arms, her head bowed over the youngster as though she could protect her child from their inevitable end. Others lay together, clutched in a final, desperate embrace, a last comfort of necessary human touch.

The nightmare deviated then, and the woman clutching her child came into the light, lifted out, together in death as they had been in life.

The woman no longer bore the darker skin and hair of the Middle-Eastern people in the lorry.

It was Katherine.

Her face taut in a ghastly, painful end, her bloodshot eyes staring at him desperately, and the child in her arms—he knew with instinctive certainty—was the child they had never managed to have.

CHAPTER NINETEEN

Several miles away, the man watched the tv appeal that night. His heart hammered with the violent torrent of fear raging through him.

Strong leads, the police man had said. Were they onto him? The papers were already spreading stories. *Michael Green had struck again*, they said. However, who knew what the police were doing behind closed doors. He had no way to know. Nausea roiled through him.

His eyes flicked to the covered upstairs windows—the curtains drawn against prying eyes. He'd been so careful to avoid the obvious places the police would turn to. He'd been meticulous so he could escape scrutiny.

Then his eyes flicked to the little girl lying next to him in the bed, clutching the teddy bear. Sleeping. Nearly always sleeping. It was just easier. They shouldn't be overheard, if she awoke and screamed, but he could not take the chance. He'd need more tablets soon to keep this up.

His attention settled upon the man on screen—DCI Martin Kipling, the insert across the bottom of the screen declared, next to the helpline number. Panic had his foot tapping on the footboard, a nervous twitch unable to be quelled.

Strong leads. The man's voice rang in his head again, a hammer blow against his confidence. Outside, something rattled—a shed, a gate, who knew—and he found himself jumping at it, half expecting the police to be battering down the door.

He couldn't go back. Not now. He'd come too far. He glanced down at Millie again. Her face was pale and slack in sleep, the colour washed out of her in the poor light of the lamp next to him.

Once more, he glanced at the curtains. Had this all been a mistake? Had he been too rash?

A horn beeped outside, and he swore under his breath, cursing himself for letting insidious fears creep in. He glanced down at Millie Thompson. She wouldn't wake for a few hours yet—not until morning, with what he'd dosed her with.

He needed to get out.

CHAPTER TWENTY

I t was dark when Michael Green stepped off the bus in Wibsey, but that was how he liked it. The darkness his shadows—but it hid him too. In the light of day, new identity or not, he felt as though under constant, glaring scrutiny. As though everyone watched him. As though everyone knew who he was and what he'd done. He'd not been able to stop looking over his shoulder since his release from prison, and now the Hunters knew where he was, it had only got worse.

A car backfired a couple streets away, and Michael jumped. He muttered a curse at himself and ducked his head further, shoving his hands in his pockets and continuing up the hill to Wibsey roundabout. He took a right onto Beacon Road, walking to the convenience store just opposite to one of the entrances to Wibsey Park. Police tape still fluttered there, now torn, the park open once more.

Green turned into the well-lit store, shuffling to the

counter to get his half an ounce of baccy and papers, and paying with his last tenner.

'You off into Wibsey then?' said the cashier, a teen lad with enough spots to crack a mirror. He looked wistful, as though he wanted to be in the pubs that night too, not stuck earning minimum wage selling fags to the likes of Green.

Green grunted in affirmation. 'Yeah.' He wasn't, but the lad didn't need to know that. He was off to score a fix from the knobhead dealing in the park. A little something extra to add to his roll ups. He needed it after the twenty-four hours he'd had in custody. And he couldn't face going home again. Not yet. Not in the dark. He was too scared of who he might find waiting there to finish what they'd started with his black eye.

Green scooped his purchase off the counter and left without a thanks or goodbye.

'Tosser,' he heard the lad mutter behind him.

Green pocketed the baccy and papers, and stepped out into the dark once more, crossing to the park entrance. That was where Saffy dealt. Green could have gone to one of the other dealers—there were plenty down Great Horton after all, though the quality of their deals varied and more times than not, he couldn't afford to be choosy—but it was need and morbid curiosity that drew him to the park.

He wandered through the deserted place. The playground was silent now, the raucous laughter and calling of children absent, though the swings shivered in the breeze, creaking, and the metal playground gates rattled on their hinges with each swirl of the wind.

Saffy normally waited by the pond, in the bushes there. Close enough to the paths to deal. Close enough to the park boundaries to run in any direction he needed to. Green followed the edge of the playground, under the line of trees that shaded it, and separated it from the skatepark.

It seemed deserted. Green coughed. Still, it was silent.

'Fucks sake,' Green grumbled under his breath. Saffy didn't come every night—sometimes, if the police had lingered too long in the area, or if he'd had the first whiff of trouble, Saffy played it cool for a while. Green supposed the heat around the park from the intense media and police attention since Millie's disappearance had meant Saffy stayed away.

Still, he approached the bushes, stepping into the pitch-black shadows.

Ahead, a twig snapped.

'Who's there?' Green said, jumping. He edged back—towards the light. 'Saffy?'

'Saffy's not here,' a low voice came back from the shadows.

'Know where I can find him?' Green nonchalantly backtracked onto the path, where the faint light of one of the park lights illuminated him more.

'Asking the same question myself, mate.'

'Right.' Green turned to leave. He wasn't about to chat to a shadow in a bush—at the crime scene he was being investigated for. Maybe he'd been stupid to come at all, and especially so to assume Saffy would be about.

'Wait. Spare a light?'

Green paused for a second. He didn't want to, but sometimes it was easier to defer. It was one of the ways he had survived prison.

'Sure.' Green rummaged in his pocket, and wandered back towards the bushes. 'Here.' He lit the flame, and held it out. There was a bloom of light that illuminated the outline of a man, his eyes flashing in the momentary flame, as the roll-up caught.

'Thanks, mate. Better luck next time.'

Green let out a dry laugh and turned away, shoving the lighter back in his pocket.

The force of the impact at the base of his skull cut off that laugh, and Green tumbled to the floor as pain ricocheted through his skull. The last thing he tasted was the well of blood in his mouth as he bit his tongue in the fall.

———

'Not that there'll *be* a next time, Michael Green.'

The man leaned down. His stomach roiled and he fought the urge to gag as the stench of Green's unwashed body reached him. He wanted to recoil—didn't want to touch the monster—but it was clear that he had been delivered a gift. One that he would not waste. He turned over Michael Green's prone form, and took in his face. It was definitely him.

Michael's attacker let out a low whistle. 'Now I am

glad I came out. You're a *much* better score than some weed.' He knew that Green had been in police custody. On the grapevine, it had spread, and quickly. If Michael Green walked free, it meant they had not charged him. It meant, the man realised, as his blood threatened to boil anew, that Michael Green had gotten away with it.

And he could not have that. So, he bent and scooped Green up, grunting at the dead weight of the man. The very touch of the monster repulsed him, every cell of his body longing to wash itself in bleach to have come so close to a paedophile and child killer.

Yet, his grip did not falter, and neither did his step, as he retreated into the bushes with Michael Green dangling in his arms. It would be well worth his time now, for he could exact the righteous vengeance he had longed to for so very long, now it seemed that the police had failed once more to bring Michael Green to justice in time to save an innocent life.

———

He had never imagined Michael Green would be sat in his kitchen. The man cocked his head. Nerves fought through him, tangling with each other. The rush of excitement, the thrill of the random chance, the fear of discovery—and a fascinated yet instinctive abhorrence of the monster before him.

It was hard not to think of Sarah Farrow. Of what she had suffered at Green's hands, hands that were now tied before him with several cable ties. He had laid those very same hands upon the girl. His eyes, now closed, had beheld her in her dying moments. Had he put that mouth upon her too? Had he touched her in other ways? Likewise, now, it was hard not to think of poor Millie Thompson, who was now tied up in this monster's enduring and horrific legacy.

The man's skin crawled. He longed to wash himself in the bleach standing ready on the kitchen counter behind him at the fact he had just had to endure so much close contact with Michael Green.

'Michael,' he crooned, leaning closer. 'Michael...Wake up.'

Green did not respond. The man slapped him across the face. His palm stung from it. He hoped Green's face felt worse.

Green groaned. The man tossed a cup of cold water across him, and that made Green gasp with the shock of it. Green's eyes blinked open, bleary at first, and then coming into focus. They centred on the man.

'Who are you?' Green asked. His tongue darted out to wet his lips.

'All in good time, Michael.' The man smiled.

Green's stomach flipped at that smile—how cold, calculating, and vicious it looked. His head throbbed where the man had incapacitated him, and his mouth felt thick and heavy. 'What do you want?'

As Green glanced around the unfamiliar kitchen, pale walls, pale tiles, aged eighties cupboards—and saw the array of kitchen knives upon the table. They gleamed. Mismatched sizes and handles—but he did not want to know if they had been freshly sharpened. He tugged his hands, before realising he could not part or move them, or anything in fact, for he had been restrained to the chair with cable ties and gaffer tape, with his hands strapped to the table. Crude, but effective. When he pulled, nothing happened. Panic spiked.

'I want you to pay for what you've done, Michael,' the man said evenly, shifting his weight until he could reach that neat line of knives and nudge one into place where it rested, out of parallel with the others.

'I haven't done anything,' Green said quickly. 'I don't know what this is, but I haven't done anything. I didn't take that little girl.' He struggled against his bonds, but the most he could do was shift the chair with a creak across the floor by an inch, if that.

The man's smile only deepened, and in the poor light of the single overhead bulb, the glint in his eye looked ferocious. 'Oh, but you did, Michael. This is all your fault...and we both know whether the police get you for it or not, you won't pay. Not *really*. You deserve so much *more* than they can give you.' The man idly ran a finger across the knives, and selected one. A large cleaver.

'First, I'm going to take the fingers you touched her with—her, and I don't know how many more...but I will find out. I'll find out every nasty thing you've ever done, Michael. You're going to tell me.'

'Go to hell!' snarled Michael.

The man only continued, his smile fading as rage tightened his features. 'Then, I'm going to take your eyes so you can't look at little children anymore and imagine your wicked ways. I'm going to take everything from you, Michael. You'll never violate anyone ever again, when I'm done with you.'

Michael opened his mouth, but the man was quicker and stuffed him with a tea towel—one hand shoving it between his jaws mercilessly, and the other fist tangling into his hair to stop him from moving away. Gaffer tape followed, strapping it to his face, half the threadbare tea towel dangling down past his chin.

'I'll show you how serious I am, and then you can decide how slowly and how far we take this, hmm?'

Michael cried out wordlessly, wrenching his hands, but they did not move, his fingers splayed upon the table and at the man's mercy. His scream intensified in pitch and crescendo, muffled by the towel.

The man brought the cleaver down.

CHAPTER TWENTY-ONE

FRIDAY

The call had come at six am on Friday. Well before DI Ward's shift was due to start at mid-morning.

The phone blared beside his head—but it wasn't the alarm he was used to. Instead, 'Barbie Girl' assaulted his ears, firing him out of sleep and off his mattress in half a second, before he was even awake or aware enough to know where he was.

A wordless, strangled noise escaped him, and then a string of curses as he fumbled for the phone, punching any and all buttons on the screen to shut the damn thing up.

Bloody Barbie Girl. He'd hated that damn song in his youth and he hated it even more at six in the damn morning.

He was going to murder DC Jake Patterson. It was never anyone else but the squad clown. The kid didn't have the temperament for the force, and it wound Ward right up—he sometimes felt like the DC was taking up a valuable place, one that Patterson seemed unable to earn. Each space on his team was limited by the merciless funding cuts the department had seen, that had halved their numbers over recent years. They had no room for jokers, only results.

Ward grudgingly had to admit, the kid had an edge with technology that he did not possess, however, and that between DC's Patterson and Shahzad, the Homicide and Major Enquiry Team's—HMET's—technological edge had sharpened.

And yet Ward was daft enough to leave his phone in reach of the lad. 'Stop leaving it on your desk, you prat,' he muttered. It made him easy prey. He should have learned from the last time already.

He sank back onto the mattress—just as the phone rang again. Daniel Ward gritted his teeth at the offense to his ears and accepted the call. 'Ward?'

'Sir?'

'Yes, Emma. Sorry. Wrong button.' He'd get her to fix Patterson's joke later. Maybe before he murdered Jake. Maybe after. 'What's up?'

'There's been a development.' There was an edge to her voice he didn't like.

'What's happened?' All thoughts of revenge against DC Patterson fell away, and he sat up, the thin duvet wrinkled around his waist.

'You need to come at once. Wibsey Park.'

A rush of ice drenched him. 'Is it Millie?' he asked hoarsely, already kicking the tangled cover off and pressing the phone to his ear with his shoulder as he stood and rifled through the pile of wrinkled clothes on the floor, looking for a clean shirt.

'No, sir. But...it's...just get here as soon as you can.'

In the background of the call, Ward heard sirens and a hubbub of unintelligible voices.

'I'll be there in half an hour.' *Shit*. What had happened that was so important to pull him out of bed at six, and that had shaken DS Nowak so much?

Ward threw himself through the shower—a cursory and functional scrub—and donned his clothes, fumbling with the buttons on his shirt in his haste. When he was dressed, he dragged a comb through his hair, grabbed his car keys and fled, with no thought for coffee or breakfast, the adrenaline focusing his mind.

Living on the western outskirts of Thornton village, it was a quarter of an hour race through the country back roads and then outer suburbs of Bradford to Wibsey Park. He pulled up to a scene of chaos on the road. Multiple police cars. The already tattered cordon from a couple days ago now replenished with extra tape—as though something else had happened. An ambulance awaited, silent, empty.

Ward pulled up behind the last squad car and made his way into the park, flashing his badge to quell the squawk of protest from the guarding officer. Officers stood in a group ahead, with the tell-tale dark green of paramedics amongst them, and an empty orange board on the floor.

'Nowak,' Ward called, spotting her amongst the crowd.

She jogged over to him. 'Thanks sir. Sorry for the early call but you had to see this.'

'What the heck's going on?'

Nowak 's face tightened. 'It's Michael Green, sir. He's dead.'

Ward halted. 'What?'

Nowak beckoned him to follow and led him to a grizzly scene. The smell hit him first. On the already warm morning, the stench of decay and the iron tang of blood was pungent, unbearable. Ward's empty stomach turned over.

At the side of the ornamental pond, where the thick stones lining the edge gave way to the tarmac, lay a body, the dark clothing torn and waterlogged and the head bound in a black rubbish bag. It had been partially torn off, enough to reveal some of the face within, though death—and the water—had already changed Green. Colder, greyer, swollen. The body was dressed in the same clothing that Ward had bailed Green in the day before.

'The body has distinguishing scars, sir, and his wallet's still in his pocket. There are a couple of bank cards in there with his new name on, so I think we can reasonably believe it's him.'

'He was scared,' Ward said. 'Looks like he didn't get far before someone caught up with him.' He glanced up at the disorganisation around them. 'When was he found? Who found him?' Ward asked.

Nowak pointed at a young man sat on a park bench a distance away with an officer stood by him. The lad looked traumatised. Discovery of a body took that toll on most people, especially the first time.

Emma said, 'The lad saw him about an hour ago on the pond edge and called it in. The responding officers—PSCO Hammond and PC Ishmael here—pulled him out and called it in.'

Ward glanced at the sodden body already drying and the half-dozen officers gathered around him with no sign of leadership. 'Right,' he said, clapping his hands together, and took a quick call of names and rank.

'You two,' Ward said, pointing. 'Man the cordon—one on the south side, one on the north. You, call in the divisional surgeon—I know, it's obvious—but we have to follow protocol, and—' DI Ward turned to Emma, who finished his thought for him.

'Crime Scene Investigation. Got it.'

As the officers attended to their respective duties, Ward carefully circled the body. Limp, like a ragdoll thrown to the floor, it was bluntly dehumanising to see a body with its head obscured by a bin bag. As though it were not really a person—had never lived or breathed—but simply a parody of life. It almost like an effigy, a scarecrow built of rubbish and abandoned just the same. It lay on its back, with one arm trapped underneath and one awkwardly crushed to the side.

'Look at the hand, sir,' Nowak prompted.

As Ward peered closer, taking small breaths to handle the rising scent of death, he recoiled. The fingers. All had been removed, just bloody stumps remaining, white bone peering through the blackened blood. One thumb remained. As he peered over the rest of the body, he could see through the generous tears in the fabric, tattered like ribbons, horrific bruising and cuts, and—he frowned—was that a burn? Like someone had tried to extinguish a cigarette on the skin?

Ward couldn't be certain how Michael Green had met his untimely end—by suffocation, drowning or torture—or something else. But it was clear the man had suffered brutally before he left this world. Green had gone from suspect to victim overnight.

Ward shuddered as a chill crawled down his spine. He could not confirm anything—not even Michael's identity—until the bin bag had been fully removed, and the identification process formally undertaken, but Ward had no doubt. The body before him was Michael Green, and, with Green's death, Ward had not only lost his prime suspect, he now had less chance than ever of finding Millie Thompson alive.

Ward spat out a choice curse and wheeled away from the body, sending a venomous glare up at the brazen blue sky.

———

Before long, the park was even busier. A white tent had been erected by the side of the ornamental pond to hide the body from view and provide cover from the growing heat. The locals and press were already clamouring like crows for a look as rush hour started, word escaped, and rumours grew.

Victoria Foster was almost unrecognizable in her full paper forensics suit and a mask, but Ward would have known her a mile off by her glittery purple spectacles. Ward had no idea how many pairs the woman possessed but he was frequently baffled by her desire to wear such gaudy frames.

Ward sighed. Twice in two days that he had to handle Foster early in the morning. He hadn't had enough coffee to deal with her, not by a long shot. He longed to ask her questions, but knew it would get him nowhere. So he paced instead, around the outside of the tent like a lion on the hunt. Already, the team were drifting into the office to the news—and he would be there to brief them soon, as soon as Victoria's team had concluded, and the body had been taken for formal identification and a post-mortem.

———

'You. A word,' Ward growled, jabbing a finger at DC Jake Patterson as he prowled into the office.

Patterson looked at him with a carefully surprised face, but the glint in his eye gave it away. 'Whatever's wrong, sir?' he said lightly, running a hand through his wavy, gelled hair and cracking a lopsided smirk.

'You know damn well what. Put it back. Fix it!'

'I'm sure I have no idea what you're talking about, sir.'

Ward grumbled. 'One of these days...If we weren't dealing with a missing toddler and a dead bloody suspect right now, I'd have you for this, son.'

'What's he done now?' DS Nowak asked, coming in the door.

'Acted like a total and complete toilet.' Ward held out his phone. 'I have the most ridiculous ringtone known to man thanks to DC Arsehole here. Would you mind?'

Emma rolled her eyes. 'You need to pay attention, sir. This isn't difficult.'

'I can't remember where it is, alright? All those settings are like a bloody rabbit warren.' He'd been fine with his iPhone. It was Katherine that had insisted they both upgrade to Android, and he still couldn't find his way around the damned thing.

'Ok, I'll fix it, I'll fix it,' she murmured, raising a hand to placate him, and firing Jake a warning look. It wasn't the day to be pushing DI Ward's buttons.

'Briefing now, everyone,' Ward snapped. 'And bring your brain, Patterson.'

Ward glared at Jake as the lad loped down the corridor to the Incident Room. He stalked after the DC, his hands shoved deep in his pockets so he couldn't ball them into fists, deeply frustrated by the new setback they had encountered.

A few minutes later, Emma entered and passed some prints to DS Chakrabarti, who prowled before the Big Board, whiteboard pen in hand.

'This morning, the body of Michael Green was found, deceased, at the site of Millie Thompson's kidnapping in Wibsey Park.' Ward detailed what he and Nowak had encountered, and the information they were now awaiting from forensics.

The room was deadly silent.

'I see you all realise what this means,' Ward said, a mix of despair and anger warring within him for dominance. 'Whatever small lead we may have had on Millie Thompson's disappearance, we've now lost. Our prime suspect is dead. We've got absolutely sodding *nothing*. We have to find out who did this to Michael Green and why. You all know what's at stake. There's no chance these two cases aren't connected, now. Finding out what happened to Michael Green might be our only lead to locating Millie.'

'Where do we go from here, sir?' DS Chakrabarti asked quietly. 'It's been two days.' The silent implications hung heavy in the air.

Ward sighed and ran a hand through his hair. 'We go back to the beginning. Go through everything again, see what we missed. Back through the forensics from the park, see if anything connects to Michael Green's murder. Check the family. You all remember the Shannon Matthews case, don't you?' The older officers' faces clouded, but the younger officers drew a blank.

Ward explained. 'In 2008, a young girl went missing without trace—just like Millie. It was the biggest police operation of its kind ever committed on home soil since the hunt for the Yorkshire Ripper. Hundreds of officers, thousands of house searches, nationwide media appeals—every resource thrown at it to find that little girl.

'She was found after four weeks. The poor lass had been kidnapped and drugged—arranged by her mother, a staged kidnapping to claim reward money for finding her.

Fifty grand at the time. She was found concealed under a bed in a house belonging to an associate of her mother's boyfriend, who was part of the plot.' Heads were shaking, faces darkening at the awfulness of it. Metcalfe and Norris had worked it. Ward had been fresh on the force then too. How close they had all been, searching for her on their own patch too, so desperately, for any trace.

'We cannot afford to let the same happen again. DSI McIntyre will have all our heads for it if we do, and if it's the case, god knows how that little girl is suffering right now.' He could not help but think of poor Shannon Matthews, drugged and hidden in plain sight. He knew they were all thinking the same—even Jake Patterson had lost his almost ever-present smirk, the smile in his eyes faded under frowning brows.

'I want an update on the mother—her movements, actions, *anything* at all suspicious. I want all the family data reviewing again—the works. Whatever you have to do to see if this is the Matthews case all over again—do it. I want park forensics re-examined. All witness statements taken—reread them. The divers' conclusions. Any phone calls, the tips that were rung in. Everything we have needs to be re-evaluated, in case there's one small thing we missed.

'Then there's Green. Go back over everything from the flat. Did we overlook anything vital? His interview transcripts—did he give us any clues? Can we track his movements on CCTV after leaving here? Any witnesses from the park from last night? Get that appeal out pronto.'

Ward took another breath and continued his tirade. 'Then there's Liam Chapman to consider. With Michael out of the picture, he's the only name left that we can connect to this. Perhaps Chapman and Green worked together to abduct Millie? He might be all we have.'

Ward paused as Kasim's tentative hand rose. 'Yes?'

'Sir, what about the Hunters?'

'Michael was almost certainly murdered—we're waiting on forensics but there's clearly foul play involved. I'd put money on the Hunters being behind it, yes. They're involved in this anyway, what with the stalking and the assault. It's time we talked to Jillian and Andrew Broadway again. Kasim, get on the forum and find out who claimed responsibility for Green's original assault.'

'On it, sir.'

'In the meantime, I'll chase pathology and forensics and find out exactly what killed Green.' He clapped his hands. 'Get to it. I want answers—today!'

CHAPTER TWENTY-TWO

'D I Ward.' He picked up on the second ring—a blessedly normal ring, thanks to DS Nowak's help—his breath hitching as he saw Victoria Foster's name flash up on the screen.

He'd been pacing his office for the last ten minutes as he waited for the call. He hadn't been able to get hold of Baker down in pathology, nor Victoria, but CSI had told him she'd ring him back ASAP with an update. He loosened his collar. It was stiflingly hot, the cracked open window offering no respite.

She sniffed. 'Hi. Promised update here. Baker's doing the post-mortem, but I said I'd speak to you—he's snowed under today with a backlog, so the full report will be a few hours yet.

'I can confirm it's Green. He died dreadfully. It was incredibly brutal.' He could hear her pursed lips, the distaste in her voice—pathology wasn't her gig. Baker must have really charmed Victoria into helping. The antithesis to Ward's cool nature, Baker was the Force's own Stephen Fry, warm and jolly. Only, Stephen Fry with a knack for slicing and dicing dead bodies. And baking.

'He was tortured before he died. He took a real beating—a lot of bruising on much of his body. Some cracked ribs that occurred before death. Burn marks indicating cigarette stubs. His fingers were removed—kitchen cleaver, is Baker's guess—before death. They're missing. One thumb remaining. Oh – and both eyes were gouged out.'

Ward grimaced. They dealt with such a different world to most people. He looked out of the window, watching a woman push a pram along the pavement far below. Under the hood, he could see a child's legs bouncing. He thought of Millie, how they had to find her, alive and well, if she were to ever do that again. Victoria's voice dragged him from his reverie.

'Bleeding and clotting around all of these wounds occurred before the time of death. His hands were bound together with cable ties at some point, which cut into his wrists. There are signs of a struggle. There's foreign DNA under his remaining fingernail. If whoever that belongs to is on the database, we'll have a lead. Also, he...' She trailed off for a moment and Ward's heart sank. How bad was it for matter-of-fact Victoria Foster to not want to say it?

He heard the swallow. Victoria's voice held the slightest shake before she firmed up once more. 'The victim was castrated shortly before death. His testicles and penis were cut off—quite cleanly. Baker suggests a different weapon here, a standard large kitchen knife perhaps. Those body parts are missing. The victim was also violated with some kind of sharp, barbed implement in the rectum, though the instrument was not present when he was found. Significant internal damage...A stick is Baker's best guess, because the cuts are messy, and there were plenty of splinters. There's some nasty bleeding from it all.' By now, Foster sounded positively nauseated.

Ward let out a low whistle. What could he say to that? Whoever had killed Green intended to cause him as much pain and trauma as possible. This wasn't just a robbery gone wrong – it was absolutely personal. And he could think of no one who had it in for Michael Green with more vehemence than the Hunters.

Who else would have targeted him in such a precise way? A child-killer who had potentially raped Sarah Farrow...the revenge was beyond motivated. Jillian Broadway's angry, defiant face swam before him. Oh yes, the Broadways had plenty more information to yield.

'Just be grateful you didn't have to actually see it all. I had to go down to collect the victim's clothing for forensics and there he was, all laid out.' Ward had never heard Victoria Foster, queen of composure, lose her signature coolness.

'Cause of death?'

'Well, there's a mighty wound on the back of his head. But Baker says that occurred first. It didn't kill him, only incapacitated him. Probably how the murderer over-came him. No, the cause of death was asphyxiation.'

'He drowned?'

'Did you not just hear me?' Victoria snapped. Ward's lips twitched in the hint of smile. Victoria Foster was still herself then, brutal death or not.

'You just sai—'

'I said *asphyxiation*, did that sound like drowning to you? No. There was no water in his lungs, so he died *before* he was dumped in the pond—that's Baker's assess-ment. He was gagged—there are abrasions around his mouth, and fibres in his mouth to match, but we don't think that's what killed him. We reckon he was suffo-cated with the bin bag, because there are traces of it in his lungs, so he must have been breathing when it was put over his head.'

Suffocated. Just like Sarah Farrow had been. There could be no doubt. Ward's blood was beginning to chill with the dawning realisation that Green's murderer *must* have been one of the Hunters. It screamed of their involvement, for Green's murder had been symbolically carried out to mimic and exaggerate what had happened to the girl. Whether she'd been raped or abused before her death was forever inconclusive, due to the state of decomposition when her body was discovered...but Ward could hazard a pretty certain guess that in the killer's mind—or killers—for it could likely have been more than one —they believed they had repaid Green amply for his crimes.

Fuck.

Victoria had not finished. 'One more thing. Based on the state of the body, Baker believes the victim died somewhere between midnight and three am last night, and was dumped in the pond soon after.'

'He would have been murdered fairly close by, then. He's a small man but even so, it takes strength to lift a corpse.'

'That's your area of expertise, not mine—but yes. Based on the evidence, the park was not the kill site. We combed around the pond and focused on the woods where it would have been easiest to conceal what happened...nothing. Again, with the park being so well used, it's hard to distinguish a killer from every Tom, Dick, and Harry that went through. That being said...'

'What?' Ward said eagerly, as he heard the tell-tale smugness in her voice—the itch to *know* things.

'We checked the nature trail for prints. It's been closed for weeks for repairs, so the chance of anyone being there are slim to none, unless you perhaps had nefarious intent...'

She was brimming with it now, building up to her crowing epiphany. 'Go on?' He stood to attention, listening, waiting.

'We found evidence of *very* fresh movement in the area. Someone used that path recently. A male, unusually heavy—perhaps heavy enough to be carrying a body— who left plenty of scuff marks in the gravel, and partial prints where it thins out to dirt. I'd estimate we're looking at a size eleven shoe from the partials we took. It might be nothing, but—'

'It might be everything,' Ward breathed.

'Exactly! I still have some of the team up there checking for any blood spatters, or other evidence we might find to corroborate that that was indeed the murderer transporting Michael Green's body. We're still working backwards to establish if there is a particular point of entry to the park, and where the tracks stop.'

'There weren't any witnesses who heard anything unusual last night,' Ward said. 'Nothing was rung in, and nothing has come in from the door-to-doors yet.'

'I reckon that might be significant then. What the murderer did to Michael Green was barbaric—if he was able to scream, you'd have heard him a mile away.'

'You did say he was gagged, though.'

'Hmm. Yes. Still though, I imagine he would have made some noise. There are houses backing onto those woods, and there's no obvious kill site. I don't believe he was killed in the park.'

Ward sighed. More and more questions seemed to be mounting, but no concrete answers. 'Alright. Well, thanks for that, I appreciate the heads up. Let me know as soon as you find anything else.' Ward hung up.

'Shit,' he breathed out, standing utterly still for a moment in his office, letting the awful details replay in his mind.

Michael Green hadn't just been murdered. He'd been *annihilated*. There was only one direction DI Daniel Ward planned to head in right now to start finding out those missing answers. The Hunters.

He stormed back to the Incident Room to brief the team on Baker and Foster's findings.

'Any update on those Hunters?' he growled in the direction of DCs Shahzad and Patterson.

'We're still working on tracking the forum members who claimed responsibility for the attack on Green.' Kasim said.

'Then work faster,' Ward glowered. 'We've got a murder now – aren't they crowing about it? There must be something!'

'We're looking, sir' said Jake quickly.

'They wanted this son of a bitch dead. Not only that, but if they were watching him, they'll know his movements and might lead us to Millie. This is a double enquiry now. It all connects. I need you on this *now* and I need it done yesterday.'

'Understood,' chimed Shahzad and Patterson. They turned tail and left.

'Where are we?' Ward turned his full attention to DC Chakrabarti, who was updating the Big Board.

'We're pulling everything together, sir. There's no CCTV of Green in the village that we've seen yet, but the local shop at the top of the park did say a member of staff recognised him. He went in last night to purchase a pack of cigarettes at approximately eleven fifteen—which can be backed up by their security footage—and he told them he was off to the pubs.' Wibsey was known for the street of pubs that usually led the locals on a crawl from one to the next, from the top of the village to the bottom.

'So, he never made it to the pubs?' Ward frowned.

'And he only had a fiver in his wallet when he was found —less than a tenner if you count change.' Green didn't seem like the type of guy who would pay by card, not when he carried a phone older than half the kids who frequented the bars in Bradford those days, and his closest thing to technology was a laptop which he seemingly only used to access pornography.

Priya shook her head. 'It doesn't appear so, sir. We are still following up but none of the staff recall seeing him. I have a couple of officers going from door to door there to see what they can find. DS Metcalfe is touching base with the family liaison officer so we can dig deeper into Stacey Thompson and any potential family involvement.'

'Blimey—you managed to prise Scott away from his desk?'

DS Chakrabarti let out a dry chuckle. 'Well, it is an emergency, sir. All hands on deck.'

'Where's Emma?'

'DS Nowak's out in Leeds now checking out Liam Chapman's address and making initial enquiries.'

'Who with?' Ward's conscience twitched. He ought to have been out there with her—he'd been so concerned with getting the results from the autopsy back, she had been gone before he'd even realised. His sixth sense was uncurling deep in the pit of his stomach.

'Alone, sir.'

'Right, I'll follow her out there—'

'Hold on, There's also the matter of the press, sir.'

'What about them?'

'Well, with the tent in the park, we're getting a *lot* of enquiries as to whether Millie's body's been found.'

'Damn it.' Ward chewed his lip, thinking. 'We can't tell them Green's dead—not yet. And we have the square root of naff all to give them on Millie.'

'What do you want me to do, sir?'

Ward grinned as a wicked idea unfurled. 'Delegate it.'

'I don't follow.'

'Well, we're only grunts, aren't we? Let DCI Kipling into the loop. If he wants to run press, let him. We can trust him not to give away anything that he oughtn't and he's a better bullshitter than any of us are when it comes to the press.'

Priya's lip twitched. 'I don't think the press will take too kindly to being told to eff off.'

'They shouldn't be a nosy, immoral set of dicks, then.'

'They *are* helping with the Millie Thompson case.'

'Are they?' he said irritably. 'Because so far, TV appeal or not—which, we have *no* useful leads from yet—all they've given us is a wildly damning article with no basis of truth, that has most likely contributed to Michael Green's death and the loss of our most promising lead.'

Someone out there was so sure of his guilt, they acted on it, not even forty-eight hours after the girl had gone missing. 'The press can shove their sense of entitlement up their arseholes until their involvement proves the slightest bit of actual help in this.'

'Alright boss, just saying. The appeal is going national

today. DCI Kipling pulled some strings—every network is taking it up.'

'Hmm.' As much as he hated to admit it, with no other leads, Ward knew it was the best thing to do. Millie Thompson could be anywhere in the country by now – or even out of it. If she had been targeted by traffickers, as unlikely as the scenario was, she could be hundreds of miles from Bradford. He turned his thoughts away from Bogdan Varga and the lorry full of bodies.

'Anything else?' He prayed for any other piece of golden evidence that she had somehow forgotten or saved until last.

A mute shake of Priya's head, and an apologetic glance, were his only answers. He gritted his teeth. His instinct still lurked and it was not to be ignored. 'Right, I'll go after Emma. We might need to bring Chapman in, and something tells me he's not going to like it.'

CHAPTER TWENTY-THREE

D I Ward didn't take an official car, preferring to fly under the radar in his Golf. In Armley, even unmarked cars stuck out like sore thumbs. On the way to the vehicle, a text pinged through. Victoria Foster had obviously deemed him utterly intolerable to speak to and had preferred instead to dispense with any pleasantries.

DNA results back from under MG's nails. Male. No match on database.

Ward cursed loudly. He had hoped the DNA would lead to at least someone known. It was clear that Green had been associated with other known criminals past and likely present whose details would be on file.

He slid into the driver's seat, rested his phone in the charging cradle and waited for it to hook to the Bluetooth after turning over the car before he slid out of the parking space, thumbing the volume button on the steering wheel to turn up the radio. Nothing of interest, just background noise to keep the chatter in his head focused on the case. Noise helped him focus. Silence was unbearable.

He raced along Croft Street—the bridge crossing the Bradford Interchange train lines—following the road as it swept past the city's central cinema complex. Ward turned right up Leeds Road, one of the arterial roads out of Bradford city centre. It would eventually take him to Armley, a rough area of Leeds near the city centre home to an infamous Yorkshire prison—and Michael Green's lover and possible accomplice, Liam Chapman.

Ward had just hit the Leeds ring road when the radio cut out and his phone rang, loud over the car speakers. 'Ward.'

'Sir, it's DS Nowak. I'm at Chapman's. I've found... well sir, I think I've found Millie Thompson's shoe.'

The pit of Ward's stomach seemed to drop away. 'Are you certain?'

'As certain as I can be, sir. DS Chakrabarti sourced a photo of the shoe—the make and type, as described by Millie's mother. She verified it was the same.'

'And you only found one? Where?'

'It's in a wheelie bin outside Chapman's place. The number scratched into the bin matches his flat number. I wouldn't have seen it, except the lid was propped up by bags of rubbish. I just saw the flash of red—it stood out—so I took a closer look, and...' She trailed off, and Ward could hear the wobble in her voice. This case was so important. It was life and death for a defenceless little girl.

'Have you seen Chapman yet? Have you gained entry?'

'No sir, I bagged this and took it straight to the car—sat inside it now.'

'I'm on my way. Don't move until I get there. Keep an eye out—and be careful.'

Ward sped up, slowing for each of the speed cameras. He was minutes away from Emma's position by Chapman's flat, at the bottom of Armley near the giant gyratory that funnelled traffic in and out of the busy city of Leeds, overlooked by the giant prison that perched upon the hill.

Arriving, Ward spotted Emma on a street nearby—she'd smartly parked the unmarked car away from Chapman's so as not to risk scaring off their suspect, but if the man had connections in the area, the entire neighbourhood would probably be well aware the coppers were sniffing about.

He pulled up behind her, jumped out of the car and approached the driver side door, just as she cracked it open.

'You alright?' he asked.

'Yeah. Here it is.' She didn't look happy to have the shoe and Ward couldn't blame her. But at last, finally, they had a tangible clue to Millie's location. She had been here, or somewhere nearby. She was certainly now connected enough to Liam Chapman to have reasonable grounds to bring him in for questioning and search his flat.

'We need a warrant.'

'Already on it, sir. I let Priya know but it could take hours. I've asked her to monitor the calls from the TV appeal in case they bring in any sightings of Liam Chapman that place him anywhere significant—or *with* anyone significant.'

Ward nodded. 'Hopefully it'll turn up something. Two as shady as Green and Chapman couldn't take a two-year-old in broad daylight without being noticed. Come on. Let's see if we can flush Mr Chapman out in the meantime, and ask him why he has a missing girl's shoe in his bin.'

———

Ward and Nowak walked along the deserted streets and along to Chapman's flat. That alone was information enough that their presence had been noticed by the immediate locals, for all they could hear was the dull thunder of Friday afternoon traffic hitting the gyratory. Someone had clearly got the word out that coppers were in the area. Trouble lay a stone's throw away in any direction round there.

They approached Liam Chapman's flat, on the ground floor of a council block, with peeling pebble dashed facades.

Emma stepped forward to rap on the door. 'Police,' she called sharply.

There was no answer. She tried the handle—locked. 'What do we have here?' Emma said, leaning in closer. The paint on the door was scratched down to the wood underneath, and there were gouges to the frame as though someone had put a crowbar to work. The lock was brand new, the plate unscratched. 'This door's been kicked in very recently I reckon, sir.'

Ward nodded his agreement. He stepped back, eyeing the flat above—they were in a private nook, the way the two-storey building had been laid out. The only view on their position was from the flat upstairs, but the curtain didn't even so much as twitch. He circled the building, using the slim paved path that cut between the wall and the grass of the shared gardens, trying to peer into the windows, but it was too dark within to see anything.

'Damn it.' He returned to Emma. 'We need that warrant.'

He could feel his blood pressure rising—Millie Thompson could be inside, alive or dead but without the risk to life clear and the evidence strong, they had no right to kick down the door until a warrant arrived.

A scrape sounded behind them—something catching against the brick wall. And then a clatter as something heavy landed. Ward didn't need to turn—his instinct sounded loud and clear again. Nowak's too, for they both bolted for the gate at the same moment, realising that someone had just vaulted the wall out of the apartment complex.

Nowak—younger and fitter—reached the gate first. 'Think it's Chapman!' she called to Ward, and breaking into a sprint, she went after the figure pulling away ahead. Ward dug deep and forced himself to run—too old, too slow, he felt, as Nowak and Chapman drew away.

'Stop!' DS Nowak called at the man, who did not listen and instead sprinted across a road, earning a horn honk from a passing vehicle that had to brake. Emma sprinted in front of the halted vehicle, and Ward too, before it roared into life and off again behind them, over-heavy on the accelerator. Down another street Ward chased them both, to see Nowak launch herself at the man and tackle him to the ground.

They rolled over and then the man was on top, swiping a fist at Nowak to keep her down. It glanced off her cheek as she scrambled to rise. The man staggered to his feet, but Nowak grabbed him round the knees, holding on doggedly as he stopped again. She was atop him in a flash.

With a knee on his back, she grabbed and twisted an arm until he cried out. 'Liam Chapman, you're under arrest for attempting to evade the police and on suspicion of child abduction!' she gasped as Ward caught up, his breath bellowing as he fought to catch it. 'You do not have to say anything, but it may harm your defence if you do not mention when questioned something you later rely on in court. Anything you do say may be given in evidence.' She slipped a pair of cuffs on him, and hauled him to his feet, helped by Ward, who glared at the man as they stood him up.

'It's him, sir,' she gasped, regaining her breath 'Recognised his face from his files.'

Anger built in Ward as he saw the red mark on Nowak's cheek. 'Are you alright?'

'I'll be fine.' She glared at Chapman.

Dust and dirt covered the front of his grey tracksuit, and he'd scraped his own cheek in the fall. 'My face! You've injured my face—I'll press charges, police brutality! Pigs!' Liam spat a globule of milky saliva at Emma, who dodged out of the way.

Ward launched himself at the man, spinning him around and crushing him face first against a wall. There were a few passers-by on the other side of the road—a raucous catcall launched at the police, but Ward ignored them.

'Don't you do that again,' he growled. 'Call for a van, DS Nowak. And a spit hood. I'm not having my DS assaulted by the likes of *you*.' His dark tone told Chapman exactly what Ward thought of him.

The reek of something familiar reached Ward's nose. 'Do you have anything on you that you shouldn't have, Liam?'

'Fuck off.'

Ward repeated the question.

Sullen silence was his only reply.

'Liam Chapman, I'd suggest you change your tune. You've been arrested in connection with the disappearance of Millie Thompson—I shouldn't need to tell you how serious that is. If you've got anything on you—drugs, needles or any knives—I need to know right now. You will be searched.'

'Dunno what you're talking about.'

'Fine,' Ward ground out. 'We'll do this the hard way.' He nodded for Nowak to approach, whilst he held Chapman firm to make sure the man could not spit at Nowak, lash out, or escape. 'Stand still.'

Nowak ran her hands across Liam's back and down his sides, then padded down his arms and legs, then ran her hands past his groin, stilling when she found a lump that ought not to be there. 'Front of his pants, sir.'

Ward hauled Liam around and, pulling aside the waistband of his pants, lifted out a clear sandwich bag filled with pungent green cannabis.

'Lovely. You're also being arrested for possession of Class B drugs.'

'Nothing else, sir,' said Nowak, having completed her search. Ward could see the relief on her face that the man hadn't had a knife. They always made stop and searches so much more dangerous.

Whilst they waited for the van to arrive, Nowak phoned the station to update DS Chakrabarti. 'Sir?' Nowak held out the phone to Ward. 'She wants to speak to you.'

Ward took the phone. 'Ward.'

At the other end, DS Chakrabarti cleared her throat. 'Got something very interesting, sir. Logged this morning from the TV appeal. A man matching Liam Chapman's description was reportedly sighted with a little girl matching Millie's description on the day of her disappearance, close to his home location.'

Ward stepped a few feet away from Nowak, who was

still watching Chapman with eagle eyes. 'Who reported it?' He said quietly.

'Tip came in anonymously to the appeal hotline. A man, that's all they could tell me. But if it checks out...'

'Bollocks. What use are they to us being anonymous? Look, we've just bagged Chapman. So maybe we have another piece of the trail to pin on him. An accomplice at the very least, perhaps co-conspirator, perhaps even orchestrator...we have to crack him, and fast. I need to get into that flat. How's the warrant coming along?'

'Nowak's find and the tip-off meant I could give a nudge that was more of a shove, if you get me. I'm expecting the warrant any time now, they found someone to review and sign it. I'd get yourself to the property and ready to enter. I've let Foster know. She'll be on her way too.'

Ward could hear the emotion swelling in Priya's voice, the desperate hope that they would still find Millie before it was too late.

'We'll be there,' he promised grimly. They would reroute the police van to Chapman's address and send him off from there to Bradford nick for questioning. Then attend to the most important matter at hand—finding Millie Thompson inside Liam Chapman's flat.

———

When the van arrived, Chapman was loaded into it with more than a few vocal protests, especially when it came to the spit hood that the two PCs fitted to him.

'Thanks,' said Ward grimly, eyeing Chapman through the bars before the van was sealed shut. The man had refused them entry into his flat and refused to give them the keys. Ward couldn't be sure what he was hiding but he loathed Chapman for causing any delay, given the stakes. 'We'll meet you back at the station after we're done here. Can you book him in and get an interview room ready?'

'Aye,' promised the PC.

At that moment, Ward's phone rang. 'Got the warrant,' Priya rushed to say. 'Get in there!'

Ward hung up without replying and nodded to Nowak 'We're good to go. Let's do this.' He charged to the front door and stepped back a pace. Raising a booted foot, he slammed it into the wood. The pain in his knee was blinding, but it was worth it. The door bounced in its frame, dust falling. The new lock was the sturdiest part of it, it seemed, somewhat ironically. Two more kicks and the door couldn't hold up. It creaked open, falling off its hinges, and Ward elbowed the wooden carcass aside.

'Police!' Ward yelled, charging into the flat. It was dark compared to the bright sunlight outside, and Ward halted, his eyes adjusting to the gloom, his nose taking in the assault of stale sweat, cigarette smoke, and weed.

The flat was silent. Ward glanced around. A short hallway led into a lounge to his right and as he ducked his head in, he saw a small kitchen beyond. Ahead lay a door, to a bedroom, he assumed. 'You take the lounge and kitchen, I'll take back here,' he called to Nowak.

'Yes, sir.' Her voice was grim.

They pulled on gloves but Ward realised he hadn't brought boot covers in his haste to charge after Nowak earlier. With a missing child possibly somewhere in the flat, Foster's forensics would have to suffer his bloody footprints on the floor just this once.

He marched along the short hallway and pushed open the bedroom door. It was a pigsty inside, with dark curtains obliterating all the natural light. Ward flicked the switch. A pitifully dim lightbulb flickered into life—it would have to be enough. He had to disturb as little as possible for CSI.

There was not much to disturb in any case. It looked like Chapman didn't care much for homely touches. A dirty mattress lay on the floor, with a greying sheet crumpled on top. An ashtray sat on the floor beside it, piled high with old cigarettes and joint stubs. Beer cans were littered everywhere, and grubby laundry piled up by the wall.

Ward smelled sex there too, the stale remnants of presumably Chapman and Green's dalliances...hopefully nothing involving those of more juvenile ages. Ward's stomach turned at the thought. There was no wardrobe, no furniture—not much room for anything besides the mattress. He backed out carefully, trying to follow his own footsteps, and pushed aside the door next to the bedroom.

Another flick of a switch and a small bathroom jumped into light. Grimy, as though it had never been cleaned, the grout between the tiles was black from floor to ceiling. It stank of stagnant water and shit. Ward peered into the shower, past the curtain that had once been white and was now covered in brown stains, then—reluctantly—down the toilet. He jerked backwards sharply, regretting it at once. That had clearly never been cleaned either. Ward was spotting a pattern here. Green and Chapman were none too big on personal hygiene or any form of cleanliness, it seemed.

'All clear,' he called out to Nowak. He glanced around again, but there was nowhere else to be found, nowhere to hide. He got to the living room just as Nowak emerged.

'All clear here too, sir,' she said. 'Not a trace of the lass.'

Ward itched to leap past her, to search again, miraculously find little Millie Thompson hiding. It wasn't that he did not trust DS Emma Nowak, he had simply been so certain that this was the end of the trail. And now what? The only other option they had right now was to search places where she couldn't hope to be found alive. The woodlands, scrubland, bins...places where a body could be disposed of, since Wibsey park's pond had turned up empty.

'What are we missing, Emma?' he said, meeting her gaze dead on. In the narrow hall, they were crammed together and it was like a window into each other's souls. She mirrored his own uncertainty and utter lack of ideas.

Emma broke the stare first, casting her glance at the floor. 'I don't think we're going to find Millie Thompson alive, sir,' she said quietly.

She couldn't have articulated his worst fear any

better. His fingers flexed into a fist as he resisted punching the stained magnolia walls of the property.

Turning, he stormed outside, relieved to be in the fresh air. He could breathe again, think, see. But why couldn't he connect any of the dots? 'What are we missing?' he asked no one in particular, as though he expected the sky to answer. It was despicably humid now—thunderstorms were on the way. It would give them the break from the relentless heat that they all so desired, but it would also make forensics more difficult. Already, his mind was in the woods, watching clues wash away in a deluge. They had to beat the storm.

But first, they had to wait for CSI to arrive. Ward already knew one thing—Victoria Foster would find no answers in Chapman's flat. Not because she couldn't but because—Ward knew in his heart of hearts—that there were none there. He doubted Millie Thompson had ever set foot there, alive or dead.

It took all his willpower not to crumble now. Because he was surer with every passing second that they were too late. Michael Green had kidnapped Millie Thompson, just like Sarah Farrow, so long ago. Perhaps he and Chapman had had their despicable fun with her, and then together, they had worked to erase the evidence. Ward and his team had been chasing—one step behind, nipping at heels but they were too slow.

———

When Foster turned up with her CSI team, Ward greeted her with little more than a terse 'She's not here. We're too late.'

Victoria took one look at him and then, and her face blanked, paled. She nodded, a frown growing.

'Anything you can find...call as soon as you can. We may be looking for a body now. DS Nowak found her shoe in that bin.'

A breathless Nowak had run to her car to fetch it, returning to hand the bag to Victoria. Victoria waved one of her colleagues over to begin examining the bin.

Ward turned away.

He beckoned to DS Nowak. 'Let's go and question this scumbag.' His voice emerged as a guttural growl that made Victoria take a half step back. Ward stormed away from Liam Chapman's cesspit of a home, back to the car. Back to the station, where he wanted to carve Chapman to pieces for answers.

CHAPTER TWENTY-FOUR

The team was tense and fraught when DI Ward and DS Nowak arrived back at the station. All of them had reached the same conclusion—that the Millie Thompson case was no longer a missing person inquiry, but a murder investigation. They each took it on board with the same personal weight that Ward and Nowak did. Each one feeling as though it was a personal failure.

Ward stood before a silent Incident Room where any detectives not out in the field were gathered. He updated them in as few words as possible on the recent developments. 'Let me be clear. We are still looking for Millie Thompson,' he said, looking at each of them in turn. 'We are still finding out what happened to her, and we are still bringing her *home*. We are still going to find out who is responsible and we will still bring them to justice, whatever has happened to her. Understood?'

'Yes, sir,' rang out sombrely across the Incident Room.

'Where are we, DS Chakrabarti?'

'Our main lead is now Liam Chapman,' she said. Her voice was subdued but clear. 'You're to interview him with DS Nowak now—he's been booked in, but he says he won't speak to anyone without a lawyer, so we —'

'Son of a...' cursed Ward.

Chakrabarti nodded. 'We're getting a legal aid lawyer here ASAP. As you know, CSI are at Liam's flat, and I have word that we have his smartphone in custody downstairs. A tablet has been seized at the property. They're doing the usual sweep and have examined the rubbish in the bin—unfortunately, no further clues from it so far.'

Ward's heart sank. Not that he had expected the two men to dump Millie in with the rubbish, but after finding the shoe there, he had hoped they would find something else.

'We've been combing back over everything sir, but nothing yet, I'm afraid.'

Ward looked around until he spotted Kasim and Jake stood near the back of the room. 'You two. What about your dark web stuff on those Hunters?'

Kasim cleared his throat. 'Promising, sir. I'm close to tracking down some of the more vocal users who might be connected to what happened to Green. So far, there's still no chatter on there about his death.'

'That's odd, don't you think?'

'Exactly. If they were responsible...you'd expect it to be off the charts.'

'Keep on it. Good work. Have you an address for the Broadway's too? I haven't forgotten them.' They would be his next port of call after Liam Chapman.

Liam Chapman awaited DI Ward and DS Nowak in Interview Room Two. He sat huddled at the grey table without handcuffs, quiet, though Ward was not entirely sure of his compliance given the man's posture—folded arms, legs clamped together, head bowed—he could just see a scowl of magnificent proportion marring the man's gaunt face.

Beside Liam—with her chair edged away, as though she did not want to be close to him—sat his young lawyer, a bone tossed from the court as his Legal Aid representation, whether she liked it or not. In her mid-twenties, she was a similar age to Nowak, but looked ill at ease in her attire—a too-large pinstripe skirt suit, polished black heels that glinted in the harsh strip lighting of the room, and a poker straight bob framing her round face.

At their entrance, Liam looked up, open dislike brewing on his stubble-covered face. Dark hollows ringed his eyes as he evaluated Ward and Nowak. He crossed his legs, the cheap grey fabric of his tatty, dirty tracksuit slithering together, and his folded arms tightened.

Very cooperative, Ward wryly thought. He crossed to the empty chairs opposite and sat down with Nowak, who placed a brown manila folder on the table. The lawyer eyed it. Nowak said nothing, meeting her stare with a steely expression.

DI Ward cleared his throat and spoke for the benefit of the recording, and the cameras above them, confirming the date, time, names of those present, and reason for interview.

Immediately the lawyer jumped in. 'My client denies the charge. He has no knowledge of Millie Thompson and you have insufficient evidence to charge him further.' She sniffed and sat taller, her back ramrod straight. 'I've already lodged a complaint to overturn the warrant with which you illegally searched my client's property, and filed for his personal effects to be returned.'

'The warrant was entirely legal,' Ward said flatly, 'So let's not waste time. We had very reasonable belief to arrest Liam Chapman on the basis that we did and the warrant was exercised to the letter.' He turned to Chapman and gave him a dark smile. 'Don't worry. I kicked down your door the moment it was legal to do so and not one second sooner.'

Liam swore and made to stand, his face flooding red.

'Sit down!' his lawyer hissed.

He sank back into his chair, glaring venomously at her, before turning his ire on Ward and Nowak.

'Listen to your legal counsel,' Ward suggested. 'Wouldn't want you tripping up now, would we.'

'I want my stuff back,' Liam snarled.

'And you'll get it,' said Ward, leaning back in his chair, his tone casual. 'When we've had a good look through it all.'

'My client is needlessly in custody. Are you planning to actually ask him any questions?' interjected the lawyer pointedly.

'You better not break anything,' snapped Chapman. 'I'll have you for it.'

Ward smirked. 'I told you. You'll get it back when we're done—if it's clean.' He turned stony eyes upon Chapman. 'And we *will* be going over every inch of it, believe me. I wonder what we'll find? But, as Miss Roper here has kindly pointed out, that's not why we're here. We have something far more important to discuss.'

Liam Chapman visibly squirmed in his seat as Ward stared him down.

'Where is Millie Thompson, Liam?'

'How would I know?'

'We have multiple sightings of Michael Green around the area at the time she was abducted, and a sighting later that day of a man matching your description, with a girl matching Millie's description, in Armley. Her shoe was found in your rubbish bin today, Mr Chapman. We know you and Michael abducted her. Tell us where she is. We've already searched your shithole of a flat.'

Chapman scowled. 'I. Don't. Know.'

'Not good enough,' snapped Ward. 'I want to know what you've done with her. Is she alive?'

'No comment.'

DS Emma Nowak pushed a photograph of Millie across the table. The toddler stared unblinkingly up at them all, innocent and unknowing. Next, Emma pulled out a photo of Millie's shoe, on a white background next to a tape measure.

'How can you look at her face, and not tell us where she is?' Ward demanded.

"Cos I don't know! I told you.' Liam snapped.

Beside him, his solicitor turned to give him a warning glare, but the callous look he returned it with had her paling and turning back to face DI Ward and DS Nowak, her lips clamping together in obvious discomfort at the client she had to represent. She eyed Ward and Nowak anxiously.

'Ok, Liam, I get it. I understand.' Ward leaned forward, clasping his hands together, and placing them on the table. 'It was all Michael's idea, wasn't it?'

'Ask him yourself,' came the surly reply.

Ward and Nowak shared a glance. *He doesn't know.* Ward cocked his head. 'We would, but we can't. Bit difficult to ask a dead man anything.'

That got his attention. Liam's head whipped up, his wild glare piercing Ward. 'What?'

Ward shook his head.

Liam's hands fell into his lap as, in a moment, the fight in him vanished for a moment before it returned in full force. 'You're lying! I saw him the other day—we texted yesterday. Once he left here. He was fine—gonna come over mine today, 'cept he...never showed.' His voice slowed. As the penny dropped.

'Michael Green was murdered last night,' Ward said. 'Terribly sorry to be the bearer of bad news.'

Liam shook his head, visibly distressed. 'How? Who?'

Ward sighed. 'I'm not at liberty to discuss an ongoing inves—'

'It was those bloody Hunters wasn't it? Those bastards have had it in for him a long time.' Chapman's jaw set in a vicious snarl.

How ironic, Ward thought. *The criminal sees himself as the victim.*

'I can't discuss an ongoing investigation,' Ward repeated, 'but we are connecting the murder to the disappearance of Millie Thompson. The evidence is stacking up that you and Michael were involved in that.'

Liam started to speak, but Ward spoke louder, flattening his protest. 'Let me help you out here, Liam. This is bad enough as a missing person investigation, but if we find out that that little girl is dead because of your actions, or your attempts to evade justice, the consequences will be far worse for you, I can promise you that.'

'I don't have anything do with it!' Liam protested desperately. 'What Michael got up to was his own business. I'm not a kiddie fiddler, that's fucking monstrous.'

Ward let out a boom of cynical laughter. 'Great to hear you have some principles, Mr Chapman, but your conviction record is hardly glowing.'

'I've *never* seen that little girl. You've got to believe me!' Liam's gaze was frantic as he searched Ward's face for any sign of sympathy, understanding, acknowledgement.

He did not find any.

Ward leaned forward and tapped the picture of Millie's shoe. 'Then why was an exact match for her shoe found in your wheelie bin, Mr Chapman? Explain that.'

Slowly, Liam sank back in his chair. The seriousness

of the interview dawned on him—that the drugs possession wasn't the serious part of his arrest after all. That
they were no longer looking for a missing girl but a
murdered one. That he was the prime suspect. And his
lover was dead.

CHAPTER TWENTY-FIVE

'DI Ward. Sir!' Kasim's voice echoed along the hallway. Ward turned.

'Sir, Green's death is out. I don't know who leaked it, but the T&A have picked it up, the *Yorkshire Post*, *Bradford Herald*, *Halifax Courier*, *Leeds Star*...it's everywhere. Every time I refresh, it hits another outlet. It's spreading like wildfire.'

'Shit. What's the story?' Ward hoped they didn't have all the gory details—that no one inside had leaked it.

'Not as much as we know, thankfully. Only that Green is dead and was found in Wibsey Park. They have pictures of the forensics tent, nothing else. Oh, and they're wondering if it's connected to Millie Thompson's disappearance. There's not much to speculate but our press office is already being hounded for updates. We're not issuing a statement, are we?'

'Damn right we're not,' said Ward with a scowl, but relief surged. It must have been a public tip, and the press had tied the two stories together. Michael Green and Millie Thompson. 'Never feed sharks. They only keep coming back for more. Ask DS Metcalfe to pass this on to DCI Kipling. He can beat them off with a stick. We have more important things to do.'

'There's another thing too, sir.' Kasim was visibly uncomfortable.

'Yes?'

'The Hunters are lit up about this, sir. Whilst you were in the interview with Chapman, details of Green's death were posted on the forum by an anonymous user—didn't even have a username. And they know more than the papers. They know things that no one would know, unless...'

'Unless they killed Michael.'

'Or were party to the knowledge, sir. And if they're using a completely anonymous front on an already hidden, anonymous forum...I reckon we *are* looking at the culprit, or one of them.'

'Are they taking credit for the murder?'

'No. I think they're being very careful not to. Unfortunately for us, anyway. I'll keep looking.' Kasim held a hand up as Ward made to speak. 'Oh, it gets worse, sir, sorry. As far as the Hunters are concerned, this is the best thing since sliced bread. There are calls for what happened to Michael to happen to others too. There's a lot of excitement about this. They're whipping themselves into a frenzy.' Kasim frowned.

'Right. So, keep monitoring that chatter. Stay on it,

don't miss a thing. If you see any whiff of a credible threat, you know what to do.'

'Do you want me and Jake on that, sir?'

'Put DC Patterson onto it as a matter of urgency. I want you honing in. We need names, and fast. Who are these people? Where are they? What involvement do they have with Michael Green's targeting?' He was more certain than ever now that the Hunters were responsible for Green's death. But where did that leave Millie?

Damn them! He cursed. The Hunters had cost them what little chance of finding Millie Thompson alive—or dead—that they had. He would make them pay for it, when the time came.

————

The news did not improve as the day went on, and the storm brewed outside, the once blue skies now clogged with cavernous clouds of steel and thunder that rumbled ominously, hiding the light and deepening the gloom inside the station.

The press were unrelenting—and a statement by DCI Kipling had done nothing to placate them. The DCI was on the warpath, and Ward had already taken a ribbing for not having more answers. Ward had almost retorted but he stopped short. It wouldn't help Millie Thompson if he lost focus now. And so, he took DCI Kipling's flak with unusual silence, until the DCI had done berating him and turned him loose to try and make sense of any of the mis-fitting pieces of evidence they had.

Ward had only one hope of salvation left. Victoria Foster. He'd never admit it to her, of course, but she held the key to their success that day. 'She has to have something on the bastard,' he muttered to himself as he stalked down to her department in answer to the cryptic voicemail she had left him whilst he had been getting his dressing down from Kipling.

The interview with Chapman had yielded nothing. Questions with no answers, statements without comment. If Chapman knew anything, he wouldn't crack with the evidence they had so far—and nor could they charge him without anything more. Ward couldn't contemplate what might happen if Chapman truly was as ignorant as the man claimed—if he was a dead end. Their best, and only other lead was mutilated and stone-cold dead in the morgue.

Ward let himself in and Victoria waved him over. Her office was impeccably tidy, filing cabinets lining one wall, all neatly labelled in her scrolling script, her desk clear of papers or any personal touches. A vase of fresh Stargazer lilies was the only decoration. They cast a pungent scent over the room that made his nose itch.

'We've done, and we've got what we can. I'm sorry—you're probably not going to like it.'

Ward's shoulders sank. He was too deflated to snap at her—she truly had been the last hope they had. He needed Victoria to come through to give them a next step. Anything at all.

'Go on,' he forced out the words.

'We dusted his flat for prints. All adult prints—matching Liam Chapman and Michael Green. Couple of other locals on our files too. Nothing child-sized, I'm afraid—and there are no signs anything has been cleaned or scrubbed—' Ward could well imagine that from the state of the dump, '—to conceal someone else being there. The only physical piece of evidence we have is the shoe inside Liam Chapman's bin, which *has* been scrubbed clean. So clean, in fact, that there's no DNA on it at all.'

'It was deliberately cleaned?'

'Yes.' Victoria looked at him, like him, clearly speculating, but only that. If they had nothing more than speculation, it wouldn't help one jot.

'What do you think?' He levelled with her. He respected her professional opinion after all. She mirrored his folded arms and leaned back in her chair, chewing on her lip.

'It's odd, is what I think. Doesn't make sense. You've seen how Chapman and Green live. Honestly, I don't think either of them even own any cleaning products, let alone know how to use them. That's the only thing I'm stalling on. We have no trace of Millie Thompson. None whatsoever. She was not at Green's flat. She was not at Chapman's. But...the shoe. It ties at least Chapman to her. And you say Green had been staying with him?'

'Apparently. They were both sighted too. Green near the scene of her disappearance. Chapman later that day, with a girl matching Millie's description.'

Victoria shook her head. 'So they *had* to be involved. Evidence or not.'

Ward nodded grimly.

Victoria whistled. 'Well then. The shoe fits—no pun intended. Perhaps they're not stupid after all. Not in the forensics sense. They knew to clean any trace off the shoe, but I'm surprised they figured out how to do such a good job, to be honest. They're both criminals, Chapman more so than Green, arguably, if you go by conviction counts alone, but they're not exactly *clever*.'

'You've been digging.'

'I like to know what I'm dealing with.' She met his eyes with a challenging fire in her gaze. He didn't disapprove, in fairness. Thoroughness was one of the traits that made her so good at what she did. She spotted everything there was to spot. 'I'm one hundred percent certain, Daniel. Millie Thompson was never at either of those flats.'

'So where did they take her—and where is she now?' he asked quietly.

Victoria's reply was soft—softer than she normally spoke to him. 'That's your job to determine—not mine.'

Ward ran a hand through his hair and exhaled. 'Alright. Well, I suppose, it might not be what we wanted to hear, but it's useful. We can discount the flats. We just have to find a needle in a haystack elsewhere. Do you have anything else?'

Victoria wrinkled her nose. 'Just a disgusting porn collection to put Michael Green's to shame.'

Ward grimaced.

'Tech Forensics said the laptop was full of it. Chapman moves in darker circles than Green—or perhaps they used his device together. Who knows? He uses the dark web to connect with a network of other known parties in the sexually *deviant* community, shall we say. The content on the laptop is mostly above board. Some homemade adult stuff directly on the hard drive, and well-known providers on his web history. However, there's some indecent items you'll want to question him about.' Her mouth thinned into a hard line.

Ward waited for her to continue.

'There looks to be underage content on there. Boys and girls, younger teenagers. *Maybe* he could argue that he believed some were overage—it's harder to tell these days, isn't it? But plenty are absolutely *not* overage. I'm not sure whether he's making it or just consuming it, but he shouldn't have it either way, so I'll leave it with you. I'll email you the relevant details and files.'

'It's proof that he—they—had sexual motives that could have linked them to Millie Thompson's disappearance though, isn't it?'

'Yes,' said Victoria heavily, and when she glanced up at him her eyes were haunted. 'It does. His phone is much the same. Smartphone, unlike Green. A colourful web history on there, and a contact list that probably matches a list of people you'd like to lock up, to be quite honest.'

'I wonder if we're looking at a whole network, not just one or two,' Just like Varga, who had a spider's web weaving across an entire continent. 'Perhaps we haven't found her because someone else has her.'

Victoria pondered for a moment. 'Maybe. But Daniel, you need to find that little girl. These are *awful* people.' Her hard voice wavered ever so slightly, a sign of the inner turmoil behind her flawless mask.

'We will.' Ward turned away, his next step already firmly in mind—going back over Green's—and now Chapman's—phone records. There could be a paedophile ring at play here that they had only just uncovered. And he had to find the rest of the players—before the Hunters did.

As he left, Ward knew Victoria would be thinking the same thing—that Millie Thompson could still be alive, or dead, at the hands of a gang of child abusers. It did not bear thinking about—if she had been passed around them like a toy. He'd seen it before, the depravity to which humankind could descend. And he prayed to a God he did not even believe in, that it was not true for Millie Thompson's fate.

CHAPTER TWENTY-SIX

'You don't think DI Ward will, y'know...' DC Patterson trailed off.

'Fire you?' DC Shahzad answered. 'Oh, God, yeah. But not for this, if that's what you're asking.'

Jake shot Kasim a glare, as he spun side to side in his office chair. Then, he leaned forward, and hit the button. 'Alright. S'done. No going back.'

'Welcome to the dark web,' Kasim said with a sinister wink from under lowered brows.

'Don't,' Jake groaned.

Kasim chuckled.

'What're you two knuckleheads doing?' DS Metcalfe appeared from nowhere, and leaned on both the lads' chairs, causing them to tip back, and for Jake to spit out an entirely not office friendly curse as he went off balance.

'Just signed Jake here up as a Hunter, sir,' Kasim replied.

Metcalfe raised an eyebrow. 'Come again?'

'Well sir, gotta think like them, be one, if we want to find them, right?'

Metcalfe's eyebrow rose higher, like he didn't follow, but gave Kasim a chance to continue.

'We can't access most of the forums—gotta have a username. There wasn't another way that we could think of, sir. But, we knew if we could get in, we could maybe find something out.'

'Kasim,' Jake interrupted, and pointed at the screen. 'Look!'

Kasim turned and Metcalfe leaned in, squinting at the screen.

Jake grinned. 'Bingo.'

Metcalfe grumbled, 'Can one of you young whipper-snappers please tell me what on earth I'm supposed to be looking at?'

'This, sir,' said Kasim, choosing his words with careful relish, 'is the Hunters' inner sanctum. There are extra boards in this user-only forum. Look at that—coordinating upcoming attacks on identified figures...shit. This is important. We have to pass this on. Staffordshire, London, Kent, Cornwall, Northumberland, Manchester...They're pumped about Michael's murder, and they're going to strike hard and fast and follow it with violent action across the country.'

Metcalfe gaped as he realised the gravity of what they had uncovered. Then he set to it. 'Right, lads. Get on this, *now*. I want all the information collected and sent to the relevant forces within the hour. Keep monitoring it for any updates. I'll fill Ward in on this.'

'On it,' Kasim vowed grimly, and turned back to his keyboard, his fingers already flying across the keys in a blur.

'Oh, and lads?'

'Hmm?'

'Any closer to identifying the Hunters who claimed responsibility for Green's attack or murder?'

Kasim sighed 'Sort of. We're waiting on a warrant to request IP addresses from the user's VPN servers. Trouble is they don't see it as high priority, finding out who attacked a guy who's now turned up dead, especially dealing with international VPN firms, who aren't exactly the most compliant.'

'Put pressure on them—tell them what you've just found out. We now have active leads of impending harm to multiple persons and the intent to cause fear and incite violence. We could classify this as domestic terrorism. We have details of some of the attacks, but there's nothing to suggest other users might not be inspired to carry out their own initiatives off the grid, so to speak. That should get your warrant actioned. This is now your top priority—understood?'

'Yes, DS,' Kasim and Jake replied.

———

By the time Ward returned to his tiny flat, he had entirely forgotten the photos in his kitchen drawer and the threat of Varga hanging over the place. In truth, it was out of sheer exhaustion.

Despite hours of interviews, Liam Chapman had given them nothing. They had enough to keep him in overnight, and they could charge him for possession of the indecent underage content as well as the drugs, but it wasn't what Ward needed. It wasn't what Millie Thompson needed.

Ward moved automatically, retrieving a microwave lasagne from the fridge, peeling back the plastic, and setting the timer on the microwave, the beeps punctuating his mental fog. He stood, eyes fixed on the microwave and the spinning plate within—yet, seeing nothing of it.

What were they missing?

Neither Green or Chapman had any forensic connection to Millie Thompson. The anonymous sightings couldn't be verified. All they had was a damn kid's shoe, all too conveniently placed and clean as a whistle. They needed more. But aside from the contacts in Chapman's and Green's mobiles and the history on Chapman's laptop, Ward had precious little else. He clenched his jaw in frustration, just as the microwave pinged. He rescued the meal, hissing when the carton burned his finger as he juggled it out.

Tipping the meal on to a plate, he headed for the creaking sofa and plopped down, going back over the remains of the day while he waited for his food to cool. 'What are you missing, Ward?' he challenged himself. His police instinct had never led him wrong, and now, it was screaming that he was looking in the wrong place. How could it be, when common sense told him they'd likely uncovered a ring of dangerous sex offenders and paedophiles?

Ward turned his attention to the window. Darkness had fallen at last. What time was it? He checked his phone. 'Christ', he muttered. Half past ten. No wonder he was so tired—he hadn't stopped until Metcalfe had insisted he pack up and go. He probably wouldn't have, had Scott not intervened, so immersed in the case was he. Metcalfe had invited him for dinner—not that his wife would have liked it. To her presumed relief, Ward had turned him down. The five minutes he'd promised he'd stay after Scott's departure still turned into another two hours before he did at last realise the time with a start and call it a day.

Car headlights raked past outside, below in the car park, and with a chill, Ward remembered the photos. All of a sudden, the window didn't seem like a welcome bringer of light, a vantage onto the outside world. It became an eye, focusing on him with unbearable scrutiny. Ward launched off the sofa and yanked the beige curtains closed, his heart racing. His attention slid to the otherwise innocuous kitchen drawer—as though its contents somehow perceived him too with a malicious sentience of their own.

His phone was in his hand, he realised, and he hovered over the unlock button. Should he warn Katherine? He warred with himself internally for a long moment. No. Better not. Varga was after him, not Katherine. Besides which, he didn't want to speak to her. Couldn't face hearing the same old accusations flying. 'You're obsessed! You're so paranoid! Why can't you drop this nonsense?'

Slowly, his finger retreated from the unlock button, and his hand dropped to his side.

No.

Best not for either of them if he didn't tell her about that photo, taken in front of their former home, on the very day he had left for good.

It was nothing.

Probably.

Ward gave the windows and door one last check before he flicked off all the lights in the living area and made his way to the bedroom to get ready for bed.

It wasn't thoughts of Millie Thompson that hounded him into slumber. It was Varga and Katherine. And, as he at last sunk into sleep, the wraiths awaited him deep in his nightmares, welcoming him back into the wretched depths of the lorry filled with death and despair.

―――――

Daniel Ward was one of them, this time. This was the very worst of his nightmares. He laid upon his back and the cold floor of the lorry shuddered under him, in motion as it sped towards its final, fateful destination.

Above the rumble of its engine, he could hear the choking, gasping, desperate moans of those around him. The stench of their acrid fear and the excrement in the van choked him as much as the lack of air to breathe, and his chest tightened in panic, the nightmare as real to him as any of them.

In the faint light of a tiny lamp fixed to the inside of the truck, they were nothing but shadows lumbering over him. They clutched at each other, some clawing at the door behind his head until their nails bled, dripping hot blood on him, some hammering the walls with broken down crates—each strike becoming weaker, slower, than the last.

Bang...bang...bang...

He could not move, his limbs leaden. Weighed down by his own fear and the bodies piling upon him. One by one they fell, never to rise again, covering him in limp limbs, slack faces falling into his periphery, contorted by suffering and terror, their bloodshot eyes seeming to bulge out of their sockets.

Ward struggled under their dead weight, but his limbs would not obey—it was as though he were clamped there by force, unable to move at all, command of his limbs having fled. He could only endure as the dead mounted, with him at the very bottom of the pile, until they crushed him to the floor so deeply that he could not even expand his chest to fill his lungs with the life-taking air.

And then, they compressed him further. Through the very bottom of the lorry, they all seemed to sink with him still buried under them, a great mass of tangled limbs and bodies, into blackness and cold and silence. The faint light inside the truck faded away, and with it, so too faded Daniel Ward, with his last, gasping breath.

CHAPTER TWENTY-SEVEN

Haunted by the cold, clammy hands of the dead in the night, the spectres of his imagination, Ward was glad to get back to work the next morning. It was a weekend—overtime, technically—but he didn't care. The whole team was in and the swell of pride at their dedication banished the last of Varga's spectres into the recesses of his mind, as, in the cold light of a dreary, rain-soaked day, Ward focused on the case at hand with fresh determination.

More details of Green's death had leaked to the press overnight, it appeared. DC Shahzad flagged Ward first with an update, having seen the growing chatter on the forum, then backing it up with articles from all of the major local news outlets.

Ward followed Kasim to his computer to scan quickly through it all. 'There's no way they could have speculated this. Someone who knows what happened to Green fed them this.'

'Agreed, sir. It was on the *Bradford Herald* site first, then spread to the others, so I think they got the tip first—just like last time. There's no one claiming direct responsibility on the forums we've accessed so far, but there are some other areas of the site we can't access. Jake's still working to get in.'

'See that he does. I'll handle the paper.' Ward would be damned if they protected a source now, when a murder investigation could be compromised by their omission. The leak could have only come from two sources—his own team, or the murderer and their accomplices.

He stormed to his office to find the editor's details, and rang through at once. 'James McCreary?'

'I'm sorry, Mr McCreary is busy right now. Please may I take a message?' a young man's voice replied.

'I'm Detective Inspector Daniel Ward from the West Yorkshire Police. I need to speak to Mr McCreary as a matter of urgency.'

'I'm sorry, Detective. He's in a meeting. I can check his calendar and book a meeting in, but it won't be this week, as he's very busy.'

Annoyance spiked. Ward knew exactly the type of arrogant peacock he'd be dealing with. But he could also take them down a peg or two when it counted. 'I can bring him into the station for questioning today, if he prefers. Song and dance. Big fuss.'

The man on the other end of the line stuttered. 'Uh, um, no...I'll see if...that won't be necessary I'm sure. Hang on, just let me try...Please hold.'

The line went silent, the sound of static clicking in Ward's ear as the ruffled secretary clearly tried to get hold of his boss while Ward waited. After a couple of minutes, the young man's breathy voice returned. 'Mr McCreary will take your call.'

'Of course he will,' muttered Ward. A call from the police tended to make people free up their schedules pretty quickly.

'Hello?' A much older, more confident voice said, one with the impatient bite of someone who did not like to be dictated to.

'James McCreary?' Ward said as pleasantly as he could.

'Yes, who's calling? You pulled me out of a very importa—'

Ward cleared his throat, cutting McCreary off. 'Detective Inspector Daniel Ward of West Yorkshire Police's Homicide and Major Enquiries Team. I have a few questions regarding some articles you've been sharing about Michael Green and Millie Thompson.'

'What about them?' McCreary's voice immediately closed up with hostility.

'I need your source.' There was no point beating around the bush.

'I'm afraid, Detective, that we don't give up our sources. A matter of respect, I'm sure you understand.'

'I think you'll find I don't, Mr McCreary. You received a tip that led to an article being published linking Millie Thompson's disappearance to Michael Green quite unnaturally soon after the girl's disappearance—and that article, I might add, led to a violent assault on Michael Green and then his subsequent murder, due to your paper's uncovering of his whereabouts.'

'Yes, well, we can't help the timing of our sources. Journalists need to be quick off the mark, so we acted swiftly.'

'You didn't publish the story we asked for—which was to highlight the search for Millie Thompson. You printed an entirely self-serving, profit grabbing, clickbait pile of slanderous drivel that led to a man being assaulted and murdered, and an ongoing police investigation seriously impeded.' Ward couldn't keep the contempt from his voice.

'Freedom of speech, Detective,' replied McCreary smoothly.

'Well, you're free to say whatever you please when we charge the paper with offences relating to the matter. Especially since you may now be protecting a murderer.'

McCreary spluttered. 'I beg your pardon?'

'Your latest tipoff about Michael Green was regarding his murder. There's nowhere else you could have gotten those details—and the ones you've since published, which, I might add, are subject to a highly sensitive investigation—except the murderer or their accomplice.'

McCreary's response, stuttering when it came, was incomprehensible as he tried to refute the implications of Ward's statement.

Ward continued. 'So, unless you'd like to visit the station to enlighten us, or have however many of your staff brought in for questioning on the matter, I'd suggest you give up that source now.'

'Well, I mean, I'm afraid that I don't handle news *personally* here, you see—'

'—Rubbish,' Ward scoffed. 'The biggest story you've had for the last three weeks is bin collections running late because there's an outbreak of food poisoning at the depot. If a child-murderer dropped into your lap, I'm betting you'd know *all* about that, Mr McCreary, and, whilst I'm at it, I might as well remind you what's at stake here, and what's truly important,' Ward continued, grinding out every word, 'because it damn well isn't your bottom line. It's the fact that out there, a little girl is missing and with each passing hour, her safety and well-being are compromised and the likelihood we'll find her alive *shrinks*. So do the right thing, Mr McCreary, or I will do everything in my power to let the good folk of Bradford know that at your paper, your bottom line means a lot more to you than a little girl's life. And you can watch all your readers switch to the *Telegraph & Argus*.'

'Now there's no need to be like that,' Mr McCreary replied indignantly, and in his mind's eye, Ward could imagine the man. Middle-aged and portly—well-endowed after a lifetime of fat pay checks—not to mention puffed with his own sense of self-importance. He had met plenty of men like him. Cowards, hiding behind egos and bluffs.

'Give me the source and we don't have to go any further. No harm to your reputation, or your paper's.'

Silence greeted him.

'McCreary? If you don't like that, remember, you're always welcome at the station for a chat.'

'Alright, alright!' snapped McCreary—and now, Ward could picture a rounding face with generous quivering jowls going red with annoyance. 'I'll get you the details.'

'Now, if you don't mind. Time is very much of the essence.'

'Leave your details with my secretary,' was the only reply McCreary gave him, curt and clipped, before the line went silent again. The receptionist picked up once more.

Ward left his details and gave the young man crystal clear instructions on what to do when McCreary obtained the information he needed—although he stopped short of telling the lad to pass on to McCreary to shove his details up his self-important arse.

It wasn't long before his phone rang. McCreary had not deigned to ring personally, and Ward was hardly surprised by that, when the young receptionist's voice spoke instead to pass on the details. Just a number.

'That can't be all of it,' Ward said, his pen hovering in the air above the Post It note he'd jotted the mobile number on.

'Mr McCreary said you might say that. He told me to tell you that's all we have—no name, or any other details. Just a man's voice, he called from that number.'

Ward muttered a curse under his breath. 'Right.

Thanks.' It was better than nothing. He would pass it straight to Patterson and Shahzad to investigate.

He strode to the Incident Room, where they'd created a nest of paperwork that looked a total mess but Ward recognised as organised chaos. A bleary-eyed Nowak looked up from the midst of a folder of photos from Chapman's flat. She was searching frantically amongst them. Patterson and Shahzad weren't there, so Ward continued straight on to the main office.

Ward blinked back the crushing tiredness. Whenever the nightmares came, they trapped him in a sleep he couldn't escape—and yet restfulness was the last thing they brought. He couldn't have them affecting the rest of his waking life too.

'DC Patterson,' he called over to the two lads huddled together in the corner across the shared office. 'Can you run a number for me, please? Might be connected to your Hunters.'

Patterson lifted his head, attention piqued. 'Course, sir.'

Ward explained where the number had come from and Patterson whipped the Post It note out of his hand, then typed the number into a window on his screen. 'Right. I've got the network. I'll get in touch and request details. Shouldn't be long hopefully, if they're playing ball.'

'Great. I'm off to interview Chapman again now. I'll see you after. Have you seen DS Metcalfe?'

'Yeah. The old grizzly bear's holed up in his office

grunting about being hauled in on a Saturday or some such thing. Wouldn't poke him if I were you, sir.'

Ward snorted. 'I can handle Metcalfe.' Though Ward now commanded Metcalfe, Ward always deferred to his experience. Metcalfe was a father figure to them all, in many ways. He'd helped more than one of them through a life crisis, with a steady, kind hand.

As Ward entered his office, Metcalfe grunted at Ward in a decidedly *not* fatherly way. 'It's too early to see your face,' he groaned. 'Go away. I need at least two more cups of coffee to deal with today.'

'It's nearly half nine—what's wrong with you?'

'It's called getting *old*, Danny-boy, and some day, it'll happen to you, so wipe that smirk off your face. I can't run around like you young whippersnappers, you know. Five days in and I'm done—I've done my years of overtime and they're long behind me.' He let out an enormous yawn.

Ward chuckled. 'I need you in with me to interview Chapman. Come on, grandad. I reckon if you snore at him for long enough, he'll crack under the pressure.'

Metcalfe shook his head in disbelief, snagging his half-full coffee cup as he walked around his desk. 'You know, they just don't teach respect to you youngsters these days.'

Ward grinned. Metcalfe always lightened his mood. 'Nowt to do with that, Scotty. It's just impossible to respect anyone from Lancashire, that's all.' He clapped Metcalfe on the shoulder. 'Come on. Let's get this bastard.'

CHAPTER TWENTY-EIGHT

An hour later, and, with the evidence, they had enough to charge Liam Chapman for possession of indecent images of minors, but still nothing in connection with Millie's disappearance. Ward's better mood had vanished with every refusal to cooperate.

'What do we do?' he mused aloud to Metcalfe outside. 'We'll have to bail him, but if we do...'

'Then he might go the same way as Green, and we lose our only lead,' finished Metcalfe grimly.

'Exactly.'

'We can't keep him in any longer for this—at best we might be able to drag it out a little whilst we charge for the indecent stuff, but we can't get him for anything more serious.'

Ward ran a hand through his hair. 'Hands tied, again.'

'Do you think he did it?'

'You know what, Scott, I'm not sure what I think any

more. A wise man once taught me that stupid criminals get caught. And these two...they're not the smartest tacks in the box, let's face it.'

Scott chuckled dryly.

'Nowak's already been through all the bus CCTV footage we can find for Green, and there's no clues there. He gets on and off the bus along highly populated routes. There's no sign of Millie with him in the city centre, and we can trace his route back to Great Horton, where again, it's too built up for him not to have been seen if she had been with him. I can't believe that they're clever enough to pull this off. If they had anything to do with it, we would have found *something*.'

'And the shoe?'

'It's the only piece of the puzzle that doesn't fit.' Ward shook his head. 'I'm going to give Victoria a call.'

'It's her day off. That's brave.'

'Foolish, more like. Quite possibly suicidal. But, she examined the shoe. I have to get her take on this. The moment we cut Liam loose into the wind, we're out of options.'

'I disagree, sir,' Emma Nowak's voice piped up from behind them.

'Oh?' Ward left the invite to elaborate hanging.

Emma frowned. 'They aren't the most stupid criminals I've ever met, I'll give them that, but they're not clever enough to pull this off with no clues—I feel that in my gut. That shoe *is* what ties them to it, so don't over-think it. It's an oversight that they shouldn't have made. Maybe a trophy they decided to keep, then had a change of heart on, but they didn't go far enough to conceal it. Why else would it be there if they're not involved?'

Ward shook his head, grave, as he considered her view, but he had no answers, only the same instinct that they were missing something glaringly obvious. He just didn't know what.

Metcalfe halted. 'I can see you've got a bee in your bonnet about this. Look—call Victoria. I'm sure she'll understand. Follow your gut. Always the best way, right?'

'All the way to the kitchen.' Ward couldn't resist.

'One of these days, I'm going to stop being so nice to you, Daniel.' Metcalfe gave him a sharp glare that crumbled after a moment, the man's warm eyes lighting up with mirth once more. 'I'll handle charging Chapman. You follow your nose.'

'Ta, mate.'

'I just need a moment of your time, sir,' Nowak piped up.

'Go on?'

'Just a heads up, more than anything. There's growing unrest across the country—several violent incidents that couldn't be stopped in time and one in critical condition in hospital—as a result of the Hunters.'

Ward stopped dead, and fixed her in a stare.

'Yes, it's become that serious,' Nowak replied gravely, answering his unspoken question. 'All police forces are aware, thanks to DCs Shahzad and Patterson, and they've stopped a number of assaults on the basis of the intelligence, but this is shaping up to be an act of coordinated violence, that seems clearly instigated from the incitement on the forums. We can't be everywhere at once to predict or stop every single incident.'

'Any round here?' Ward asked.

'A couple of incidents in West Yorkshire, and we're on high alert in Bradford for imminent threats. That's all DCI Kipling mentioned.'

'We have to identify these idiots *fast*. Before we have another dead Green on our hands.'

'We're on it, sir.'

'Let me know if you find anything.' Ward returned to his office and shut the door. For a moment, he stood still, considering the uncomfortable prospect of having to ring Victoria Foster on her personal mobile, on a weekend, no less. But it had to be done.

He looked at the last email she had sent him and dialled the number below her name.

'Hello?' Victoria's voice was cheerful—and it threw Ward for a second, because he didn't think he'd ever heard her sound so happy, or seen her smile.

'Uh, hi Victoria. It's DI Daniel Ward. I know it's the weekend, sorry. I need your help.'

Her voice was cooler immediately. 'Is this about the Millie Thompson case?'

'Yeah. I wouldn't have called, but I think it's important.'

Her sigh rustled down the phone. 'Fine. Don't make this a habit but this time...ok.' Victoria might be cold towards him, but she wasn't made of ice.

'You know the shoe you examined?'

'Mmhmm?'

How did he ask? 'I need your honest opinion on it,' he said finally. 'Look, I just have a niggle that something's not right. Most criminals are too stupid to pull a murder off without getting caught. There's nothing concrete pinning these two—Green, Chapman—to Millie's disappearance, or her possible murder, except that shoe. And we found it so easily. Maybe it's as simple as that. Maybe that's where they got cocky and slipped up, thinking we couldn't trace it back to Chapman, but I'm not so sure.'

'You think they didn't do it?'

'I'm not sure about that...but I don't know if I think they *did* do it anymore. From the interviews, the forensics, all the other data we have there's just...nothing to really *pin* it on them beyond any doubt. We're either missing something huge, or they didn't have anything to do with it. You examined the shoe. What do you think?'

Victoria was silent for a moment. 'It was clean.'

'And...?'

'It was *too* clean, if you ask me.'

He waited for her to continue.

'There were no cleaning materials in any of the bins there, nor in either flat. Sure, it might not have been cleaned there, but why clean the shoe away from your home, and then bring it back to dump it—without any of the cleaning material containers? That doesn't stack up—and it struck me as odd. Not impossible—perhaps they were trying to scatter any evidence—but odd.

'The shoe itself was impeccably clean. I'd expect, even with decent cleaning, that there'd be biological evidence on it, maybe a speck of blood, skin cells lodged under the clasp, dirt, fingerprints...It's pretty damn hard to get every single trace of forensic evidence off an item. It didn't even have any dirt on the sole. That shoe was cleaned with expert precision and industrial strength cleaners.'

'Which doesn't match Tweedledum and Tweedledee.'

'Not at all. I combed over every inch of those flats. If you'd have given me the flats and the shoe separately? My professional assumption would be that they weren't in the slightest bit connected. The pattern doesn't fit.'

'The shoe doesn't fit,' Ward said grimly. 'Thanks.' She had helped nudge him in the right direction—to follow the unease in his gut, as usual. Now he just needed to see if Shahzad and Patterson had traced that number.

———

Ward cursed loudly. 'Another dead end then?'

'Aye.' Patterson looked as miffed by it as he.

The number had been a burner, not registered to a known address or individual, and inactive since the last tip had reached the paper—either destroyed or the SIM card removed to make sure it couldn't be triangulated by any local cell towers.

Ward sat in a chair next to Kasim and Jake, playing over everything they had—and the doubts rolling through his mind.

'Lads,' he said at last.

'Sir?' They both looked up.

'This investigation is stalling.' He briefly filled them in. 'I have a hunch—and it's nothing more than that—that Green and Chapman had nothing to do with Millie's disappearance. I think the Hunters may be behind it—may have framed the pair of them, and possibly several as yet unidentified others—to seek vengeance for Sarah Farrow's death and Michael Green's past crimes. It may not be the first time this has happened and if it's true, it may not be the last. Right now, it's nowt more than a hunch, because the shoe points straight to Green and Chapman, but Foster agrees with me that the shoe doesn't fit where it was found.'

Kasim eyed him thoughtfully. 'Well, we'll look into the account that claimed responsibility for the assault on Green. Maybe they're connected. Now we're into the private end of the forum, we can check out posts made by specific users, like the ones who claimed responsibility for the attack on Green.'

'Have you managed to trace them yet?' Ward shot back at him.

'No, sir, not yet.'

'Why not?' Ward bristled.

'We're still waiting for the warrants to be signed off—Priya said it should happen today, that there's a backlog somewhere or other—then we can apply pressure to the Internet provider to get the customer details.'

'Damn it. Right—can you check something else in the meantime?'

'Go on?'

'Check the sightings of Green and Chapman reported to the anonymous helpline. We won't have names, but there'll be numbers. The sightings are the only other things tying either of them to Millie. I'm betting the Hunters are behind those calls.'

A spark ignited in Jake's eyes, and, closest to his computer, he wheeled the chair around and was flicking through various screens faster than Ward could compute. 'Now then...' he murmured. 'That's very interesting.'

'What is it?' Ward said, leaning forward.

Jake frowned. 'I recognise one of the numbers.'

Ward wanted to reach across the desk and shake him. 'Spit it out, then!'

'Well sir, one of the numbers belongs to the Broadways, the pair you and Nowak collared outside Green's place. Nowak dug into them and passed over the file when she realised we were focusing on the Hunters. I remember it, because it had '8876' in one of their numbers, just like mine does. It's their landline, by the looks of it. They must have made one of the calls about Michael being spotted near Wibsey Park on the morning of Millie's disappearance.'

Ward's blood chilled. 'They were at Michael Green's after Millie's disappearance, but there's nothing to say they weren't at Wibsey Park beforehand.'

'You think one of the Hunters took Millie to frame Green?' Kasim asked, sharing a troubled glance with Jake.

'You've seen how far they'll go,' replied Ward. Violence was erupting around the country at that very second, due to the group's persecution of whoever they perceived to deserve punishment—innocent or guilty. But it took on an even more chilling turn when he considered it. Would they abduct an innocent little girl just to punish someone?

He got up. 'We need to have a word with the Broadways, *now.*' Faced with Green's murder, and Chapman's possible involvement dangled like a carrot before them, he had put it off for too long, trying to juggle their stretched resources.

He had bugger all to go on except a hunch and a potentially fake tip—it wasn't enough to search their home for Millie, or put the pressure on, not truly. However, if Jillian and Andrew Broadway had orchestrated the entire damn thing, a hoax, to incriminate Michael Green and put a little girl at risk of harm, they would feel the full force of the law like a ton of bricks.

'Sir, wait!' said DC Patterson. 'There's something else.' When Ward turned back, the young man's face had paled. 'The sightings. The second one for Green at the park, and one for Chapman with Millie in Armley. They were made from an identical phone number. And, sir...' Patterson rifled through some papers on his desk, before he nodded. 'The phone that made those two calls...it's the same phone that was used to tip off the *Bradford Herald* on both occasions, to leak the Green stories.'

Ward stilled. The Broadways had called in one tip on Green. Someone else had made the second Green tip *and* the Chapman one—and whoever was responsible for those two tips was also the *Herald's* source.

The burner phone. 'Fuck!' Ward said, punching the door. 'We've wasted so much time.' He shook his head. How could they be so stupid? But of *course* they'd jumped on it. A child killer and paedophile? A convicted sex offender? Why on earth wouldn't they have easily assumed the two of them were responsible, believed them guilty? It was so obvious, it was blinding. Except...they had been duped.

Now, the pennies were beginning to drop. This was what he'd been missing. This was why Green's and Chapman's involvements didn't make any sense. They had never been a part of it. They had been victims too, however unsavoury, playing a convenient cameo to distract from the real culprits. Puppet masters who thought they were too clever to be caught, no doubt.

'Where are you going sir?'

'I'm going to pay a visit to Mr and Mrs Broadway. Get me every detail on them you can. I want phone numbers, previous addresses, jobs, car registrations and any ANPR hits. Hell, I want to know when Andrew Broadway last went to the bog and whether it was a shit or a piss,' Ward growled, his clenched fists twitching as he strode out—as though they had a mind of their own to lamp anyone that got in his way.

CHAPTER TWENTY-NINE

W ard and Nowak pulled up outside a nondescript detached house in the leafy suburb of Clayton Heights. On a hill in the south of Bradford, it was a world removed from the city centre bustle at the police station. The estate was only a couple of decades old, built on the site of the former Westwood Hospital at the turn of the millennium, but already, it showed signs of wear and tear, with faded fascias and dirty stone taking the new shine off it.

Not Jillian and Andrew Broadway's house, however. Ward pulled up in front of the place, checking that the number—marked by shining brass digits—was correct. The windows sparkled and the fascias were bright white, not a hint of moss growing on their roof, unlike the neighbours to either side.

Behind the house, at the edge of the estate, a strip of trees crowded, blocking out light from the west. The small lawn was lush and green, with neatly trimmed laurel bushes to the front bulging with glossy emerald leaves, while hanging flower baskets drooped with the weight of bright blooms.

'The window', Ward said quietly. But the twitching voile was already falling back into place and Jillian Broadway appeared in the doorway a moment later, looking both excited and aghast at the car daring to park across the bottom of her driveway. Ward and Nowak got out of the car and approached her.

'Detectives,' Jillian said with a smile, her eyes remained cold, and tight. 'What can I do for you? I do apologise, I can't recall your names.'

'Detective Inspector Daniel Ward and Detective Sergeant Emma Nowak.' Ward said. 'It would be better if we had a word in private. May we come inside?'

'Of course, come in,' she replied, glancing round the street before ushering them in. 'We saw the news, of course. About that monster's death. Terrible.'

That man whose house you stalked, Ward thought, noting that the woman looked positively thrilled about the news, her lips twisted in a sneer, a glint in her eye. He did not reply—could not—and forced the fury inside him to simmer down. Forcing the rush of his own blood pumping through his ears to quiet—so he could listen for any signs of Millie Thompson, perhaps concealed some-where in the residence.

He heard nothing—but that didn't mean the girl wasn't there.

'Please, do sit,' Jillian said, inviting them to perch on a

plump cream leather couch that dominated the living room. 'Tea? Coffee?'

'Coffee please, milk, no sugar,' Ward said, keeping his voice neutral. This one was too important to mess up by going in all guns blazing.

'And you?' Jillian smiled at Emma.

'Tea, milk, and a sugar, please.' Emma's answering smile was deceptively warm and genuine. Ward admired her ability to assimilate in any situation, she was a true chameleon.

He heard gentle clinking in the kitchen after Jillian shouted through, to her husband's muffled reply. Jillian looked through the voile again and then settled in an armchair, just as Andrew brought out a plate of biscuits and left them out of reach of everyone on the coffee table in the middle of the dingy lounge.

Ward eyed the lace doily on the table, and the porcelain ornaments that stood upon it—and dotted around the room. Flowing, shiny sculptures of Jesus, Mary, Joseph and Christian symbology adorned the living space, right down to the hand-stitched cross hanging in a frame above the fireplace. Ward did not lean forward to take a biscuit.

'To what do we owe the pleasure, detective?' Jillian asked. 'Can we help with the investigation? I assume this isn't a social call.'

Ward eyed her carefully. 'We're here for a chat, yes, Jillian. We hope you can help us clarify a few things.'

'Oh, of course,' she gushed, puffing with self-importance, a poorly hidden smile lighting up her face.

At that moment, Andrew entered, balancing four

china cups on a tray. He nodded a greeting, his focus on not spilling a drop, and doled them out on the lace doily too.

Emma reached forward to take hers, admiring the delicate handle, the gilding on the dusky pink roses painted onto the cups.

'They were my mother's, and her father's before her,' Jillian said. 'Brought all the way from India during the Empire. My grandfather was a very important military man out there, you know.'

Emma smiled politely and put the cup back on the table so she could slip out her notebook and pen.

Ward tried not to shuffle. He didn't have the patience for this placating nonsense. 'We'll get right to it—we don't want to keep you.'

'Of course,' said Jillian, with a beaming smile.

'We need to ask your whereabouts at eleven AM on the Wednesday this week, when Millie Thompson disappeared.

Jillian's smile flickered. 'I beg your pardon?'

Nowak looked up from her notes. 'Standard procedure in an investigation of this nature, I'm afraid, Mrs Broadway.'

'Oh, yes...of course.' But Jillian's smile was fading. 'Where were we Andrew? I can't really recall.' But she didn't give him a chance to respond before she opened her mouth once more. 'Oh—of course. We went shopping that morning, didn't we? To Lidl on Halifax Road.'

'And what time was that?' Nowak prompted, a frown crinkling her eyebrows.

'Gosh, about half ten, I should think? We were done for about quarter past eleven, and then we came home.'

Ward stirred. The time frame didn't put them out of the picture. The supermarket they mentioned was a stone's throw away from Millie's home and a mile away from the park. It was not inconceivable that they had abducted Millie, used a burner phone to report all the sightings, and killed Michael Green. They had the motive, the means, and the opportunity on all counts. The moment the burner phone came back to them in any way, shape, or form, Ward had them. But what he didn't have was Millie Thompson.

'Then, you were in the area where Millie was last seen, around the time she disappeared,' he said, staring flatly at Jillian. From the corner of his eye, he could see Andrew squirming. They didn't look like murderers, but then, few people ever did. Just last week, there'd been a piece in the paper about one distinguished surgeon stabbing another highly respected practitioner in a well-to-do area down south. It was being treated as attempted murder. Ward could never see inside people—but his instincts were rarely wrong.

Jillian gaped. 'Wh-what is this?'

'What this is, Jillian, is a friendly chat for now, but there are a few holes we need to patch up,' Ward said affably. 'Do you know the Thompson family?'

'No!' Jillian drew herself up with affront. 'We don't know anyone from *Buttershaw* Estate.' The sneer upon her face spoke volumes. Westwood Park—the newer, affluent estate—sat across the main road from Buttershaw, a former council estate that had never managed to shake its bad rep, despite being no better or worse than half of the city.

Snob. Annoyance spiked in Ward. He'd grown up on Buttershaw—back in his day, it had been a lot less savoury than it was now—and clawed his way out of it. It was a matter of pride, not shame, that he'd come from those roots. 'But you knew Michael, didn't you?'

'Knew *of* Michael,' Andrew interjected to clarify, earning him a scalding glare from his wife that soon saw him quiet.

Jillian said, 'I thought we'd been over this before, Detective Inspector.'

'When we met you stalking his flat, do you mean? For the Hunters?'

'We haven't done anything wrong.' said Jillian. 'Why are we being questioned? Do we need a lawyer? Is this even legal?'

'You're not being arrested at present, Mrs Broadway, and this isn't a formal interview, so no, you do not need legal counsel, though of course, you are free to do whatever you wish.'

Ward kept his expression carefully blank as he asked, 'How long have you been members of the Hunters?'

'A few years.' Jillian's voice had changed—the open, enthusiastic tone lost to a brusque, darker note.

'And you participate on Facebook—as group administrators?'

'Yes.'

'Do you participate on any other forums?'

Jillian hesitated.

'Again, Mrs Broadway, this is a polite chat until we feel like you're not telling us the whole truth,' Ward said, his own tone hardening. 'But we can take you down to the station and continue formally, if you like.'

'No,' she replied sharply. 'That won't be necessary. Ok, yes. There are other...more private forums. We're members there.'

'I'll need your usernames.'

'That's private.'

'Not in a murder investigation, or an abduction, for that matter.'

'You think we had something to do with the girl's disappearance? And that monster's death?'

Ward's silence gave Jillian the answer she needed.

'Fine. *Fine*. I'm 'HandsofGod' and Andrew is 'BroadieBoy50' on a forum on Reddit.'

Nowak jotted the usernames down, no doubt already as desperate as he was to get them cross-referenced back at the station. 'And what about the dark web or the deep web?'

'The what?'

'Do you use any forums that aren't available on the public Internet—any special browsers, that sort of thing?'

Jillian looked utterly blank. 'I don't know what those things are. We didn't do anything,' she protested. 'We're not connected to any of it—we just volunteered to watch Michael's place, everyone locally did, we were taking it in turns, to make sure he didn't hurt anyone again like he did before...'

'Then who was watching him that morning while you were at the supermarket?'

Jillian shared a glance with Andrew. 'We weren't supposed to be,' she admitted quietly. 'But we were drafted in last minute after someone else fell sick. We needed to go food shopping, and Michael hadn't been spotted all week...we left, and returned later.'

'Not very dedicated of you, was it? You didn't see him returning?'

'No.' Jillian's scowl at the floor was directed at herself, Ward realised. And he understood.

'You called in the tip—of seeing Michael Green near to Wibsey Park.'

Jillian looked up, aghast. 'What? No!'

'Yes,' said Andrew, suddenly. Ward's attention flicked to him. 'I did.' Andrew sat up straight, his chin up, more dominant than Ward had seen him yet.

'Why would you do that?' Jillian whispered, her hand flying to her mouth. 'Why didn't you tell me?'

'Because he was trying to protect you both, weren't you?' Ward said grimly.

Andrew nodded, his mouth set in a thin line, and he folded his arms, looking brittle perched on the edge of the chair, as though the faintest threat would shatter his resolve. 'We should have been watching Michael's place. It felt like we'd missed him, in the one moment we needed to be there. When the little girl went missing, I knew it was him. Just *knew* it.' His face contorted with a hatred so strong, it made Ward recoil. The man was unrecognizable behind the mask of fury.

'So, you rung in the tip, even though it was false, to save your own arse?' Ward asked flatly.

Andrew nodded.

'How many times did you ring in?' Ward asked.

Andrew frowned. 'I beg your pardon?'

'Did you just leave the one tip, or did you leave more?'

'I don't understand. I rang in, and said I'd seen Michael Green near the roundabout. That's it.'

'Does anyone else know?'

'No.'

'None of the Hunters?'

'No.'

Ward exchanged a glance with Nowak. Her frown mirrored his. Andrew's reaction appeared genuine.

'What phones do you have?'

Andrew frowned, puzzled. 'A mobile each and our landline.'

'Any other phones?'

'No, why?'

'A pay-as-you-go phone, anything like that?'

'No,' said Andrew insistently, annoyance edging his response.

'Where were you when Michael Green was murdered, between midnight and three AM on Friday morning?'

'Here in bed, sleeping,' said Jillian. She shrunk before them now, her eyes wide with horror as the dawning realisation took over her—she realised now why Ward and Nowak had come. Knew what they were implicated in.

The only thing Ward could not determine was whether she feared the truth coming out, or being blamed for something they had never done.

'Can anyone verify that?'

Jillian shook her head, and as she brought her hand to cover her mouth, it trembled.

'Mrs Broadway, I'm going to need to take you both into custody, I'm afraid, on the basis of the information disclosed here. You both have the means, motive, and opportunity to abduct Millie Thompson and frame Michael Green for that offence. You also have the means, motive, and opportunity to be connected to his murder.'

Jillian let out a wordless cry.

'We'll need to question you further on both matters. Andrew, I'm formally arresting you for providing false information in the form of your fabricated tip to the police, and perverting the course of justice. You do not have to say anything. But, it may harm your defence if you do not mention when questioned something which you later rely on in court. Anything you do say may be given in evidence. Do you understand?'

'We need to go to the station now,' Ward said. 'You will be given access to a phone there if you wish to seek legal assistance. I can take you by force, or we can go amicably. The choice is yours.'

Jillian looked small, her arms wrapped around herself, as though she could protect herself from what was happening. Andrew, deeply unhappy, his arms still folded and his shoulders hunched, made no move to comfort her.

'I have one more question,' Ward said, 'and it is imperative you answer honestly. A little girl's life is at stake. Your home will be formally searched once we have a warrant. Is Millie Thompson in this house?'

'No!' Jillian vehemently shook her head.

'If she is found dead and your early confession would have prevented her death, I will make sure the full force of the law comes down on you both,' Ward warned. 'Do you know where she is? Last chance for you to tell me before this is taken out of your hands.'

'No.' Jillian burst into tears, and Andrew strode across the room to wrap an arm around her shoulders.

'The girl isn't here,' he said, his face pale and his voice shaking. 'We have nothing to do with any of it except the false tip.'

'Then let us search the house.'

Andrew gaped for a moment. 'Absolutely not! We're innocent!'

Ward glanced at Nowak. 'Get onto Metcalfe. Get an emergency warrant authorised and CSI ready to move in. I'll take Mr and Mrs Broadway to the station, but I need you to stay here.'

DS Nowak gave him a nod, her expression serious. Given the new connections to the Broadways, a warrant could be granted within the hour. From their behaviour, he didn't think Millie was there, but he would leave no stone unturned. Just in case he was wrong. With the wild goose chase he seemed to have found himself on, Ward wasn't sure whether or not to trust his instincts anymore.

CHAPTER THIRTY

By the time Ward arrived at Trafalgar House police station with the Broadways, the warrant had been granted. They were directly connected to a murder and a missing child—two cases growing in interest. With Millie's safety at stake, it seemed not even the judges were hesitating on this one.

The Broadways were booked in and legal representation requested for both. Now, it was a waiting game, as the two were separated and Ward prowled to the office upstairs to catch up on any progress—in particular Kasim's and Patterson's work on the Hunters, and whatever he could find out about the Broadways' web activity under the handles they had given.

'Any joys, lads?' he said, cutting straight to the chase.

'Nothing on the two user handles you sent, sir. They're on the subReddit—' DC Kasim said, stretching in his chair.

'The what?'

'You *have* to get with the times, boss.' DS Patterson rolled his eyes. 'The forum. They're on there and plenty active, but nowt inciting—nowt that's a crime, put it that way.'

'Are they on the dark web secret thingy?'

Kasim winced. 'God, you're old, sir. Matter of fact, one of the handles is. 'BroadieBoy50'. A lurker mostly, no posts that I can find, but plenty of comments. Here.' Kasim handed Ward a handful of papers, printouts from the forum.

Nothing damning there either but enough to show that Andrew Broadway was active on the forum and knew others on there, judging by the level of banter, including comments on his stakeouts of Green's flat. 'Any mention of Millie?'

'No, sir. Nowhere on the forum, in fact. There is a Reddit thread with a bunch of conspiracy theories, Michael Green crops up regularly, as you can imagine, but nothing else we consider a credible lead.'

'Hmm.' It looked more and more like the niggle had been right, that Green had likely not been involved in Millie's disappearance, and that the Hunters, a small group or perhaps a lone wolf—the Broadways being two suspects—had abducted Millie in order to frame the man. It lent Ward hope, however small it was, if she had been abducted for a stunt like this...there was a possibility, however slight, that she was alive.

'Lads, I need you to double down whilst I'm interviewing the Broadways. If they had accomplices, if there's any evidence you can find to connect them with

Millie, or Michael Green's death—or that burner phone. Anything at all incriminating. Since Andrew Broadway found the dark web, I'm doubting they're stupid enough to post willy-nilly on Facebook, but if he thinks whatever he said is protected...you never know what people will say when they think they can't be seen or heard.'

'We're on it, sir. Sorry—Kipling kept us busy whilst you were gone, firefighting on all this violence they're inciting. We'll bring anything we find to you in the interview.'

————

At last, the interview room was set up with Andrew Broadway in first, and the family lawyer, Mr Abbas, a slender, greying Asian man with a cropped beard and a sharp suit, sat beside him at the table, facing the two-way mirror. DI Ward slid in opposite them, with DS Chakrabarti beside him to take notes.

Ward hardly interviewed with Priya, Emma being his usual partner, but he liked Priya's steady, thorough approach, and her influence. Somehow, she could ease or increase pressure just when it was needed and, older than Nowak, suspects tended to take her more seriously. She had a Masters in policing, a wicked tongue and a sharp eye. DS Priya Chakrabarti bucked every stereotype going and trod on anyone who got in her way—whilst still being a mum of two, a wife, and a proud homemaker.

DI Ward finished reeling off the details for the purpose of the recording and focused on Andrew. 'I need you to tell me once again where you were on the morning of Millie Thompson's disappearance, between the hours of ten am and one pm specifically, and then your movements later that day.'

Andrew recited the answer back to him—much the same as the Broadways had already explained—of the supermarket trip.

'So, you were in the vicinity, less than roughly three hundred metres, from Millie Thompson's home at that supermarket, and a mile away from where she disappeared, and it would have been conceivably very easy for you to deviate from your route home up Cooper Lane to visit the park?'

'We did not take Millie Thompson,' Andrew started hotly, before his solicitor cleared his throat.

'My client has come to answer charges on perverting the course of justice regarding a false tip made during the investigation.'

'And we'll get to that in due time,' Ward said, glaring at the man, who stared unflinchingly back, his poker face not wavering for a second. 'I just find it an awfully interesting coincidence that the Broadways are members of the Hunters, who knew Michael Green's identity and whereabouts on the day in question, and had the means, motive, and opportunity to abduct that little girl to frame Michael Green for a crime he did not commit. The Broadways have also confessed to making a false tip to place Michael Green in the area of Millie Thompson's disappearance, which led to his potentially unfounded arrest and may, alongside the unbalanced press coverage, have contributed to his death.'

'My client makes no comment on that.'

'I don't believe in coincidences, Mr Broadway.' Ward glowered at Andrew. 'As we speak, our Crime Scene Investigation team will be turning over every inch of your home. Every corner, every cupboard, every *drawer* will be searched. Your loft, your garden shed, your cars. Your devices.'

Andrew flinched.

Gotcha. Andrew was hiding something. 'It looks better on you if you tell me what you're thinking.'

Andrew swallowed. 'I didn't want to say in front of Jillian. She'd kill me. Not literally, of course!' He gave a nervous laugh, glanced at his solicitor, at Ward—who remained unsmiling—and then back at his hands on the table. 'I'm on a forum Jillian doesn't know about. A secret one.'

'The dark web.'

Andrew nodded.

'We know.'

His eyebrows rose. 'Oh.'

'Anything on there we should be particularly inter-ested to find?'

'No. Nothing. Look, we haven't done anything wrong —I mean...I have. The tip and all that. But we have nothing to do with Millie Thompson's disappearance. You think someone—a Hunter—took her to frame Michael? Well, it wasn't us. That's all I can tell you. Stop wasting your time combing over our house. You won't find anything.'

'Why should I believe you? Is that because you've done a bang-up job covering your trail?' Ward leaned forward.

Andrew shook his head, speechless for a moment. 'N-no! Nothing like that.' He took a moment to gather himself, and swallowed. 'That little girl is missing. We thought Michael had done it. We *knew* he'd done it—I would have staked my life on it. That's why I made the tip, to help the case against him, make sure he was placed near the scene at the right time...in case it helped.'

'It helped steer us possibly the wrong way, for *days*,' Ward fired at him, scowling. 'Days that may have cost Millie Thompson her life.'

Andrew flinched again. 'That's why there's no point searching our house,' he said, sitting up, his hands clasped on the table in front of him. 'You won't find anything there, because this has nothing to do with us. If that little girl is out there, then you need to find her.'

'And you're suddenly willing to help?' Ward eyed him, with no idea as to whether Andrew Broadway was telling the truth.

Andrew gave a mirthless chuckle. 'Michael Green is dead. The monster suffered his punishment at last—and I heard on the grapevine it was a bad one. He got what was coming to him, whether he had anything to do with the disappearance or not. But...if he didn't do it, then who did? I have to help in whatever way I can. She doesn't deserve to suffer. If she already hasn't.'

Andrew's voice dimmed, his tone grave. 'The monster is dead, and he got every ounce of what he deserved, but she doesn't deserve whatever's happening to her, wherever she is.'

'You mean he deserves it for what he did to Sarah Farrow?'

'Yes.' Andrew scowled.

'You heard about his death on the dark web forum?'

'Yeah. It was big news. Everyone was talking about it.'

'Who claimed responsibility?'

'Huh? No one I saw.'

'But you knew about Michael Green, didn't you, Mr Broadway? You knew who he was, where he lived—the Hunters uncovered his identity, and you were watching him. You *personally*.'

Andrew paled as he realised where the interview was heading. 'I didn't kill him.'

'We'll see. They all say that. Don't they all say that, DS Chakrabarti?'

'They do indeed,' Priya replied, her shrewd eyes burning a hole in Mr Broadway. Andrew looked away.

'This is pointless speculation,' interjected Mr Abbas. 'Stop wasting my client's time.'

'We'll be digging into your alibi *very* keenly.' Ward said, ignoring the lawyer. 'Being asleep with no witnesses isn't a fantastic one, as things stand. We have some excellent forensics evidence from Mr Green's remains. Fingerprints, fibres...We'll be checking them very thoroughly.' He left the suggestions hanging, watching Andrew Broadway carefully, but the man stared at him like a rabbit caught in headlights, utterly terrified and reeking of innocence.

The man was a coward, not a murderer, Ward reckoned. Maybe Jillian had done it, he wondered. She certainly had the balls of the pair of them. He wouldn't put it past her, though she would have to have had an accomplice. There was no way the slight woman could have overpowered Green by herself, nor taken his body to dump in Wibsey Park.

The cleaning, however, he would have pegged her for. By all accounts, the forensics report on Green's body had shown some sloppy fingerprint partials. He would have expected better from Jillian, having seen how utterly spotless her home was.

An idea sparked. 'DS Chakrabarti, could you get me evidence photo seventeen B, please?'

Priya opened the manilla file in front of her and pulled out a photograph. She slid it across—the single red shoe that had been found in Liam Chapman's bin. 'Do you recognise this?' she said.

Andrew looked utterly blank as he examined it, and slowly shook his head. 'I'm sorry...no.'

And, Ward believed him. He sighed, and shared a glance with Priya. She was unreadable—as ever.

The lawyer's chair creaked as he shifted his weight. 'As it stands, you really have nothing to keep my client here with, Detective. Yes, he'll most likely face the charge of perverting the course of justice—which, given the circumstances, I will fight hard to be downgraded, with every chance of success in making sure my client doesn't spend one single moment with his liberty impaired by punishing his moral fibre. But as for the rest?' He scoffed, disdain clear in his eyes. 'It's all conjecture. Any court would throw it out. You have absolutely nothing to charge my client with.'

'Yet,' Ward said, enunciating the single syllable with crystal clarity. 'CSI is combing his property now, and we're checking his Internet history and phone records. Right now, we have enough reasonable belief and circumstantial evidence to hold him for twenty-four hours, which, by the way, we shall be doing, so buckle up for a great weekend in here, Mr Abbas—'

The solicitor scowled.

'—And believe me, if there's anything to find, we will find it.' It was a promise as much as a threat.

The back and forth continued, but Ward got little else from Andrew of use in the search for Millie Thompson, or Michael Green's killer, though he did glean useful information about the Hunters that had Broadway's solicitor wincing with each fresh admission, until at last he insisted on a recess to pull his client out for a 'chat' that Ward suspected would be less than friendly.

Ward was inclined to deny the request—it felt like Andrew Broadway was finally cracking, and Ward wanted to know whatever he did, whether it could help them with Millie Thompson and Michael Green or not. It was an invaluable insight into a secretive organisation they barely had a fingertip into.

The Hunters ran a more sophisticated national system than they had realised, and it seemed DCs

Patterson and Kasim had discovered, for Andrew had, probably more by desperate accident than wilful intent, revealed that they even possessed facial recognition software in their fight against the criminals they persecuted, donated and funded by wealthy benefactors of the organisation—and that was how Michael Green's hidden identity had been confirmed.

There was a sudden braying on the door. *Bang bang bang! Bang bang bang!* And over the speaker, the static-filled voice of DS Scott Metcalfe emanated. 'Urgent update, DI Ward.'

Ward had been considering his best next move—whether or not to leave Andrew to sweat whilst he picked away at Jillian's prickly defence. He couldn't keep them without charge more than a full day. He had to play it strategically. Yet, at Scott's tone, Ward fell cold. If Metcalfe had interrupted them, it had to be deadly important.

He rattled off the spiel to close the interview, and left Priya to escort Broadway back to the cells, whilst he bolted out and nearly bowled over DC Shahzad and DS Metcalfe, who waited outside, buzzing with energy.

'Sir!' Kasim exclaimed. 'I've got something—something *big*.'

'What is it?' Ward demanded.

'You need to come with me,' Kasim was already jogging down the hallway. Ward didn't run. Ever. But, with adrenaline racing through him at the lad's urgency, he picked up the pace, loping after him, with DS Metcalfe puffing along behind him.

DC Patterson awaited them, pacing back and forth by his desk, with uncharacteristic seriousness.

'What is it, lads? Spill.'

Kasim beckoned Ward over to their computers. 'We've got someone. He's not on any of our databases but he fits everything.'

Kasim pointed to the screen. 'Look here, on the dark web forum. We have the user 'TheRealJustice' who claimed responsibility for the attack on Green alongside these other two users.'

'Now, since Jake here was able to sign up as a user, it gave us a *lot* more access to the private forums, member profiles...all sorts. When we visited the profile for this user, it also listed a previous username. 'Justice4Sarah'.'

'*Sarah*,' said Ward.

'Exactly,' replied Kasim. 'You're thinking what I'm thinking—Sarah Farrow, right?'

'Yeah. Go on.' Ward's mind was already racing with possibilities.

Priya arrived, breathless and red-cheeked, having obviously passed off Broadway and Abbas to someone else so she could join them. She darted across the office to huddle with Ward and Metcalfe over Patterson and Shahzad's shoulders.

Kasim explained, 'The profiles also list recent posts and comments. We found several alluding to this person having intimate knowledge of Michael Green's murder that doesn't appear to be from any other sources. Knowledge that someone shouldn't have.'

Kasim pointed to the other window. 'Now look here.

This is the Reddit forum. Same username. Same topic. Tamer posts. Clearly aware this isn't a private space. So, the same person, right? We've tracked the IP address that made this post. I just got back the details from the provider.' Kasim clicked on another window—the Hunters group on Facebook.

'It matches a Facebook user in the Hunter group. A man named Gavin Farrow. No profile picture, no details at all on that profile, in fact, as though it's just a dummy used to post in groups like this, we reckon.'

Gavin... 'This man's connected to Sarah Farrow?' Ward asked. It was too neat. The man had 'Sarah' in his former dark web username, and his Facebook surname was 'Farrow'?

'That's exactly what we thought too, sir, so we looked back into the Sarah Farrow case. It turns out, she had a brother. Gavin Thomas Farrow.'

'So, this guy's behind the attack on Green, strong links to his murder, perhaps?' Ward's spirits leapt. Could this be the missing piece they were looking for? He couldn't see how it connected to Millie, but if they could answer to what happened to Green...

'We think so,' said Jake.

'A revenge killing, then? Christ.' Ward exhaled. 'Did you run his details? We need to find him—fast.'

'We did, but, well...'

'Well, what?' snapped Ward, leaning forward, as if he could leap into the monitor and pull the man out.

'There's no one that goes legally by the name of Gavin Farrow, you see, sir. When we looked into the family just now, to figure out how we could trace them, it turned out that Gavin's parents divorced soon after Sarah's death. Gavin's surname changed to his mother's maiden name...and when we looked him up under the maiden name on Facebook, this is what we found.' Kasim flicked to another window, with a fully populated Facebook profile already loaded.

Ward's heart stopped. He recognised that face.

Gavin Farrow...was Gavin *Turnbull*.

Cold rushed through Ward.

Finally, it all made sense.

CHAPTER THIRTY-ONE

'Gavin Turnbull? I recognise that name,' Priya said.
'We know,' Jake said grimly. 'I just dug through the background checks in the hope it might be someone we could connect.'

'He's a family friend of the Thompsons,' Priya said, frowning. 'There weren't any concerns about him. He had an alibi for Millie's disappearance. He's been round numerous times since she disappeared, accounting to the Family Liaison officer—seems a really caring, stand-up man. As far as I could tell, he held good standing with the community. His statement to the search teams checked out, and he was squeaky clean. Is it the same person?'

'The IP address matches,' said Kasim. 'Farrow is Turnbull. And by the looks of it, he's responsible for Michael Green's murder.'

Ward said hoarsely, 'He took Millie. I'm certain of it. This has to be connected.'

Ward was back at Wibsey park in his mind's eye.

Walking over to Stacey, as she sobbed on that bench with her boy huddled close and the kindly man with his arm around her. Comforting her, turning his warm brown eyes up to Ward as he approached...He recalled chatting to the man both at the park and afterwards—and feeling no hint of his duplicity.

Gavin Farrow's—or Gavin Turnbull's—picture stared out at them from the screen. A tight smile that didn't quite reach his eyes, as though the image was taken without real want. Ward could see the resemblance now —he shared his sister's hair colour and large brown eyes.

Of course, in the heat of that day in the park, with only a fleeting glance at the man, and his attention had been focused on Stacey that day. Even after returning to speak to Farrow, Ward had never made any connection— no one would, without the context they now had. Farrow had flown swiftly under his radar.

Had Gavin taken her? *How* had he done it? How had he made the girl vanish, then doubled back to help with the search? Ward had even searched his house. Not thoroughly, but enough to see there was no child hidden there. He said as much. 'Where is she?'

No one could answer.

'His alibi checked out. He'd have had *minutes* to do this without being found. His neighbours saw him before and after Millie's disappearance. I spoke to them myself.' *Was it possible?*

Priya said, 'His house backs right onto Wibsey Park. He wouldn't have gone in plain sight.'

'The nature trail. Easy access,' Ward murmured. 'All

too bloody easy.' He remembered the gate in the back fence. And groaned. Ward chastised himself mentally. Misdirection. Just like he had pretended to throw the ball that night in the field for Oliver, they had been deliberately misdirected on the case. And fallen for it.

'He's a cleaner at Buttershaw school,' Metcalfe said as he squinted at the records on screen that Jake pulled up. 'The shoe...'

Ward groaned. 'He took Millie, and planted the shoe on Chapman—using his Hunter connections to find Green's associate, so we'd be thrown further off the trail after Green's death. He must have been spooked by the fact we hadn't been able to pin Green or keep him in custody. He took matters into his own hands to punish Green—but he still needed to get away with Millie's abduction. He has her. I'm certain of it.'

Ward cursed. 'We need to go. Jake, get all local units to Turnbull's address *now*. Kasim, you're coming with me. Scott, let the DSI know, and have Emma meet us there. She's currently guarding the Broadway's house. Priya, get a warrant *now*—I don't care who you have to poke to make it happen. We can't let Millie slip past our fingers.'

'Yes, sir!' came the answering chorus, and in a flurry of activity, they sped to work. Ward grabbed a set of keys from the board and bolted out of the door, with Shahzad hot on his heels.

Ward knew he wasn't supposed to use the blues and twos in an unmarked car, but he thumped them on, roaring the BMW out of the car park and through the back streets towards Little Horton, then up the hill to Wibsey, overtaking anyone who got in the way. The DC clung on for dear life.

Heart pumping with adrenaline, Ward ran it all through his head again. They had the pieces, yes, but it felt too little and too late. Millie Thompson could already have come to harm, accidentally or deliberately. What if they were *too late*?

However, DI Ward finally felt that he understood. Gavin bloody *Farrow*. How could he have ever forgiven the man that violated and murdered his sister? Ward couldn't blame Farrow for hating Green—who would? The man had destroyed Gavin's childhood, his family. Had Millie's abduction been premeditated? Perhaps she was the right little girl at the right time, the victim of a trauma awoken by the release of a convicted monster. As was so often the case, it was all about having the opportunity, means, and motive.

Gavin Farrow *had* waited decades for all three. Waited and then used his connections in the Hunter network—people just like him who abhorred that the death penalty was no more, that the most depraved monsters faced little of the suffering that they had caused their victims.

It must have appeared like a God-given gift when Michael Green reappeared in the very area that Gavin Farrow had settled in, far from his childhood home, far from what had happened to Sarah. Yet Michael Green had dropped right into his lap.

Maybe Gavin had thought it only a matter of time

before Green did it again. Maybe his crusade was altruistic, a genuine cause to stop another little girl from Sarah's fate. Or maybe decades of anger had hardened his need for revenge. Either way, an innocent girl—barely more than a baby—had ended up caught in the trauma. And no cause justified that.

'A bloody cleaner at the school!' Ward lamented to Shahzad, who was still hanging on for dear life as the BMW pounded the streets. 'Cleaning a shoe would be a breeze after dealing with all that sick and poo and god knows what else kids gets up to.'

'Then a quick trip to Chapman's to plant it, like you said, sir,' Shahzad nodded, gripping the seat as Ward overtook an oblivious elderly woman in a Citroen as if he were blazing around Silverstone.

'And all the while he was dialling in those fake sightings of Green and Chapman on that bloody burner phone!' The frustration burst out of Ward as he realised another missing piece that fit so neatly it had to be true. Those 'sightings' had kept his team tied up for days—crucial days—but Farrow had made a rookie error. He hadn't considered that any forensic data at the scene of Millie's disappearance or on the shoe needed to match Green and Chapman to implicate them beyond reasonable doubt. If not for that oversight, the pair would have likely both been charged with Millie's abduction—or at least still be in custody. Well, if one of them hadn't then shown up dead, that was.

Farrow had planted a trail of false breadcrumbs for the police to follow and when it had stalled, when Green had been released without charge, and Farrow's plan to see him charged with Millie's disappearance had failed, Farrow had taken matters into his own hands.

Ward saw how it had played out. The man—so familiar to the little girl—had easily lured her into the bushes. Then, he had whisked her away, perhaps willingly, perhaps drugging her to make sure she did not cry out. He'd taken her along the deserted nature trail and into his home—the perfect location—shrouded from the park by the bushes and trees, hidden from prying neighbours by the six-foot fence running along the boundary. So easy. So simple.

Yet where had Farrow hidden her? For Millie had not been at Farrow's home when Ward had visited.

The grim events that led to Michael's murder were yet to be uncovered, but Ward would pin anything on it being Gavin Farrow. The evidence they'd found of heavy travel on the nature trail couldn't be ignored. Farrow's home location was critical to it all—a chance decision he had made years before to live there, Ward assumed, that had come to serve him well. It had provided the perfect getaway with Millie. And the perfect concealment to dump Michael Green's mutilated body.

'Motive, means, and opportunity,' Ward muttered to himself.

Shahzad eyed him. 'Boss?'

'Aye,' Ward said grimly, throwing the BMW across a painted-on mini roundabout and blazing up the hill. They were minutes away. 'It all fits like a glove, doesn't it?'

'Yeah, sir,' said Shazad gravely, his eyes on the hill before them. St. Enoch's Road would lead them straight to the heart of Wibsey, then Farrow's address.

The Bluetooth in the car rang, and Ward hooked up the call. 'DI Ward.'

'What the hell happened?' DCI Kipling roared down the phone. 'He lives right next to the damn park!'

'Sir, if you'll calm dow—'

'Don't you dare,' snarled DCI Kipling. 'I want to know how this was overlooked!'

'Sir,' defended DI Ward. 'The man wasn't connected to the Thompsons by any familial means. And his alibi was rock solid. The neighbours remember talking to him at his home at the time Millie was taken and he was early on the scene to help out. The turnaround was incredibly tight. He had planned this with precision and covered all his bases. He had good standing in the community and was well-regarded.

'It's only because of DC Shahzad's and DC Patterson's extensive work on the Hunter network that we turned up any connection. Without that crucial link, we would never have known any better. All the evidence pointed us straight in the direction of Green and Chapman from day one. We had a known child-killer and paedophile recently back in the area, plus a registered sex offender, and leads pointing to both—can you really blame us for going after them?'

DCI Kipling had no answer.

'I'll take any rap you want to give, but don't criticise my team. If there's been any failings, they're my responsibility, but I don't believe there have—not on our end. We followed *every* lead.' He didn't mention that half those leads appeared to have been faked by Farrow. That could be unpicked later. Ward wouldn't stand for the DCI dressing down his team when they had worked their arseholes off to find Millie.

'Make sure you find that girl,' DCI Kipling spat down the phone. 'Local units will already be there by now. Warrant's authorised. CSI are on route. Keep me informed.'

Ward mashed the button and ended the call, wishing it was Kipling's face he was lamping. God above, the man was infuriating—a total stickler for the rules, and the first to criticise and lay blame when the slightest thing went awry.

Praying they weren't too late, Ward flung the car around Wibsey roundabout and shot past the park. He saw the turning up ahead where Gavin Farrow lived. He just hoped he could count on Gavin Farrow's skewed desire to protect being stronger than his pain for revenge. Ward couldn't see the lass carried out of there in a body bag. He just couldn't face that.

CHAPTER THIRTY-TWO

There were already three marked units outside the house, a nondescript semi on a close set back from the road by a small green. Ward pulled up in the BMW behind them, got out and headed towards the house. He didn't need to check the number. It was blindly obvious. The door had been smashed in with the big red key and PCs were already rolling out a cordon.

Ward flashed his warrant card. 'DI Ward. SIO. Where is he?'

The nearest PC looked up. 'He's not here, sir. We're already searching inside.'

'The girl?' Ward fired at him.

'No, sir.' She broke off as a shout came from inside the property.

Ward barrelled past her with Shahzad close behind. 'Extend that cordon across the square. No one in or out without my say so. Start asking the neighbours for any sightings,' he called over his shoulder to the PC. To

Shahzad, he said, 'Get me a car registration, if he's got one. I want an alert out on that vehicle.'

'Yes, boss.'

The smell of death hit Ward first—the hint of decay on the air, mixed with strong bleach—as he went through the door. To his left, the living room. Ahead, the kitchen. And with every step towards it, the smell grew.

A PC stepped aside to let him in. 'Something nasty in the bin, sir.'

'Don't touch it,' ordered Ward. He crossed to the bin and, using a tissue in his pocket, nudged open the swing lid. A collection of fingers greeted him. Ward turned away, letting the bin lid swing shut—on both the gruesome sight and the stench of rotting meat that erupted from within—before he took a gulp of breath and tried to keep the contents of his stomach inside. 'Victoria needs eyes on that as soon as she gets here.'

He eyed the room. The rest of the house gave a tired impression, dust covered and passably clean and tidy, but nothing like the kitchen, which appeared entirely out of place. Every surface had been scrubbed meticulously, the grout between the splashback tiles freshly pale and every surface free from stains. The smell of bleach was everywhere, so intense, every breath burned.

Ward looked up. 'What's that?' He frowned. And then he realised. A tell-tale speckle of blood upon the ceiling. Minute spots, sprayed upwards. Few people thought to clean the ceiling. 'We need to make sure Foster sees this.' Ward pointed up, drawing Shahzad's line of sight to the spattered ceiling. 'Blood.' *Michael*

Green's kill site? he wondered. Foster would confirm that for him.

He strode through the open back door to find another PC casting about in the garden. The youngster rattled the shed door half-heartedly.

'Kick it in,' Ward said. 'The lass might be in there. Break things first, ask questions later. Get it open now!'

The tall, gangly PC looked positively terrified at the prospect—a young, new thing on the force, Ward surmised. Sighing, he marched forward and plunged a huge booted foot through the rotting wood. He charged in first, carried by his own momentum—and crashed straight into a rusty lawnmower.

His heart hammering, he scrambled up, squinting in the faint light cast from the door. The small space was full alright. Full of junk. But no Millie. Ward backed out. He glanced around the garden, taking in the shiny new padlock and freshly oiled hinges on the back gate that seemed out of place with the dilapidated state of the rest of the overgrown garden—and the trees of the park beyond the fence.

The line of sight was covered from the neighbours houses by overhanging trees, sheds and a lean-to. Ward shook his head. There was no doubt in his mind—it would have been all too easy for Farrow to come and go unseen.

He entered the house and Shahzad joined him as they thundered up the stairs to the first floor, where the PCs were busy searching. 'Farrow has a car. Priya's sending out an alert now and checking ANPR for any hits.'

'Excellent.' They still had to make sure Millie wasn't still in the house—that Farrow hadn't fled by himself.

The upstairs bedrooms revealed nothing. Bare of any personal mementos much like the downstairs. Two bedrooms, each with neatly made beds that didn't look recently slept in. An empty bathroom.

'Mind out, please.' A PC said behind him. 'We'll check the loft now.'

The PC opened the hatch above his head, and used the pole leaning in a corner of the landing to wrangle with a set of pull-down ladders. Ward held himself back as the PC darted up the steps, a torch between his teeth, and disappeared. Every second was an age.

'Nothing up here,' he finally called down.

It was a punch in Ward's gut.

'Think, think,' he muttered to himself as they thundered downstairs.

'Sir?' a PC called up. 'Just found something in the kitchen. Not sure if it means anything?'

Ward thundered downstairs, to find the PC pointing at a set of three keys in the corner of the kitchen worktop. He peered closer—at the tag, and the handwritten label on it.

18. SPARE KEYS.

'No...' Number eighteen. The neighbours next door. Who were on holiday. They'd left spare keys with Farrow. Maybe Ward hadn't found Millie in Farrow's house because...

Ward snatched them up and dashed outside, careening past another PC and straight up next door's driveway. He tried the keys in the lock, fumbling with the first—no good. The second rotated, and he pushed open the door as soon as the lock clicked.

'Millie?' he called. The house smelled like any other —lived in. No hint of decay or death. Ward poked his head into the living room, and strode to the kitchen. The same layout as Farrow's house, only flipped. Nothing.

He pushed past Kasim who shadowed him, and took the steps two at a time, flicking on the landing light as the upstairs lay in darkness, curtains all drawn.

Ward halted dead. Shahzad ploughed into his back and bounced off the larger man with muffled curses.

The master bedroom lay ahead. Inside, a double bed —recently used, the covers ruffled and unmade— stood under the window. A pink blanket lay upon it, similarly rumpled as though it had been recently slept under. And there, on the pillow, was a stuffed teddy bear, cast aside, eyes staring up at the ceiling. A baby's bottle sat on the bedside table, milk congealing inside. A pile of nappies and wipes teetered next to it. A toddler-sized dress hung on the radiator. Gavin Farrow had been there—taking care of a young child in that room.

'She was here,' Ward said. 'Shit...' he breathed.

Farrow would know he was running on borrowed time, Ward was sure of it. The man *must* have known that eventually the police would catch up with him. But fear would make him desperate. Desperate to escape, desperate to protect himself...desperate to erase any trace of what linked him to any of it.

There were signs that he had grown sloppy in his haste. He'd neglected the blood spots on the ceiling in his kitchen, and as for leaving Michael Green's body parts in the bin...he didn't fit the profile of a killer who did such things with planning. But he was desperate, and that placed Millie in more danger. Perhaps he'd cared for her at the start but now—she was a liability...

Ward had seen the lengths that traumatised people went to. The boundaries they crossed.

And he didn't trust Farrow to stay on the right side of those boundaries.

They'd finally broken the false trail. Connected the dots. And they were too late.

CHAPTER THIRTY-THREE

Rain peppered the street as Ward and Shahzad emerged from the house and the seething mass above cast a pallor over them all, dulling even the fluorescent jackets of the PCs. DS Nowak ran across to him, zipping up a purple rain mac, while along the street two CSI vans were parking up.

'She's not here, Emma. Neither of them are, but they were,' Ward said, his voice flat.

Nowak's hopeful expression, the light in her eyes, fled. 'Oh.'

'Cordon off number eighteen—he kept her in there. The occupants are on holiday.'

Shazhad's phone buzzed and he answered at once. 'Yes? Yes. Got it. Yes.' He looked at Ward. 'Sir. Priya's found several ANPR hits for Farrow's car. He's heading towards the motorway in a silver Ford Focus. She'll give us live updates.'

Ward mobilised at once. 'DS Nowak, you're with me.

DC Shahzad—fill Foster in on what we've found. I want her to focus on that bedroom and the kitchen. Warn her about the bin. And get everyone out of there so she can do her job. I want you managing this scene.'

'Yes, sir.' Shahzad jogged towards the CSI vans while Ward headed for the car.

Emma joined him in the unmarked BMW, the car steaming up before the air conditioning blasted through the condensation.

'What's happening at the Broadways' place?' Ward asked. He shifted the car into gear and pulled out, doing a U-turn and re-joining the main road. They didn't have a direction of travel for Farrow, but it didn't matter. They could head to the M62 motorway and see which way he chose from Priya's updates. East, deep into Yorkshire. Or West, across the Pennine hills into Lancashire.

'Full search done. Nothing of significance found, though they've seized Andrew's tablet and computer so we can corroborate the evidence that he made the false tip, and make sure he had no involvement with Millie's disappearance or Green's murder. Victoria was just about to pack up and ship off when she got the call to come here.'

'Lucky you were only five minutes up the road.' He filled Emma in on the developments since he'd left her at the Broadways that morning, though it felt like a lifetime ago.

'Wow.'

'Yup.'

He glanced across, watching as she processed it all.

That Michael Green was never guilty of any of it. That he was murdered, most probably in Farrow's kitchen, all as part of an elaborate plot for revenge that had burned for decades.

Priya's name flashed up on the dashboard as the phone rang over the speakers. 'Ward.'

'West. Farrow's vehicle is heading west on the M62,' Priya informed them.

Ward had just pulled onto the M606, the short stretch of motorway leading out of Bradford that joined the city to the M62, the motorway that spanned the whole county of Yorkshire from east to west, and across the western border into the county of Yorkshire's historical rival county, Lancashire. They were less than a minute from hitting the M62.

'Where?'

'He just hit ANPR at the Huddersfield junction—Ainley Top.'

'Damn it.' He was ahead by a couple of junctions on the lengthy motorway. 'Any local units?'

'Already on it, sir. There are a few in the area. They're all heading to the motorway. I'll let you know when he hits the camera at the next junction.'

Ward floored it, ignoring the speed cameras that flashed at him, overtaking everyone at eighty-five on the outside lane, then ninety, then a hundred. He drove down to the Brighouse junction and then up, starting the long ascent over the Pennines to Ainley Top and beyond. The M62 summited the Pennines at the highest point of any motorway in the British Isles. They had just reached Ainley Top when Priya rang again.

'Can confirm, Farrow's car hit junction twenty-three —' the next one, '—but it has *not*, I repeat, *it has not* passed junction twenty-two.' At the very summit of the motorway.

'He came off at twenty-three?'

'Yes. Must have done, unless he's crashed or parked up on the motorway, but there's no reports matching it from the traffic units. We have a unit passing at Mount. He didn't take the main road.'

'He's gone to ground.' *But where?* There was nothing up there. The motorway led out into the sticks. Wild and windswept moors awaited out past junction twenty-three. No villages, barely a hamlet between there and Lancashire over the other side of the tops. A couple of reservoirs and the occasional sheep farm were about all to be found in the barren hills.

'Damn it,' Ward cursed. They were coming up to Junction twenty-two now and he indicated to pull off, sweeping down the ramp to the roundabout underneath the motorway. 'There are two roads back to Yorkshire— Huddersfield and Ainley Top. He wouldn't go back if he's fleeing.'

That left just one option. An old country road over the hills that wound beside the motorway. Ward took it instinctively. The urgency bit into him. They were running out of time. Farrow was desperate—his erratic direction, and lack of any discernible destination, showed that. Ward was growing ever more concerned for Millie Thompson's safety. If Farrow thought he was out of options, backed into a corner...there was no telling what he might do.

Ward drove through a small village—one main road all that Outlane had to its name— before crossing over the M62 on a high bridge and onto the other side. Small lanes peeled off in all directions—farm tracks, country roads, a tangled maze.

Ward drew to a halt at the side of the A-road, over-looking the sweeping valleys below them from almost the very heights of the hill. The dark waters of Scammonden Reservoir were steely and unfathomable, hiding their secrets. In those waters lay the former village of Scammonden, purposefully flooded to create the reservoir. Now, only the small church and graveyard marking the hillside revealed that anyone had ever lived there. Forever haunted, Ward always felt the deep mournfulness that flowed out of the place whenever he drove past.

Beyond, the dam itself carried the motorway, before the six lanes disappeared between the Deanhead cutting and under Scammonden Bridge, once famed for being the longest single-span non-suspension bridge in the world, now more infamous for the jumpers who plunged forty metres to their deaths below. Ward's sharp eye grazed over it all.

'But where now?' he muttered. 'Come on Farrow, where the hell are you?'

Without any further directions, they were driving blind. Every turning might be taking them closer—or further away. Ward scanned the horizon desperately.

The light was dimming, the sky brooding. Across the valley, he couldn't see any vehicles moving on the few lanes visible criss-crossing the moor.

He slammed his hands on the steering wheel, making Nowak jump.

'We're out of options and out of time,' he said. Nowak drooped in her seat, her crest-fallen expression giving him her own silent agreement.

CHAPTER THIRTY-FOUR

Priya's call had never been more welcome. Her voice was breathless as she raced to explain. 'We've found her—you need to get there now! The B6114— where it intersects with Church Lane, just before Scammonden Bridge.'

Already, Nowak was on her phone, looking up directions, then relaying directions to Ward. He pulled a three-point turn and raced back the way they had come, diving down into the valley towards the reservoir then along a small, steep lane, towards their destination on the opposite hill.

'There's a farm on the corner and a little terraced house. Five minutes ago, at the end terrace, an old fellow and his wife heard battering at the door. They opened the door to find no one there but a bundle on the doorstep. From the description of her, it's Millie.' Priya's voice broke on a sob of relief. The map showed the destination as just minutes away. They had been *so close*.

'Is she alive?' Ward demanded as he passed the head of the reservoir in the valley and chased the steep lane up the other side.

'Yes! She's drowsy and unresponsive, possibly drugged. Ambulance crew on its way from Huddersfield now. But she's *alive*. They're waiting for you to get there. All local units are aware and moving in to locate Farrow. He's vanished.'

Ward couldn't think about that for a moment. Millie was safe and *alive*. A well of warm hurt rushed into his chest, caving him in and stealing his breath. It was hope, he realised. Hope that he had forsaken over the past few days, with the growing belief that she was dead—and that it was all his fault.

And now, hope burst into life anew, like a match taken to strike. Ward pushed his foot to the floor as he turned onto the B-road, towards the buildings in the distance where Millie Thompson, allegedly alive and well, awaited them.

At the end terrace, he braked sharply, throwing the pair of them against their seatbelts, and then they were both jumping out of the car, which he had abandoned a foot into the road. Ordinarily, he'd have mocked anyone for such shoddy parking but he didn't even notice, fixing his attention on the front door. Ward knocked once, twice. The seconds felt torturously long—and then the door opened.

An old lady, bowed with age, peered up at Ward, squinting through glasses so thick they made her eyes look gigantic.

'Mrs Holdsworth?' DS Nowak said from Ward's side. Of course, she'd taken note of the name. Ward hadn't paid the slightest bit of attention, focused solely on getting them to Millie. Hoping it were true. Hoping it was the toddler. Hoping she was unharmed.

'Come in, come in,' the aged, hunched woman replied, a slight quaver in her voice. 'Derek's just looking after her now, poor thing. Recognised her off the telly, we did. What a to do!'

Ward followed her inside, impatiently hovering behind her shuffling, slow footsteps, into a small living room where a coal fire burned, casting a warm glow across the stone-flagged floor and the faded, worn rug. And the chair, with the old, bald man in, cradling the form of a limp toddler.

She was, most recognisably, Millie Thompson.

For a second, Ward couldn't breathe from the weight of it, and he sagged against the dark wooden door frame, overwhelmed by the relief that against all the odds, all the false trails and all the dead ends...they had found her.

Emma rushed forwards, sinking to her knees on the stone as she reached out to the girl. Her slim fingers felt for a pulse. She bent close—the old man regarding her with brows furrowed in concern as he held the young lass close.

Emma listened for breath—her own stilled in antici-pation and fear. She ran a palm over Millie's forehead tenderly and brushed her hair back. And then, she sat back, relief washing over her face. She turned, looking up to Ward, tears glistening in her eyes. 'She's alive.'

CHAPTER THIRTY-FIVE

Ward called Priya with shaking fingers. 'We have her. She *is* alive.'

A rush of breath on the other side blew static into Ward's ears. When she spoke, DS Chakrabarti's voice was thick. 'Thank God. Ambulance crews are five minutes out, other units the same.'

Ward hung up. 'I'm going after Farrow.'

'You don't know where he's gone,' Emma said, as Ward returned his phone to his pocket.

'I have a hunch.'

Farrow was acting exactly as a desperate man would and Ward was familiar with desperation. He'd been raised by a desperate man, and at times, he'd been one.

Ward left the cottage and slipped back into his car. The bridge was visible ahead as was the car abandoned there as he crested the hill—glinting silver, he realised, with a rush of adrenaline shooting through him. He could have run, but the car was faster, and Ward knew he had seconds, if that, to act.

Gavin Farrow was coming to the end of the figurative road. He surely knew by now that his time was up, that his actions had been discovered, and if by some miracle he really *didn't* know yet, the paranoia would almost certainly be eating away at him. He'd killed Michael, done what he set out to do, exacted vengeance—though it hadn't turned out how he had planned. And Ward was prepared to bet that he had nothing left.

Ward braked behind the abandoned car. A glance at the plate confirmed it was Gavin Farrow's. Ward's heart thundered now, the adrenaline powering through him with what was at stake. Millie was safe and hopefully well, but Farrow still had to be accounted for.

The lone figure ahead in the middle of the bridge could be no one else.

He exited his car and ran to the bridge.

They were both brutally exposed. The wind whipped across the bridge, howling and jostling as below, the traffic rumbled along the M62.

Ward pulled his phone out and dialled Priya. She picked up at once. 'Close M62 at Scammonden Bridge. *Urgent.* Possible threat to life.'

And then, Ward hung up and strode out onto the bridge. He didn't dare take his eyes off the figure ahead as it drifted closer to the edge of the bridge.

The wind buffeted him, tearing what little warmth was hiding in his jacket. Above, steel grey clouds scudded ominously, threatening the next rainfall.

'Gavin?' Ward called—and then again, louder, as the wind snatched the word from him.

'Stay away!' came the answering call. The man looked back at him. 'Or I'll jump!'

Ward edged closer. His instincts had been right. So close to the railings, Ward's stomach churned as he glanced down and saw the traffic thundering past far below. Gavin was still too far away, a lone figure in the centre of the two-hundred-metre bridge, with only a waist-high railing separating him from the drop. They'd been banging on about installing higher fences for years—and never doing anything about it, even as each fresh death was splashed over the local newspapers.

'I'm just here to talk, Gavin.'

'I don't want to talk! Leave me alone!' the man screamed back, his voice raw. He'd been crying, by the sound of it.

'I understand, Gavin.' Ward kept approaching, slow and steady, his hands in his pockets, until he was only fifty metres away...then thirty...then twenty. Then Gavin screamed and Ward stopped, as the man flapped his hands in desperation.

'Stop right there! Don't come any closer! I'm going to jump, I'm not joking!' Farrow pressed his back against the railing, clutching onto it with one hand.

This close, Ward could see Gavin's red eyes, his intense grief. The man looked old, far older than Ward remembered from their brief meeting just days before. Grief did that to people—and he could understand a shred of Gavin's.

'It's alright, Gavin. It's over. It's going to be alright.' Ward's voice was low, deep, soothing, carrying across the bridge, though a lull in the wind. Gavin was shivering, wearing only a T-shirt and jeans—no match for summer in the Pennines.

'No, it's not! You have no idea, about...about any of it!' Gavin spat. But his words were riddled with pain, not spite.

'I understand enough. I know who you are. I know you're Sarah's brother,' Ward said, meeting the man's gaze steadily. 'And I know what you've done. You only took Millie because of Michael Green, Gavin, that's right, isn't it? You didn't mean her any harm, did you?'

'No. They let him out. How could they do that? After what he did...'

'So, you had to make sure he couldn't hurt anyone again. I understand.'

'I-I had to! I couldn't let him hurt anyone else like he hurt Sarah, like he hurt us.' Gavin crumpled. 'I had no choice.'

'You thought he hadn't been punished enough.'

'He could never endure enough for what he did to her.' An ugliness contorted Gavin's face. He met Ward's eyes, his own burning with hatred. 'Do you know what he admitted to me, before I-I killed him?' He didn't wait for Ward to answer before he spat it out. 'He told me he *raped* her. He raped my four-year-old sister, and then he murdered her. He told me that she suffocated because he went *too far* in his fucking *fantasy*.'

Gavin breathed heavily, his eyes wild and glazed

over. 'I lost my mind when he said that. Then I destroyed him piece by piece and I enjoyed every scream from his monstrous mouth before I ended his disgusting, sick excuse for a life in as much pain as I could.'

Ward stood firm, but he wanted to crumble too, at the horror that anyone could inflict that upon a *child*. 'That man was beyond a monster, Gavin,' he said in a low voice. 'But it wasn't your punishment to give.' As much as he, in the same position, would have probably wanted to do the same.

Gavin laughed, a mirthless scoff. 'Like the law punished him? Housed, fed, looked after. It's a fucking joke. That demon tore my family apart. My parents never recovered. They died of grief. And then I was alone.'

Ward heard the sharp edge of pain in Gavin's voice.

'I couldn't live without her. She's haunted me all these years. She never got justice. How could she? How could anyone ever undo what happened to her? Erase the past? Nothing short of that would be *fair*. Nothing short of bringing her back to us, whole, without...without what *he* did to her.'

Gavin looked to Ward again, the fervour in his eyes gone, pleading now. 'I haven't slept for years. The night-mares—they won't let me be. I see her face, so scared... wondering why I didn't save her.'

'It wasn't your fault, Gavin.'

'I know. I *know*. It was that...that evil bastard's. But I'm her big brother. I should have been there to protect her.'

'You were seven years old. Just a child. It wasn't your

fault.' Ward edged closer, now only a handful of metres away.

'I still wanted to fix it.'

'And you did. It was clever that, going to the Hunters.'

'They had what I needed. Information. And a family, of sorts. Their quest was mine. They wanted Michael to pay for what he'd done too. We watched him for years. Tried more than once, whilst he was on the inside. And when he walked free...' Gavin paused, swallowed.

'I had to find him, and I had to end it. When he turned up, right on my doorstep...God smiled over me that day. I knew I wasn't alone—something higher had brought him to me, exactly as intended. I knew Sarah was still with me. My guardian angel. I was patient, and I was rewarded.'

Ward kept his mouth shut. There was nothing godly about any of it, he was pretty sure.

Gavin shivered with the cold, the wind biting into him. But he smiled, then, a smile that flashed with victory and vengeance before turning soft and sad. 'I got him. For her.'

'You did. But you hurt an innocent girl and tore apart her family—they didn't deserve that.'

'I wasn't thinking straight. Everything just seemed to line up right there in that moment...when I knew Green was local, and I heard Stacey was taking the kids to the park, even with the rain...I acted.'

'You must have thought it through—you even took her next door.'

Gavin looked away. 'I knew you'd be back to check on me, after we met.'

'What was the plan, Gavin. What was your end game?'

Gavin looked at him once more, his face crinkling in anguish. 'I don't know, alright? I don't know. Michael, I just wanted him to *pay*.'

'Believe me, I understand. Look, it's cold up here Gavin, I've got my car just there. How about we take a sit inside, and we can talk?'

'No!' Gavin said sharply and then, realising how close Ward was, he shuffled away along the railing a few feet. 'I'm not rotting in prison for giving him even half the punishment he deserves. I hope he burns in the fires of hell for eternity for what he's done, and then maybe he'll be close to starting to get what's owed.'

'But you took an innocent child. Would Sarah have wanted that?'

Remorse flashed over Gavin, wiping the fury from him. 'I never hurt her though. I kept her asleep, fed her, played a little bit. She was upset, wanted Stacey—her mum. That killed me, but I couldn't undo it. I'm *sorry*. I never meant to upset her. Millie's mum knows I'd never hurt her, she'll tell you.'

Ward could see the shock dilating his pupils then, as the events of the past few days began to hit home. 'Oh, God, is Millie going to be alright? I didn't mean to hurt her...'

'That remains to be seen,' said Ward gravely.

'Oh, God!' Gavin clutched his hands around himself.

'What have I done. I'm just as bad as he is, taking her. I'm so sorry. Tell Stacey I'm *sorry*.'

'You can tell her yourself.'

'No! You can't take me.' Gavin backed away again.

Ward shuffled half a step forward.

'I won't let you.' Gavin looked down for a moment, then back at Ward, his eyes wild.

As Ward looked at the motorway from their high vantage point, back into Yorkshire, he could see a break in the traffic, and flashing blue lights beyond that, holding back a surge of vehicles heading west. The eastbound carriageway was already empty. Something swooped in his stomach. Priya had pulled it off. Closed the motorway, just in case.

It wouldn't come to that. He hoped. It felt as though he and Farrow were balancing upon a knife edge.

'Gavin, you need to do this. Come on,' Ward said, holding out a hand.

Gavin recoiled and edged away another step, his other hand also finding a railing to grasp. 'No,' Gavin said softly, the word almost lost in the wind. 'I have nothing left, now. I'm going home to Sarah.'

And then he moved.

'No!' shouted Ward, surging forward.

Gavin threw himself over the railing.

Time slowed.

Ward lunged.

His snatching fingers grazed Gavin's trouser leg.

And then the man was gone.

Ward's momentum carried him crashing into the

barrier, and he latched onto it to save himself going over too.

The tramping of booted feet behind him announced the arrival of the cavalry.

But they were all too late.

Ward stared at the broken form of Gavin Farrow far below, and sunk to his knees against the cold metal of the railings.

CHAPTER THIRTY-SIX

Ward allowed himself a moment before he moved. They'd saved Millie, in the end, but Gavin had been beyond help. Ward pitied the man. To endure alone in a lifetime of pain and grief, loss and anger, must have been *unbearable*.

It was a pain he could partly identify with too, to a point, after the rougher patches of his own life. One he didn't wish on anyone else.

Footsteps pounded on the road towards him as the cavalry arrived.

'It's too late,' he said hoarsely, turning to greet them. 'He's gone over. Secure the scene, please—here and the motorway. Get me an ambulance for him.' He knew it would be too late for Gavin, but they had to go through the motion.

He walked towards his car at the end of the bridge, parked haphazardly by Gavin's—and behind both vehicles, an array of marked police cars dumped. Numbness washed over him. Ward took out his phone and dialled DCI Kipling.

'Sir. We have Millie. She's being checked over now.' He could just see the top of the ambulance over the crest in the road, outside the house where they had found Millie. 'We've found her abductor, who is also Michael Green's murderer. He's dead. Jumped off Scammonden Bridge.'

Static blistered his ear at Kipling's outbreath.

'It's a tangle to unwrap, sir, but we have all the pieces.'

'You don't do anything by halves, Ward. How big a problem am I going to have?' With the higher ups, with the press.

'We'll do our best, sir. There's clean up required here —I need a divisional surgeon and CSI, for his body. Motorway's already halted—DS Chakrabarti liaised with Traffic on that. The girl's getting checked over now by paramedics. If she's alright, I'd like to inform her mother, get them reunited as quickly as we can.'

'Yes, it's been a long enough ordeal—you're certain the mother wasn't involved?'

'Yes, sir. We've traced everything back to the deceased.'

'Right. Good.'

'I'd best go, sir. I need to see how Millie is.'

'Keep me informed.'

Ward rang Priya at once to get her and Metcalfe to coordinate the response—CSI, and managing the chaos on the closed motorway, before slipping into his car. He managed to edge it out from the tangle of vehicles without incident, and drove back to the house, parking in front of the ambulance.

'Sir?' Nowak approached as he opened the door and stepped out, rolling his neck. Somehow, suddenly, he ached all over as fatigue crashed into him. She frowned, but her face slackened as she saw his silent resignation.

'He jumped,' Ward said to confirm. 'There was nothing I could do. Is she ok?'

Nowak's face broke upon a relieved smile. 'Yes. She's started to come around. She's woozy, but her vitals are strong, and they just want to make sure she's hydrated. They've taken bloods to see if there's anything in her system that could cause long term damage from whatever he sedated her with. Aside from that, they'll keep her under observation until she wakes up and the bloods come back.'

'Where are they taking her?'

'Calderdale.'

'Can you ring Metcalfe? Have her mum meet us there with liaison.'

'Sir.'

'Thanks, Emma.' He smiled tiredly at her. 'I'll fill Priya in, she'll be chomping at the bit to know what's happening.

––––––

By the time Millie had a room at the hospital, her mother had arrived with the family liaison officer. Her face crumpled as she walked into a side room on the bright children's ward where Millie was a tiny lump on a huge bed. She raced forward and gathered the girl in her arms, sobbing.

Millie's eyes fluttered open at her mother's attention, and pudgy fists tightly wound themselves into Stacey's top. 'Mama!' Millie screeched and buried into Stacey's chest.

Even Ward had a lump in his throat and burning eyes as he watched the powerful reunion. Nowak was flat out crying beside him. He put an arm round her shoulders and gave her a silent squeeze of comfort.

'This is why we do what we do, eh?' he murmured to her.

When the sobbing had subsided, Ward could inform Stacey what had happened—the bare bones of Millie's abduction, and not the whole, gruesome truth of Michael Green's murder. That would come out later, most probably, though Gavin Farrow could not stand trial for any of his crimes now.

'I can't believe it,' Stacey said numbly, staring at the floor. Millie still clung to her as they sat on the hospital bed.

'We'll support you as best we can. We know this has been so tough for you, and there's still a lot to work through. You'll have access to family liaison for a little while, and we can connect you with any services you need to be able to get on with your lives, alright?'

'What about Millie?' Stacey held her daughter tighter.

Ward grimaced. 'She's young, and I hope she won't remember any of this soon, but you'll have access to help for her too, if she needs it. Physical or psychological.'

Stacey closed her eyes, though fresh tears continued to slide through the cracks, soaking into Millie's curls.

———

Ward soon returned to the motorway beneath Scammonden Bridge to make sure that everything had been processed correctly. The motorway had been closed for hours for the investigation and clean-up operation, and for Gavin's remains to be removed in as dignified manner as possible. The press had already picked it up from the traffic updates, though they didn't know the who or the why yet. Just another jumper to them, causing hours of inconvenience to gridlocked, stranded motorists.

Then, it had been back to the office, for a weekend lock in. They'd already worked most of Saturday, and Sunday would see them all back on shift too to get ahead of the tide of evidence they had to correlate.

DS Chakrabarti had taken point with family liaison, and Ward hadn't tried to get in her way. The family would need support, of course, and counselling, but they had each other again. Stacey was already making plans to move away from Wibsey, Priya had told Ward. Away from the trauma to start afresh, so that bad memories didn't destroy their lives.

Victoria Foster had pulled an all-weekender too. Ward had even thanked her—which had rendered her speechless—and invited her for a drink with them. It was only fair, he reasoned. She'd pulled her weight. She'd declined, of course, on the grounds of 'having to spend any more time in your unbearable company,' as she'd put it.

The report had been huge. Even without Gavin's testimony, there was enough to piece together the dots. Millie's DNA was all over Farrow's neighbour's bedroom and bathroom. One of her shoes was present there— matching the one found in Liam Chapman's bin—and contained enough of her DNA and Gavin's to connect him firmly to her abduction. A pay-as-you-go mobile had been recovered, SIM card still inside, which matched the number that had rung in false tips on Green and Chapman, along with the newspaper source material. Along with the location of his house, the access to the park and the alibis he had—it was more than enough to link Gavin to Millie's abduction and what had happened to Michael Green.

As for Michael Green's murder, no doubt his death had been *loud*, but the next-door neighbour was deaf as a post—that had been noted in the initial investigations and door-to-door enquiries—whilst the other next-door neighbours were, as Gavin well knew, on holiday.

The bin bag used to cover Michael Green's head had matched the roll under Gavin's kitchen sink. The blood spatters on the ceiling matched Green. Mark Baker, the pathologist, had pieced together the man's remains like a morbid jigsaw from what had been found in Farrow's kitchen bin. The penis, testicles, fingers, thumb, and eyes...quite the collection. And one last sliver of evidence—the DNA under Green's remaining thumbnail was a perfect match for Farrow. How neatly everything fit, when one had *all* the pieces of the puzzle.

Ward couldn't yet take DCI Kipling's inevitable tirade about that puzzle. He'd managed to avoid it so far but he knew the man expected answers, and he'd be getting a robust grilling to make sure they hadn't failed on a single point. Ward stood by his team's work. He couldn't fault a single one of them for the dedication they'd put in.

They had not understood about Gavin's past—but Millie had never been the target, Michael had. She was simply the wrong child, in the wrong place, at the wrong time. Gavin had drugged her to keep her quiet for the most part it seemed, but otherwise cared for her tenderly, keeping her fed and watered, with toys to play with.

Ward hoped Millie would simply forget the ordeal—be so young that the trauma would quickly fade, to be replaced with happier times. He did not know whether that was wishful thinking. It would stay with her mother for a lifetime. He didn't doubt that.

And they'd gotten their man in the end, didn't they, even if he didn't make it to serve out the punishment he deserved? Michael Green had suffered an unimaginable final punishment...but Gavin Farrow's only escape from a lifetime of undeserved torture was death.

Farrow had died immediately on impact. A merciful death, all told. It was his actions that tugged at Ward's moral compass most of all. Killing was wrong. And yet...

he could understand exactly what had driven Farrow. More than that, Ward sympathised. It was a question he'd asked himself over the past couple of days, one that he did not dare answer.

Would I do the same?

CHAPTER THIRTY-SEVEN

MONDAY

The new week brought no relief from the caseload. The paperwork on Farrow and Green bogged down the whole team—and there were others still to deal with. Liam Chapman and the Broadways had been processed on their relative charges and bailed. They'd face the sting of the law in the fallout from the case.

Ward, however, hadn't even gotten started that morning. Overnight, a new update had arrived, on the Varga case. He'd been so exhausted and so consumed with the Millie Thompson investigation, that he'd had a blessed twenty-four hours free from thoughts of Varga or nightmares of that lorry.

Cold settled in the pit of his belly as he looked at the photos that had landed in his inbox from CSI that morning. From the body they'd photographed and collected evidence from the previous morning. And the pathology report that had followed later that day.

It was a girl—a girl he knew from the tattoo upon her

chest. Her blue-green eyes were closed. Her top was ripped. Her body covered in bruises—a beating before death, the post-mortem said. Cause of death was strangulation. Forensic evidence: none. A contract kill. Merciless, professional, untraceable.

Once the girl's identity had been traced from a missing person's report by the refuge charity she'd failed to show up at, it had landed straight on his desk. Ward propped his face in his hands. 'Fuck!' he cursed, the word muffled in his palm.

He thought he'd saved one—thought that it might be worth *something* that one poor young woman had gotten away from that hellhole of a brothel with a chance for a fresh start away from abuse and fear.

'Sir?' Nowak crossed to his desk. She read over his shoulder. 'Anja...*no*...' Nowak had personally sought protection for the girl, Anja, and promised her a better life.

'I'm sorry.'

Nowak swallowed audibly. 'I thought she'd be safe there.'

'It's not your fault, alright? We did what we could for the lass.'

Nowak gritted her teeth and shook her head, fury darkening her eyes. 'Not enough. The bastard had her killed, and we both know he's gotten away with it. Again.'

Ward looked up from his hands, at the photos of the young woman's battered body lying in a heap of fly-tipped rubbish on waste-land. His own anger already reared at the injustice of her death—yet another at

Varga's hands or on his orders—and the impunity with which Bogdan Varga operated.

'I'm not giving up on him,' he said, meeting Nowak's gaze. 'Kipling's warned me off, but I won't stop. Not until we have him.'

'You can count on me, sir.' Nowak's attention flickered, grazing across the photo before meeting Ward once more. The young DS steeled herself, straightening—presenting a tough exterior. But Ward knew her better. He could see the aching vengeance for injustice seething inside her, at how the young woman, a young woman like her, had been treated. 'Promise me we'll get him.'

'You know we'll do our damn best and then some, Nowak.'

It wasn't enough. How could it be? But he couldn't promise, because he didn't know if they would ever get the bastard.

As evasive as smoke and slippery as oil...Bogdan Varga would be the hunt of their careers.

Ward feared that it would consume them all, before the end came.

His thoughts slipped to that innocuous envelope of photos still sat in the top drawer of his kitchen. Between him and Varga, neither would give up the hunt—but who would destroy the other first?

CHAPTER THIRTY-EIGHT

D I Daniel Ward nursed a pint, quiet for a moment, as his team raucously bantered around him. He'd treated them all to a pint, essential downtime after the weekend they'd had, after the case that had wholly consumed them. They were holed up in a trendy gin bar in the refurbished Sunbridgewells, though, with it being a Monday, Ward reckoned it wouldn't be a late one. Except for DC Patterson, maybe, whose liver seemed to be made of steel. Though, true enough to DI Ward's claim, the lad hadn't been able to beat DS Metcalfe's six-second pint, or even come anywhere close. The older man had a miracle gullet and a few decades extra practice.

Ward sighed. At the end of the rollercoaster that had been the previous week, he felt drained by it all—by how much poison was in society. Maybe he did need a break. Maybe DCI Kipling had been right. He'd worked too hard, gotten in too deep and too close. Was he really still doing his job as well as he expected of himself?

'You alright there, boss?' Patterson clapped a hand on his shoulder as he sat down with a packet of peanuts.

'Aye, lad.'

DS Scott Metcalfe gave him a grin. 'Give the man some sympathy. He's getting long in the tooth and he can't hack it!'

'Says the old man who has slippers *just* for work under his desk!'

'Hey, that's a medical condition, you know.'

'Bone idleness isn't a medical condition, Scott.'

'I have chilblains. Doctor said I have to keep my feet warm.'

'It's called *moving*. You should try it some time.'

'Yeah, might lose the gut that way,' piped up Patterson.

Both Ward and Metcalfe turned as one to glare at him and he froze—the glint of 'deer in headlights' flashing across him.

Metcalfe puffed up. 'Now then, lad, steady on there. You might be a young fit thing, but one day, you'll have a barrel of your own to cart about, and then you won't be laughing.'

Patterson relaxed, then smirked. 'Yeah. In about a million years when I'm as ancient as you two, maybe.'

'Right, that's it,' Metcalfe heaved out of his chair. 'Next round's on Patterson.'

'Hey! I can't afford a round in here on a Constable's salary!'

'Should'ha thought of that before you insulted your seniors, lad. Come on. Pay up.'

'Orange gin and tonic, please,' piped up DS Nowak.

'Elderflower lemonade,' said DS Chakrabarti. 'Ta!'

'Pint of pale ale for me,' said DI Ward with a wink at the gaping, spluttering Patterson.

'Coke for me,' said DC Shahzad.

'And I'll have a bitter,' DS Metcalfe said with a nod. 'Get yourself something too, lad.'

Patterson loped off, his head hanging and his thin wallet in hand, to the sound of everyone's laughter.

It wasn't just the alcohol. Ward felt warmer and lighter inside—like the night he'd played with Olly in the field. Like the evenings he'd watched his mother paint. Home wasn't a place. Home was a feeling. Home was the people you called family—blood or not. And crowded around the table—alright, with the possible exception of Patterson, who Ward still thought was a first-class prat—the detectives there were the closest thing to family that he had.

And, Ward knew in his heart of hearts, that there was nowhere he would rather be.

THE END

A NOTE FROM THE AUTHOR

Hello readers, and thank you for coming on a journey with DI Daniel Ward, his team, and I through West Yorkshire.

All of the locations within the book are based on real settings, though some details have been fabricated. I'm not sure if there really is a Gavin Farrow/Turnbull living at 20 Park Square in Wibsey, for example—if there is, it would be an almighty coincidence!

I was born and raised in and around Bradford, and have spent my life working and living in West Yorkshire. These wild and windswept hills are my beloved home, and it has been such a pleasure to write about some of the places I know and love.

I visited Wibsey Park as a child, and I now play there with my own son, which feels like a poignant marker of the passage of time. It's a beautiful park, and the pond is a lovely place to feed the ducks—though thankfully, I have never found any bodies there, and hopefully never will!

Buttershaw, Wibsey, Clayton Heights, and all the areas mentioned, are areas I have deep connections to through work, family, and friends over the years. I worked in Great Horton for several years, and taught myself some Slovakian to be able to converse with some of the locals there—it was a great pleasure to make friends with a Slovakian colleague of mine (*Ahoj Patrick!*), who helped me along, and was very encouraging of my probably terrible accent!

Scammonden Bridge, the setting for the climax of this novel, is a local landmark, marking the border between Yorkshire and Lancashire, which sits just a short distance away on the motorway. Whenever I come to the Deanhead Cutting from Lancashire, and Scammonden Bridge soars overhead, I know I'm coming *home* to my beloved Yorkshire.

If you enjoyed this story, I'd really appreciate if you could leave a review on Amazon or Goodreads. If you want behind the scenes sneak peeks and information on upcoming books, please join my Reader's Club at my website www.megjolly.com).

So, for now, '*si thee later*' as we say here in Yorkshire. DI Ward returns next in *The Revenge We Seek*.

Warmly yours,
Meg Jolly

ABOUT THE AUTHOR

Meg is a USA Today Bestselling Author and illustrator living amongst the wild and windswept moors of Yorkshire, England with her husband and two cats. Now, she spends most of her days writing with a view of the moors, being serenaded by snoring cats.

Want to stay in touch?

If you want to reach out, Meg loves hearing from readers. You can follow her on Amazon, Bookbub, or sign up to her newsletter. You can also say hi via Facebook or Instagram.

You can find links to all the above on Meg's website at:
www.megjolly.com